T0402350

ALSO BY ANN Y. K. CHOI

Kay's Lucky Coin Variety

All Things Under the Moon

A NOVEL

Ann Y. K. Choi

Published by Simon & Schuster

NEW YORK AMSTERDAM/ANTWERP LONDON
TORONTO SYDNEY/MELBOURNE NEW DELHI

A Division of Simon & Schuster, LLC
166 King Street East, Suite 300
Toronto, Ontario M5A 1J3

This Simon & Schuster Canada edition September 2025

Manufactured in the United States of America

1 3 5 7 9 10 8 6 4 2

Online Computer Library Center number: 1487551481

ISBN 978-1-9821-1456-5
ISBN 978-1-9821-1460-2 (ebook)

For Phyllis Bruce, who told me women
need other women to survive

All Things Under the Moon

PART I

village

Monsoon

Daegeori, 1924

The monsoon rain was at its worst that July. The day the sun came out, the women of Daegeori headed for the river with loads of white shirts, white pants, and other white clothing in hand. White had been the colour that commoners wore long before the Japanese empire seized control of the country. From a distance, the laundry looked like melting snow along the riverbanks as the women laid out their wet clothes.

For generations, the remote village had been isolated by the surrounding pine-wooded mountains. In the ancient principles of pungsu jiri, mountains and rivers were key to a balanced and prosperous life. Mountains harnessed the wind and the rivers moved water. This constant movement from the sky to the earth transported energy, qi. In Daegeori, the highest mountain at the rear of the village blocked the wind and protected the fields, and the rivers that flowed from the mountains enriched the many rice fields and allowed for lush fruit and nut orchards to thrive.

It was already late morning by the time Na-Young reached the river. Carrying a straw basket filled with her and her mother's dirty clothes on her head, she bowed to several of the women and exchanged the usual courtesies. Like them, Na-Young wore a hanbok, the traditional long-sleeved jeogori worn over a full-length wraparound skirt, the chima. The soft pink colour of her clothes reflected her status. Her father was a prominent landowner with the second-largest walnut orchard in their village. Not that that meant much these days. Since the Japanese had taken over Korea fourteen years ago, many landowners across the country had been forced to pay more than half their crops as rent to Japan, effectively making them tenants on their own land. Even Sang-Hoon, Na-Young's oppa, her older brother, had to abandon his plans to attend university to help out. He had wanted to be a doctor and was crushed. Things were different when Korea had a king, he had told her. Now a Japanese governor-general oversaw control of the country, and the Japanese emperor ruled over the empire of which it was a part. But all of that felt far away on this bright day that came after weeks of rain.

Na-Young spotted her friend Yeon-Soo nearby. Her naturally red highlights, the same colour as wild omija berries, seemed to sizzle against her coal-black hair, which she wore in a bun close to the nape of her neck.

As Na-Young picked her way towards her friend, she passed Su-Bin, Yeon-Soo's only child, sprawled on the dirt. His blue pants, made of the finest silk, were stained brown and green, and there was a tear in one knee. He was shooting pretend stones into the air with a slingshot.

"Anh-yong," Na-Young greeted him.

Su-Bin sat up and motioned for her to come closer. He opened his mouth to reveal that he had lost another tooth.

"Soon all your teeth will be grown-up ones, and you will be a man."

"I'm already ten years old," he said. He winced when she patted his head, and lay back down on the ground. Na-Young continued towards his mother. "Good morning," she said, dropping her laundry. "Is your boy doing all right?"

"Good morning!" Yeon-Soo shielded her one good eye from the sun as she peered up. Na-Young noticed her friend's hands were swollen and bruised.

Yeon-Soo caught her looking. "Su-Bin fell, hit his head, and tore the new pants that his grandmother got him. She was furious," Yeon-Soo said. "He was chasing a dragonfly."

Everyone in the village knew that Lady Lee had a temper, and that she looked down on Yeon-Soo because she had worked as a servant before Lady Lee's eldest son, Jung-Nam, fell in love. When Yeon-Soo became pregnant, a marriage was arranged. Because she had been born blind in one eye and had unusually red hair, all her parents got for her were three bags of potatoes and a large bag of walnuts. "I wasn't even worth a single grain of rice," she often said to Na-Young. "You won't have to worry about that when your family arranges your wedding."

When Yeon-Soo gave birth to a son, her status in the house was secured, but, like his mother, little Su-Bin had trouble seeing well. He also was prone to repeating sounds he heard around him, and his head often jerked to one side. Lady Lee considered these impediments and felt that Su-Bin was not the heir she'd hoped for. This was just one more reason for her to hate Yeon-Soo, although Yeon-Soo's husband shielded her from the worst of Lady Lee's anger. But when he died from a sudden heart attack two years ago, Lady Lee made Yeon-Soo the target of her grief and began to lash out, often beating her for the smallest infraction. As her friend was older, it wasn't Na-Young's place to comment on the abuse she endured, but Na-Young knew it probably hurt Yeon-Soo's hands to do the laundry. Thankfully, she only had Su-Bin's clothes and her own to wash.

"Let me help you," Na-Young said, rolling up her sleeves. "How did your son fall?"

Yeon-Soo sniffed the shirt she had been washing and dropped it back into the water. "I got the smell out, but grass and bloodstains are another matter. He was playing with a dragonfly when a bird suddenly appeared and attempted to feast on it. He attacked the bird with his slingshot, running after it until he tumbled over some rocks."

"He thought it was his father again?" Na-Young whispered.

"Yes."

"How exhausting it must be for him to believe his father's spirit still lives in other forms."

"I don't think there's any harm in believing that someone is watching over us."

"I suppose it's a bit of a survival instinct given his . . ." Na-Young stopped.

"Oddities?" Yeon-Soo said. Her lips parted, but she said no more.

Na-Young tugged at her jeogori to allow some cooler air to reach her skin.

"How's your mother doing?" Yeon-Soo asked.

"Not even the sunshine can draw her outside." Na-Young sighed as she thought of her mother, cooped up in her room. It started when Na-Young's older sister, Mi-Young, died seven years ago. They had all grieved the loss, but Mother had retreated into herself. It didn't help that Na-Young's father had taken a second wife.

Yeon-Soo nodded in understanding and the two fell quiet as they turned back to work. Na-Young took a shirt from her friend's basket and soaked it in water, then used a heavy wooden washboard to scrub it. Once the shirt was rinsed and wrung out, she moved on to the next garment.

The water was cool, but soon she was sweating under the heat of the sun. She dipped her braided hair into the river and used the tail to splash water over her face.

In the distance, a dog barked, and Su-Bin mimicked the sound, letting out a high-pitched squawking noise. The dog barked again. So did Su-Bin. The other women began hushing him, calling, "Quiet, Chicken Boy."

Na-Young had not been there to witness the "Great Chicken Miracle" that had given Su-Bin his nickname. As the only son, Su-Bin had been given the task of killing the chicken that would be the special dinner to mark the one-year anniversary of his father's death. He was told by the cook to chop the head off at the neck, but he'd botched the task, the axe's blade landing just below the chicken's ear holes. Without a head, the bird flew about the yard before Su-Bin could collect it and wrap the open wound with some rags. The headless chicken eventually recovered and now spent its days preening and strutting around like a peacock. Lady Lee was disgusted at first, but then she proclaimed it a miracle. Seeing the financial opportunities, she praised her grandson as a hero: a saviour of all things, including chickens.

Like everyone else in the village, Na-Young was in awe of the Chicken Miracle, and so she was deeply disappointed when her brother told her that it was only because the brain stem, which controlled an animal's reflex actions, was intact that Headless Chicken was able to keep living after the clotting had stopped it from bleeding to death. As Oppa had been the closest thing to a doctor available when the unfortunate accident happened, he'd been asked to treat the chicken. He had been clever enough to leave a small opening in the esophagus so that the bird could be fed.

But no one was interested in the science or a rational explanation for the headless chicken. Word spread throughout neighbouring villages. Soon everyone came to see Headless Chicken, each willing to pay money they did not have to see the miracle for themselves.

Su-Bin rushed towards them. "I need to go back," he said. "I need to feed Headless Chicken."

"You go ahead," Yeon-Soo replied, "then come back to help me carry the wash."

Su-Bin showed Na-Young the gap in his teeth again before he dashed off, barking each time he heard the dog.

"I was terrified of having a girl," Yeon-Soo whispered. "I prayed so hard for a boy; I never thought to pray for a normal one."

"It's good to have a son," Na-Young said to her friend as she watched Su-Bin go. Without Su-Bin and his chicken, things would be a lot worse for her friend.

Farther up the river, the elder women began to sing of their plight. "What, what do we have to live for? Hard work, hard work, hard work—life as a grasshopper would be gentler. Please, may I return as one in my next life?"

Or a headless chicken, Na-Young thought, envisioning it seated at the head of the table as everyone toasted its greatness.

After a while, Na-Young's hands were wrinkled like prunes in the water. She used her braid to splash more water against her face. The sun was unbearably hot, and she longed for a cool breeze to bring some relief. She could use a nap, she thought. She'd been having bad dreams again, but this time, she kept them to herself. The last time she told Oppa and Mother about her dreams—talking spiders that took over their land or dead chickens falling from the sky—Mother ended up consulting with the village apothecary, who had made wild predictions about an early harvest or a family member's imminent illness. It was easier to keep her dreams to herself rather than burden her family with such preposterous fantasies.

Yeon-Soo passed her friend a rice cake. "Eat," she said, indicating that she needed a break. They stepped away from the river and sat on the grass.

Another old woman, this time with a deep, raspy voice, had taken over the singing upstream. The song was more upbeat, and others joined in: "Mountain rabbit, mountain rabbit, where are you going? You hop around all day long."

"Do you suppose laundry was ever men's work?" Yeon-Soo asked, leaning back on her elbows.

Na-Young shook her head, although she hadn't ever thought of the possibility.

"Do you ever wonder what life would be like if you were a man?"

"No, that's silly," Na-Young said. She waved her hands lazily at the small bugs that buzzed about.

Yeon-Soo got a faraway look in her eyes. "When I was a child, I wanted to be a hwarang and serve the queens of the ancient kingdom of Silla. There were female warriors, but I always wanted to be a hwarang."

"A what?"

"A hwarang! They were young male warriors sworn to bravery and loyalty. They were devoted to their family, and, of course, the king."

Na-Young couldn't help but laugh.

"I was only a child. Serving a queen just seemed so much better than serving a husband. Serving a queen as a brave warrior seemed best of all. I would have trained to fight in battles with a sword, and learned the art of seoye using the finest brushes and paper." After a long pause, she went on, "Girls can't even go to school and learn properly like the boys. The world is unfair to women. That's why women need other women to teach them how to survive."

"At least your husband taught you to read and write," Na-Young said.

"Not that it helps in any way." Yeon-Soo ran her fingers over the stitch marks and stray threads of her chima.

"You should teach me."

"I can teach you other things," Yeon-Soo said. Na-Young knew why her friend had said this: Na-Young's parents would never agree.

All Na-Young wanted was to learn to read and write, but her mother always told her that no man wanted a wife who was smarter than he was. That didn't stop her from daydreaming about going to school where there were no clothes or dishes to wash, just books to read and lessons to learn. She had never actually seen a school, but it sounded like a magical place, much like the king's palace, which Oppa had told her had wooden floors, golden ceilings, and rooms full of books.

"I bet I could have been a doctor," Na-Young said, "if only I were allowed to go to school. All I have waiting for me is marriage."

"I miss being married," Yeon-Soo said more to herself. "I miss how my husband protected me from his family."

How sad, Na-Young thought, *that we should need protection from our own families*. But then she thought of Father's second wife. Unlike most second wives, who took direction from the first wives, Second Mother had dictated the terms of their relationship, her arrogant confidence fuelled by Father's obvious affection for her. Although her parents' marriage had been an arranged one, Mother said she had made the mistake of falling in love with her husband. Love, she warned Na-Young, seduced with the fragrances of magnolias and gardenias, but all flowers eventually died and rotted away. Yet marriage was inevitable: She was already seventeen years old.

A series of piercing screams suddenly cut through the air. Everyone turned around. Several servants from Yeon-Soo's house were running towards the river, their arms flailing. "It's Su-Bin! Come quickly!"

Yeon-Soo leaped to her feet. Na-Young ran after her, holding her long chima up as much as possible to avoid tripping. They ran past the farmers with their knees buried in the rice fields, past the open barley fields, and through the orchard of walnut trees before they reached the estate. There, by the inner courtyard, lying on the dirt again, was Su-Bin. His head was turned to one side, blood oozing out of his ear.

Yeon-Soo dropped by her son's side and started shaking him violently. Na-Young stood watching, her heart pounding, unsure of what to do. Yeon-Soo screamed louder than Na-Young had ever heard, but Su-Bin didn't move. After several minutes, two houseboys carried Su-Bin's body inside, and Yeon-Soo went with them, refusing to let go of her son's hand. Na-Young tried to follow, but Lady Lee stopped her.

"There's nothing you can do here," she said sharply, and gestured Na-Young away with her hand. She headed inside, stepping on Su-Bin's slingshot along the way.

Stunned, Na-Young turned. There in the courtyard, Headless Chicken strutted. Blind and deaf, she had been spared the sight of her lifeless master's body sprawled on the ground and the piercing cries of his mother. Na-Young couldn't even think of what was to become of the bird. Her thoughts were on poor Su-Bin.

Funeral

Straw hats dotted the paddy fields as Na-Young walked amongst the funeral procession. Men dressed in white shirts, with their pant legs rolled up to their knees, worked ankle-deep in the murky waters. Lush, green rice plants poked up row after row until they reached the base of a nearby hill. Su-Bin would be buried next to his father and grandfather on a steep hill overlooking the family's estate. The field-workers looked up, removed their hats, and lowered their heads. The funeral song that an old woman sang was so loud and mournful that even the birds stopped chirping, seemingly to pay their respects.

Representatives from all thirty-five families in the village were there. Na-Young caught Yeon-Soo's eye as the procession began, and her blank stare suggested that Lady Ko, the apothecary, must have given her some very powerful herbal concoction to get her through the day. Na-Young's heart broke for her friend. Su-Bin had been the centre of her universe after her husband died.

Although a doctor had determined that Su-Bin's death was the result of his head injury, some of the villagers insisted that there were other reasons. Na-Young lingered near the end of the procession, her mother at her side, listening to the villagers talk.

"It was no doubt the evil spirits," Lady Shim said, "taking revenge for the family's treatment of Headless Chicken."

"But he loved that chicken," Lady Cho said.

"Still, what dignity was left when half its head was lopped off and people paid money to see it flopping about like a mad devil?"

"I wish I could get my hands on that chicken," Lady Ko said. "What potions I could make with the blood of a magical headless bird!"

Mother stayed silent, but her arm was wrapped tightly around Na-Young's for support. Her loose hanbok emphasized her frail body. She squinted to see under the blazing sun. Mother hadn't left the house in nearly a year. Na-Young knew it pained her to be out in public where everyone could witness how Father rejected her as he did now, walking near Su-Bin's family with Second Mother and Old Man Rhee, the village's unofficial leader. But Mother was terrified that Su-Bin's young spirit would roam aimlessly about, possibly making its way into her home by accident. She'd had the same fear when Mi-Young, Na-Young's older sister, passed away seven years ago from pneumonia, and so she was determined to join the procession today.

"Children wander," Mother said now. "That's what they do. They get lost. How can dead children be any different? It's only natural that I worry. You'll understand one day when you become a mother."

Na-Young kept her eyes forward and tried not to think of the knot growing in her belly. Mother had made her pray fiercely to prevent Mi-Young's spirit from getting lost in the forty-nine days that it took a spirit to reach heavenly realms or to be reborn into a new life. Although Na-Young didn't understand what happened when one's soul separated from the body, the idea that Mi-Young would return in some way did little to comfort her. Instead, she followed her mother's cue, praying when her mother did and doing her best to perform during the series of gok, the ritual wailing, that demanded mourners cry out their pain and grief with such violent passion that many ended up passing out.

Na-Young imagined Su-Bin's corpse laid on a table, his hands and feet bound together in preparation for burial. Na-Young hadn't actually seen his body since he had collapsed three days earlier, but she was familiar with the burial rituals, having gone through them when her sister died.

Although Na-Young was only ten years old at the time, she still had vivid memories. Mother had taken great care to ensure that the bathwater used to cleanse her sister's body was rich with scents of soothing jasmine and roses. She hadn't understood many of the rituals involved in caring for a dead body, but she watched, with great fascination, as Mother dressed her sister in a simple white hanbok, clipped her fingernails and toenails, and carefully combed and braided her hair. She collected the nail clippings and the fallen hair from the comb and put them into a white silk pouch, which was later tucked under Mi-Young's hand. Finally, Mother placed three spoonfuls of rice and several coins inside her sister's mouth, so that her spirit would not be without food or money as she journeyed to the next world. Later, when Mother thought no one was watching, Na-Young saw her stuff more money into a different white silk pouch, with a pink lotus design embroidered on it, and pin it to the underskirt of Mi-Young's chima to conceal it. Na-Young nodded to herself in understanding; it was good to be prepared to appease the unknown.

Wiping the sweat from her forehead, Mother stopped when they reached the hill with the burial plot. It was a gentle incline, and although the graves were still not within view, they were close now. Halfway up, Mother turned and made her way to some nearby trees.

"I need to sit a moment," she said. "No one will even notice that we're gone."

Na-Young was relieved to escape the direct sunlight. Her eyes traced the path they had walked and gazed out at the field in the distance. Su-Bin's family owned the largest amount of land in their village. Despite his oddities, Su-Bin would have been the legitimate heir. Her thoughts turned to Oppa, who, as the eldest son in her family, was destined to take over their father's estate. "Your brother is very intelligent," Mother had repeatedly said. "He passed all of his exams with the highest scores! And how he managed to learn Japanese as well as he did, I'll never know. Too bad that he has to rot here instead of going to the city and becoming the doctor he wants to be. But we cannot escape our fate."

An individual's birth year, month, day, and hour were considered the Four Pillars that determined their fate. Although Na-Young had grown up believing this was how life unfolded, she struggled to accept that her own life could already be charted for her. What would be the point of living if she didn't have some say in the direction it took?

Na-Young thought of Su-Bin's body, wrapped tightly in hemp cloth and bound with rope in his coffin. How many coins had Yeon-Soo stuffed into his mouth? How unbearable it must feel. Or maybe not—maybe his spirit had escaped already, and he was down by the river, bathing naked, laughing at them as they baked in the sun, labouring up a hill to bury a box full of nothing. This would be his revenge on the tiny village that had mocked him his entire brief life.

Stones

Had Oppa not insisted on their presence in the main room within the inner quarters of the big house, Na-Young and her mother would have retreated into their room upon returning from the funeral. Mother's pride kept her away from Second Mother as much as possible, even though it meant she and Na-Young had to live within the servants' quarters.

Why had Oppa asked the family to meet here? Na-Young wondered as she took a seat next to Mother on the red and blue silk cushions on the floor. Second Mother, who, since claiming ladyship of the house, had been unfailingly proper and in command, wilted to a heap in the sticky heat and fell to the floor. Mother gestured for Na-Young to look at Second Mother, whose closed eyelids fluttered like she was fighting a demon in a dream.

"That's the face she hides from the mirror and your father," Mother said under her breath.

Na-Young shifted in her seat and patted on her chima, but her cotton slip had already absorbed all the moisture it could and clung against her flesh.

The large room, with its fancy, floral silk wallpaper, served as both a living and dining room. A large, ornate, tiger-legged dining table, made out of ginkgo wood, sat low to the ground in the middle of the room. Two black-and-white portraits framed in glass, one of Na-Young's father's father and the other of his mother, hung on the east wall. An elegant yet broken folding-screen panel with brush paintings depicting the four seasons rested against the far wall. Painted by a famous Chinese artist, Wu Changshuo, and delivered all the way from Shanghai, it had been an anniversary present from Father to Second Mother. When Mi-Young's health had almost completely deteriorated, Mother had taken a knife and slashed through the first panel, tearing in half Wu's image of spring with its flower blossoms and songbirds. Oppa and Na-Young had watched it happen, too stunned to stop her.

"Our daughter lies dying, and instead of sending for the best doctors, he buys his concubine this!" Mother had cried uncontrollably. They all had. Mother would have destroyed the entire folding panel if Oppa hadn't finally restrained her. Because Mi-Young had died the next day, neither Father nor Second Mother said anything about the damaged gift. It could not be repaired but was considered too precious to throw away, so it continued to rest against the wall in the west where all things, like the sun, went to die.

Second Mother's four boys came rushing in, demanding something to eat. Na-Young thought of Su-Bin. The familiar yet unique pain that came with missing someone caused a sharp ache in her chest. Her thoughts turned to Yeon-Soo. Losing her husband had been like losing part of herself, she had told Na-Young. How in the world was she now that she had truly lost part of herself?

Second Mother cursed Sarwon, one of the house servants, for not having cold barley tea and something to eat ready for her upon their return. "That girl is even lazier than she is stupid," she hissed. "Her brains must have escaped through the gap in her teeth."

When Sarwon arrived, Na-Young watched her, noticing the large sweat stains under her arms and the beads of sweat on her forehead and nose. Sarwon was beautiful and tall, with shiny black hair and a lovely complexion. Her only "flaw" was a big gap between her front teeth, which had earned her the nickname "Gap-Mouth" from Second Mother. Na-Young suspected Second Mother was just jealous of the servant girl, because no amount of imported face powder would make Second Mother match Sar-won's natural beauty.

The youngest of the boys dumped a small sack of stones on the floor. Soon, they were each trying to stack the highest number of stones. Although it was a harmless game, it unnerved Na-Young to watch the stones grow higher, knowing that as soon as the stones toppled, the silence in the room would be interrupted by a cacophony of whining and cheering.

Na-Young couldn't wait until Second Mother's boys reached the age of seven; then, one by one, they would be encouraged to spend more time amongst the men.

Na-Young was grateful that Mother had given birth to Oppa, and that he was strong and wise, fully capable of running the farm when Father passed on. Because the law recognized only the first marriage, her brother was the legitimate heir to the property. Although his heart longed to escape and be a doctor in the city, Na-Young was secretly happy that he needed to stay and watch over Mother and her.

"What do you think will become of Yeon-Soo now?" Na-Young wondered aloud.

"She can still have more children with Jung-Su," said Mother. He was Yeon-Soo's dead husband's younger brother. Although Yeon-Soo had so far avoided this fate, it now seemed inevitable, since she was both childless and husbandless. "Yes, if she married now, she could still bear Su-Bin's family more male heirs and ensure a better status in that household."

Na-Young knew, though, that Yeon-Soo loathed the idea of

marrying her brother-in-law. She claimed he smelled like old ginseng root.

"Yes, but who's to say that the next child would be a healthy one or even a boy? Some women are simply better off being childless," Second Mother said.

Mother's hands, which had been resting on her lap, closed into fists at the hidden barb. They were talking about Yeon-Soo, but it appeared as if Mother took offence at the mention of a healthy child, since Mi-Young had been sick all her life.

A stone flew across the room, followed by another. One landed by Na-Young's feet. She noticed its uneven edges as she picked it up. It was slightly cool to the touch, and she recalled how doctors placed cold stones on Mi-Young's face, chest, and arms to help revitalize her spirit, but also to help relieve her fever. Na-Young popped the stone in her mouth. Perhaps it could help ease her current discomfort. Second Mother yelled at the boys to sit silently facing a wall, punishment for their unruly play. Na-Young grew annoyed wondering where Oppa was. Surely, he wasn't stalling because he had bad news?

Mother patted Na-Young's leg and indicated the door. Na-Young nodded; she was done being in the same room with Second Mother and wanted to go back to her room, even though it would be twice as hot with the kitchen nearby, the spicy smells of pickled cabbage clinging to the walls and ceiling.

The sliding doors opened, and Father and Oppa walked in. The women looked up, surprised. Father rarely came into what was generally considered the living quarters of the women and children. He believed in the strict separation of males and females, so that the men, who lived separate from the women on the estate, spent their days working out in the fields, while the women tended to the housework. Even Oppa had stopped coming into this part of the house now that he was considered a man. Something told Na-Young to worry: Father only came when he had bad news to share. Had the Japanese made more demands?

Second Mother, who had transformed back into her usual composed self, rose and offered Father a cushion. He was dressed in a grey hanbok, the jeogori and pants made of ramie, which was breathable and more comfortable to wear during the muggy summers than the cotton worn by commoners. As always, Father kept a carefully trimmed beard that covered his chin and wore a hat over his topknot.

As Na-Young removed the stone from her mouth, she noticed that his forehead creases had deepened and that the circles under his eyes had darkened.

Second Mother sat back down next to him, fanning both of them with a fancy, flower-decorated paper fan that she told everyone used to belong to a famous geisha. It annoyed Na-Young that Father would allow her to possess something made in Japan, since he complained relentlessly about the Japanese.

Her brother slid the door closed and sat on the floor. Oppa, unlike their father, had had short hair ever since he attended school as a young boy. He sat cross-legged, his spine firmly upright, his eyes cast downward. A lump stuck in Na-Young's throat. Then, to her surprise, Father's eyes alit on her. He had largely ignored her and Mother since his second marriage. She shrunk under his gaze.

He surveyed the room. "I have come because I have news. The timing is poor with the funeral, but one cannot anticipate death and thereby plan life around it."

He stopped when Sarwon entered the room, carrying a large tray of cups and cold tea. No one moved to help her as she poured cup after cup and handed them around to everyone in the room, except for Second Mother's sons, who had since fallen asleep, their bodies sprawled out by the far wall. When she retreated, Na-Young noticed the red welts on the back of Sarwon's ankles, another beating from Second Mother.

Everyone drank their tea in silence as they waited for Father to continue. The heat and the smell of their combined bodies had made the air thick and increasingly unbearable. Mother rocked in her spot impatiently.

"The Park family in Anyang has agreed to a marriage with Na-Young in fourteen days," Father said. "The father is a longtime friend, and the family is highly respected. The boy's name is Min-Ho. The match is a good one."

Na-Young raised her hand to her cheek as if she had been slapped. There had been no talk about marriage, not a hint from Oppa or Mother. She looked over at Mother, then at Oppa, but neither made eye contact. Had they known? Had Father even bothered to consult Mother?

"Well, that hardly gives me much time to plan," Second Mother said, sounding annoyed. "Can't the wedding be postponed? After all, it'll take at least seven days to get the right silks—"

Father cleared his throat. "The arrangement is final," he said, then he nodded to indicate his departure and left without another glance at Na-Young.

That was it? Her whole future decided in one moment? Na-Young felt lightheaded and pressed her hand on the floor to steady herself. An unexpected pain startled her. She looked down at the stone. It hadn't caused any injury, yet her hand throbbed, as did her head.

"This is good news, Na-Young," Second Mother said. "Your father was very kind to make this arrangement on your behalf. Yes, it is a little soon. And as far as I know, he hasn't consulted with any matchmakers. The dear man obviously knows nothing about how to plan a wedding and how this will reflect upon me."

"You?" Mother's voice was full of contempt now that Father was gone. She rose. "Don't you forget, Concubine, she is *my* daughter."

Second Mother remained sitting, a barely suppressed grin on her face. "Yes, of course, but for appearances' sake, you'll want me to take the lead—"

"Yes, we'll need all the help we can get, I'm sure," Oppa interrupted. "Let us not fight over such a joyous occasion."

Na-Young wanted to punch him, disgusted by his attempt to maintain peace between Father's wives. He'd once told Na-Young that it was his way of protecting Mother, but Na-Young thought that standing up for Mother was his duty. Nothing she could do would help, but Oppa was Father's favourite and outranked all of Second Mother's four sons because he was the firstborn.

She couldn't leave home. When would she see Mother again if she got married now? Her mother had seen her own mother just a handful of times in all her years of marriage. The duty of a married woman was to her husband and to her husband's family. Taking time away from them was frowned upon.

Na-Young took Mother's hand in hers. Mother needed her. Na-Young had witnessed her slowly lose the will to do anything. First, she had lost her husband to another woman, then her eldest daughter had died. Now this.

Second Mother called for Sarwon. "Send for a tailor," she said. "I'll need a new hanbok. And get me some more cold tea. I'm dying in this heat."

"Yes," Oppa said, "it's as if the red-hot sun has bullied its way into the very air that we breathe. It makes keeping a cool, level mind almost impossible." He led Mother and Na-Young out of the room.

★

Na-Young held her tears in until she and Mother reached their hut. The room was sparsely furnished with just the two floor mats they slept on, a small chest in which they kept their clothes, and a wooden table, which was still Mother's most prized possession. A wedding present from her parents, it had an oxhorn plate cover depicting images of ducks, tigers, and dragons. As small as the space was, it was theirs. Beyond providing them with some privacy, it was the one place they felt safe and comfortable.

To Mother's disappointment, the boy Father had chosen for Na-Young was only two years her senior, born in the year 1905, making him a Wood Snake. Na-Young's ideal companion would have been a Water Rabbit, a good match for a Fire Goat.

"Wood Snakes are secretive and proud! Goats are prone to depression. That's a bad match. The stars are already against you," Mother insisted. "And in the year of the Rat! That's one of the worst times for the Goat! This is what happens when you take a matchmaker's job into your own hands."

"I don't want to get married. I don't want to leave you." Na-Young's voice faded. Her eyes watered.

"You're a girl. You can't escape marriage." Her mother looked at Na-Young with no sign of sympathy.

"I don't know the boy. I don't even remember his name."

"You must do as your father says."

"But you just said he was wrong."

"It doesn't matter."

She wondered whether Mother still thought about her old room in the main house. She hadn't wanted anything brought from there when they moved. Na-Young's eyes fell on some combs on the table. Next to them was a red lacquer jewellery box etched with the image of two cranes. The only thing in it was a gold necklace with a mother-of-pearl flower pendant—a gift Father had given her on their first anniversary. One of Na-Young's earliest memories was of her mother telling her that cranes symbolized fidelity, because they mated for life.

"I want to marry for love," Na-Young said. She did not really know what this meant, but it had been the reason Yeon-Soo had gotten married. "Can't I at least meet him? What if he looks ugly, like a goblin?"

"How is it possible for you to marry for love? Besides, it's not up to you to decide whom to marry; that's not how marriage works," Mother said through tight lips.

"But don't you want me to be happy? You were once happy, yes?"

"Yes," she said. "But that didn't last. And now I'm rotting away here."

"That's why I can't leave you."

"No, that's precisely why you must marry and leave. The only true lasting love is the bond between a mother and her child. And only a husband can give you a child."

"You have a child—me. And this will separate us."

"Apart and together are companions to each other, like sorrow and joy, empty cup and full cup. We must accept them as partners. We have no choice."

Na-Young had no response. Instead, she closed her hand, the

small stone from earlier in it. The urge to squeeze her fist became so intense that she got up, opened the door, and threw the stone as far as she could.

★

As daylight started to fade, Na-Young left Mother in the hut and went to the stable to talk with Oppa. The stable had become their safe place, the noise of the sheep and oxen helping to camouflage their voices from nosy servants who reported everything back to Second Mother. Privacy was hard to come by with so many people around all the time.

She found Oppa brushing his favourite horse, a gift he had received from Father during the last Lunar New Year.

"How is it that you get a horse when I never get anything?" Na-Young asked. It was a weak attempt at levity but rang true to her.

"You're getting a wedding," he replied. "Don't stand there. Unless you want to be kicked again."

Na-Young flashed him a quick, annoyed look before moving to stand next to the horse's flank. "I don't want a wedding. Why didn't you warn me?"

"I was just told that Father had news to share, nothing more." A beat of silence stretched between them as Oppa continued to brush his horse. "But I suspected that's what he might say," he admitted. "It's sooner than I imagined, but I'm not surprised. At least you'll be escaping from Second Mother's claws and getting out of here." There was a hint of longing in his voice.

"What about Mother?" Na-Young said. "Who will take care of her if I'm not around? You? You're too busy in the fields."

"I'll do what I can. And Sarwon will help, too, of course."

Images of fierce red welts on Sarwon's ankles flashed through her head. She looked helplessly back at Oppa. Second Mother would surely inflict more pain on poor Sarwon if she was left to care for Mother.

"I can't leave her," Na-Young said.

"You have no choice," Oppa said. "Father has spoken."

"So what?"

Oppa swore softly. "Na-Young, it's not like when you were a little girl. You can't go wandering off because you don't like something."

She sighed. How many times had Mother sent Oppa looking for her because she had left home after getting upset or was curious about something? Once, when she was six, she'd gotten as far away as the next village. Old Man Yang had told her that a goat there had given birth to a baby with two heads. Sadly, it had died before she'd gotten there. But she always managed to return home safely on her own. Every bit of news the villagers received was often months old and secondhand, relayed mostly to them by Old Man Yang, who came once a month hauling a large wooden pull-cart full of merchandise, everything from paperback novels to Western-style sandals. Na-Young had known him her entire life, and adored him because he always gave her hard candy even if she never bought anything from him.

"You need to talk to Father. Tell him that now isn't the time," Na-Young pressed.

She had never been able to confront Father. When she'd wanted to go to school, Oppa had tried to convince him, but Oppa's weary eyes when he told her about Father's reaction conveyed that it was hopeless. He had the same look now.

"You're old enough to realize that we don't get to choose our path," Oppa said. Turning back to the stall, he added, "It's easier to ride with the wind against your back than in your face."

"What's that supposed to mean?"

"Don't make things harder if you can't change the outcome. I'm going for a ride."

Na-Young's heart sank. He sounded just like Mother. Oppa was the only person who might have been able to intervene on her behalf, and any hope of delaying her fate fled faster than his horse could run.

Bile rose in her throat. She fought the growing panic threatening to seize her. Eyes closed, she imagined herself walking under the trees' shadows, the fragrance of pink azaleas drifting from the patches of flowers scattered amongst the trees and open meadows. She could hear rushing water from streams and the humming and buzzing of insects, birds, and other animals, along with the rustling of leaves. She was happiest when she was out wandering in the woods or exploring the nearby mountains.

When she opened her eyes, the clouds were catching the last orange-red rays of the setting sun. Her thoughts turned to Yeon-Soo. Her friend's fate was no better than Na-Young's, especially now that her precious son was lost to her forever. They might both be forced to marry men they either despised or did not know. Was this truly the fate of all girls?

Masu Boxes

Mother was braiding Na-Young's hair when Sarwon came rushing in.

"Second Mother has ladies visiting. She wants you to come say hello. She's telling everyone how stressed she is because the wedding is less than fourteen days away."

Leave it to Second Mother! She had a way of inserting herself into any situation by playing the indispensable saviour.

"Who's there?" Mother asked.

"Lady Shim and Lady Cho, and a woman I've never seen before."

"No Lady Ko?" Mother asked.

"The apothecary? No."

It pained Mother that her rival had befriended some of her old friends. Na-Young knew Second Mother was fond of Lady Ko, and the woman's absence seemed to please Mother. "Go pay your respects," she said to Na-Young. "Tell them I'm under the weather and taking a nap."

You just want me to spy for you, Na-Young thought.

The four ladies were sitting on mats around a table in the main room. The tabletop was covered with some of the most beautiful pieces of paper Na-Young had ever seen. They were cut into squares of different sizes.

"My dear friend, Lady Jin, is showing us how to fold paper into boxes!" Second Mother said.

What that had to do with wedding preparations, Na-Young did not know, but she said nothing.

Lady Jin told everyone to choose a piece of paper and to follow along. Na-Young picked a red sheet with black dots.

"We'll start by learning to fold the traditional masu box," Lady Jin said.

Lady Jin folded the corners of her sheet to the centre and unfolded them again.

"Make creases here and unfold. And repeat," she said. She stopped to help Lady Shim, who seemed confused, before continuing with her directions to open the paper and reverse the fold on the other side.

"Where did you learn to make such fancy things out of paper?" Lady Cho asked.

"I spent a year studying in Japan," Lady Jin said. "Paper folding is very popular there. You can make almost anything out of paper. These boxes can store your most precious keepsakes."

What would Father think if he found out that his second wife had befriended someone who not only had studied in Japan but also taught his daughter how to make Japanese boxes?

"Fold the flap down and press here," Lady Jin continued. "And done!" She held up her blue box.

"This is much harder than it looks!" Lady Cho said, creasing her paper into the wrong fold.

"You said this would be fun!" Lady Shim tossed her pink misshaped box onto the table.

"Forgive me for trying to bring some culture into our lives," Second Mother said, and laughed. She held up her perfectly folded box for everyone to admire.

"Why, that's almost as good as Na-Young's!" said Lady Cho.

Na-Young didn't need to see Second Mother's face to know how much such a compliment would bother her. Instead, she smiled and kept her eyes low. The red dotted box was lovely.

"You're a natural!" Lady Jin beamed. "In the West, families don't use wrapping cloths. Instead, they use pretty boxes like these. Why, they're fancy enough to serve food in at a wedding."

"Speaking of weddings," Lady Cho said, "what can you tell us about the groom?"

"It was her father's doing," Second Mother said. "He didn't even consult with a matchmaker. Ladies, you don't know what I'm up against."

"Oh! Speaking of up against," Lady Cho cut in. "You wouldn't believe the state that I found you-know-who in the other day! Without the poor boy, who knows how much longer that headless chicken will live. And then what would Chicken Boy's grandmother have left to boast about?"

Na-Young's jaw dropped as she saw Second Mother suppress a smile. How could they be so cruel? Overcome with grief, she no longer heard their conversation. Her thoughts became flooded with the need to save herself, her friend, and her mother. Suddenly, an idea came to her.

Roots and Bark

Na-Young lay still on her sleeping mat, but she could not sleep. Beside her, Mother began to snore. Instead of her usual one cup, she had drunk several doses of her sleeping potion, a combination of herbs, roots, and bark. Na-Young figured it was her way of saying that she didn't want to talk.

As soon as she thought it was safe, Na-Young crept out of her room. Once she felt the night air on her skin, she began to run towards Yeon-Soo's house. What if someone saw her and demanded to know what she was doing out in the middle of the night? *Plotting a great escape*, she thought as she ran parallel to the dirt road, avoiding it in case someone was out, despite the late hour. Moonlight filtered through the walnut treetops and dimly lit the path.

The air was rich with night sounds, birds echoing, the chirping of crickets coming from all directions. It was then that she heard a giggle—a female voice—in the distance. She froze and pressed herself against a tree. She could hear people approaching. They weren't whispering but spoke normally, as if confident in the darkness, and were walking along the path towards her.

"The Japanese are relentless. They want to quadruple the amount of rice they got last year." It was Oppa. "At this rate, we'll all end up losing our land or becoming tenants. The irrigation costs alone are driving us all under. I'd rather die than end up working for the Japanese." His tone softened. "I wish things were different, and I could marry you now."

"There's no way your father would allow you to marry a servant girl." Na-Young recognized Sarwon's voice and suppressed a gasp. She peeked from behind the tree to see the pair stopped in the middle of the path. The semidarkness wrapped them like a fine silk scarf.

"He can't live forever," Oppa said, facing Sarwon, who was almost as tall as he was. "One day I'll be the master and I will take you as my wife." He took Sarwon's chin in his hand and kissed her.

Na-Young looked away, ashamed of witnessing such intimacy. A ball of envy coiled in her stomach as she imagined their long walks in the dead of night. She wondered about the boy she was supposed to marry. Was he in love with someone else already? Or was he just as stunned and confused as she was? She took a deep breath and took in the night sounds. The starlight encouraged her to rest her head against the tree.

Her eyes opened to a pink-and-orange sky that hinted at early morning. Angry at herself for having fallen asleep, Na-Young quickly made her way towards her friend's house. The whole household would be up soon. She reached the inner courtyard of her friend's estate and tiptoed up the stone steps that led to Yeon-Soo's quarters. Su-Bin used to play with Headless Chicken on this veranda, she recalled. He had once invited her to pet the bird. She could still remember the feel of its feathery body. She'd been half intrigued and half repelled by its grotesque appearance.

A sparrow passed, sweeping above the treetops in the garden. Na-Young gently slid the door open a crack. A soft light glowed from the lantern resting on Yeon-Soo's writing desk.

"It's me," she whispered. "Are you sleeping?"

Yeon-Soo was slouched against the wall. When the lantern's light caught the shiny blade of a letter opener, for a split second Na-Young thought the worst—that her friend had harmed herself—but Yeon-Soo stirred and attempted to sit up.

"What're you doing here?" she said. "Is it morning already?"

"It's just before dawn," Na-Young said, trying to sound calm despite her racing heart. "I have something important to tell you." She struggled to put into words the urgent need for the two of them to run. What if Yeon-Soo refused to leave the one place that housed all her memories of her son and husband? She eyed Su-Bin's slingshot on the floor and lost her breath. His small hands would never touch it again. *I never thanked him*, she thought, *for teaching me to use his favourite toy*. Even though his body jerked often, he aimed with great accuracy. A bang echoed in her mind as she recalled the first time she'd hit a target using his slingshot.

"You did it!" he'd cheered.

"Because you taught me well." She had laughed then, but now, that memory brought waves of pain.

Na-Young moved towards the desk where a small stack of papers was piled next to the letter opener. Unable to find the right words to convey the urgency of her plans to run away, Na-Young pretended to admire the elegant crystal flower design on the handle. "What's all this paper about?" she asked finally.

"I've received offers from people who want to buy Headless Chicken," Yeon-Soo said, picking up the letter opener. In one quick move, she slid the blade through the top crease of an envelope and pulled out a folded piece of paper.

"Another 'condolence' letter. How thoughtful," Yeon-Soo said sarcastically. "Of course it's another offer!"

Na-Young suddenly felt embarrassed, since she, too, had wondered what would become of Su-Bin's pet. Headless Chicken had somehow learned to follow Su-Bin around. Now that she was without a master, how was she coping?

Yeon-Soo rubbed her temples with both hands. "It's all my fault," she said.

Na-Young was about to protest but closed her mouth, attempting to stay calm. She loathed that her friend was prone to blame herself for almost everything, and she knew this tendency only encouraged Yeon-Soo's mother-in-law to mistreat her. Na-Young realized more than ever the need to get away from the village. Yet her friend clearly needed time to grieve. A dull ache was working its way from her shoulders to her back. Although she had slept earlier by the tree, both her mind and body felt fatigued now. She placed an elbow on the table and rested her head in her hand.

An image of a stone flying through the air caught her off guard. Was she dreaming? She liked the state between waking and sleeping, when she was aware enough to control what happened in her dreams before she woke entirely or fell into real sleep. What could a flying stone mean? She imagined herself outdoors, hoping to maintain lucidity by focusing on the slanting rays of early-morning sun and the cool air against her neck and cheeks.

"Why are you here so early?" Yeon-Soo asked, tugging on her arm.

Irritated to be pulled from her dream state, Na-Young kept her head down, hoping to be lulled back to sleep. The sharp, aching spasm in her chest returned. What if she was having a heart attack? Would illness get her out of a marriage? Surely, no man wanted a wife with a weak heart.

"If you're going to sleep, go home." Yeon-Soo sounded annoyed. As she got up, the table jerked when she bumped it. A pungent smell of boiled ginseng roots, dried mushrooms, and animal organs escaped the teapot as its lid tipped over.

Na-Young gagged and snapped out of herself. She blurted, "I'm getting married."

Yeon-Soo sat back down, her face as tight as Na-Young's. When she finally spoke, her voice was gentle. "Why didn't you tell me?"

"Father just made the announcement."

"When's the wedding?"

"Thirteen days."

Yeon-Soo reached out for Na-Young's arm again, but this time, her hand trembled slightly. Nearly faint with relief that someone else was finally acknowledging that the marriage was a mistake, Na-Young burst into tears.

"I don't want to get married," she said. Then, recalling her earlier plans, she said, "Let's run away. Surely you want to leave here, too, with both your husband and Su-Bin gone? We can go wherever you want." The flying stone in her dream stirred her imagination. "We can go deep into the mountains and live off lotus roots, mushrooms, and rabbits. We can climb to the highest point and be as far away as possible. No one would tell us what to do there."

Yeon-Soo stopped her with a gesture of her hand. Then, as if focusing on the light of the lantern, she said nothing as she tapped the teapot with a finger. She pulled a long smoking pipe from under the table. When had she taken up smoking?

"New habit," she said, as if reading Na-Young's mind. She lit it. In silence, they watched smoke fill the space between them. With each passing moment, Na-Young grew more encouraged at the possibilities of her big plan.

A gunshot echoed in the air. Na-Young froze a moment before they both scrambled to their feet. Just as they got through the door, Na-Young caught a blur of movement. Headless Chicken was running in circles, no doubt spooked, despite not being able to hear. Yeon-Soo's brother-in-law, Jung-Su, who was standing just outside their door, shotgun in hand, took aim to shoot at the bird again.

"What are you doing?" Yeon-Soo demanded. She tried to grab the shotgun from him. He pushed her back. Unfazed, Yeon-Soo charged at him. In their struggle, the butt of the gun smashed into his face. Stunned, Jung-Su touched his nose with his fingers, then looked down at the blood on his hand. Na-Young thought he was going to hit Yeon-Soo, but seeing Na-Young standing in the doorway, he seemed to change his mind. "Stupid chicken," he hissed, and spat blood on the ground before storming off.

"Quick, get inside," Yeon-Soo said. She grabbed Headless Chicken and the two dashed back into the room.

"Why was he so angry?" Na-Young asked.

"He's drunk. He's more drunk than sober these days. He's always hated all the attention Headless Chicken got, especially from his mother. Su-Bin's death can only buy me so much time. I suspect my mother-in-law won't support me for much longer. She wants another grandson." Her dark eyes suddenly seemed too large for her thin, pale face. A few drops of Jung-Su's blood that had splattered on Yeon-Soo's hands reflected in the blade of the letter opener.

Outside, the commotion of voices and shuffling feet grew louder. Someone barked orders to go check outside the main gate.

Na-Young worried about what Jung-Su might do next. She cringed. His breath and body reeked of an odour fouler than Yeon-Soo's medicinal tea.

They froze when they heard footsteps outside the door.

"Who's there?" Yeon-Soo said, holding it closed.

A male voice replied, "There was a gunshot. We're checking to make sure everything is okay."

"I'm fine," Yeon-Soo said. "Leave me. I'm getting dressed."

They sat a long while until they were sure the man had left. Soon, the outdoor noise of morning activity, from the shuffling of feet to birds chirping, filled the silence.

Yeon-Soo reached for Na-Young's hand. "Are you sure about running away? You're about to betray your family. Your father—your brother . . ."

Na-Young thought about the men in her life. While she adored Oppa, he was busy living his own life, and was willing to risk their father's wrath by loving the woman of his choice. What if her husband was like her father? A man she could never get to know? A man who only spoke to express orders or to punish anyone who defied him? Or even worse, a man like her brother—in love with someone else and forced to marry her? Did a woman always need a man in order to live her life?

"I'm not worried about them. It's my mother. I don't want to leave her behind," Na-Young said.

Yeon-Soo nodded. "Do you think she'd come with us?"

Na-Young thought for a moment. Given the chance, would Mother leave her husband? It would be cruel, but she would remind Mother that Father had left her first by taking up with Second Mother. "I'll ask," she said.

"Where would we go?"

"The mountains. We can head north, like birds in summer."

"Birds are good omens for peace. When should we leave?"

"As soon as we can—tonight," Na-Young answered. "Although I don't have any money."

"That's not a lot of time to prepare, but luck is on our side. It will be a full moon. Plenty of light to guide us."

"I'll meet you by the river in our usual spot," Na-Young said.

"I'll have to figure out the best way to carry Headless Chicken," Yeon-Soo mused.

Na-Young was about to protest bringing the bird along, but the depth of sadness in her friend's eyes deepened. Instead, she asked, "What about your mother-in-law? Won't she be livid when she finds out that you've stolen her golden bird?" She was worried. The greedy old woman had made so much money over the years by charging people to catch a glimpse of Headless Chicken.

"She's all I have left of Su-Bin."

Na-Young looked over at Headless Chicken as she wandered the room, occasionally bumping into a wall. She showed no signs of slowing down in spite of losing her master, then almost being shot to death. Perhaps having Headless Chicken along wouldn't spell disaster for them after all. Perhaps she would bring them as much luck as she had had so far in life.

Gold and Jade

It was midmorning by the time Na-Young reached home. Mother was still sleeping so she lay next to her, playing out different escape scenarios in her mind until she fell asleep. She woke up to see Mother lying on her back, looking up at the ceiling. A ray of sun shone through the open window.

Na-Young sat up and crossed her legs. "What are you thinking?" she asked.

Mother continued to stare at nothing. "That even thinking about the weather has become too much of a burden for me now," she said finally.

"Please try to get up."

Mother put an elbow on the mat and slowly pushed herself up, struggling until she was sitting. Na-Young looked at her frail body. Her once smooth, white skin was now the same colour as the fading paper on the walls of their room. Thin blue blood vessels were visible on her neck, chest, and hands.

"Let me comb your hair," Na-Young said.

She took her time, gently working through the knots before fastening Mother's hair with a band, careful to prevent any loose strands from spilling over her face. After she helped her mother change into fresh clothes, Na-Young turned to her and explained the plan to leave.

"Crazy talk!" Mother's thin eyebrows, which rested in straight lines across her forehead, arched upwards. "Where would we go?"

"Anywhere we'd want to." Na-Young tried to keep her voice light.

"Crazy talk," she repeated, tapping the comb on the floor. "How far do you think two foolish girls will get running away? You know nothing about the world. With both your luck, you'll end up dead somewhere."

"You should come with us," Na-Young said. "There's nothing for you here. I'm sure Second Mother will do a great job of stealing your spotlight at my funeral, too." As soon as the words came out, Na-Young knew that she'd crossed a line. But rather than angry, Mother seemed lost in thought.

Then she said, "I have a cousin, Mi-Ra, who got out of her engagement by staying at a temple. It wasn't her intention to become a monk but that's what happened. My aunt was livid because she believed it was every woman's duty to marry and have children, but I was secretly pleased to see my cousin defy her mother and do what she wanted. Maybe not every woman is meant to marry."

"You've never said anything about this cousin before," Na-Young said, surprised.

"Both my mother and aunt forbade us from ever mentioning Mi-Ra's name again after the shame they believed the broken engagement brought to the family," she explained. "I suppose you two could head to Pyeongchang and stay with her. She's at Woljeongsa, a highly revered Buddhist temple. Maybe seek her advice. For all we know, she may send you back and tell you to get married."

Na-Young stared at her mother as she walked over to the chest and removed something, wondering at her change in heart. She'd have never expected Mother to cross Father.

"Take this," she said, placing a gold-and-jade lotus-blossom brooch in Na-Young's hand. "It's a gift Mi-Ra gave me when I was a child. She'll surely remember it. Jade is a living stone. It will protect you on your journey." She closed Na-Young's hand over the brooch. Then her eyes seemed to gaze beyond her daughter, to some distant, faraway place.

"Mi-Ra is a wise woman. It's her job to help others."

Na-Young searched deep into her mother's eyes, looking for any trace of other secrets they might hold.

"But what about you?" Na-Young couldn't stay, but she didn't want to leave her mother behind. "You won't come with us?"

"I have your brother. And in spite of what you see, this is still my home. I am, after all, the first wife, the only legal wife."

"And Father?"

"What can he do to me? I've already lost one daughter. There was nothing I could do to help her; at least I can try to help you."

Na-Young nodded her head, because she didn't know what else to do. The afternoon heat seemed to grow thicker, and she wiped beads of sweat from her forehead.

Mother patted her back. "We'll get Sarwon to help us prepare for your journey. You'll need food and money." She stopped. "But we cannot tell your brother. He would not understand. Promise me—I know you two are close, but his loyalties will always remain with his father."

"What about Sarwon?" Should she tell Mother that Oppa and Sarwon were in love? If Mother told Sarwon, she might tell Oppa, who might, in turn, tell Father.

"She's the only one who has stayed loyal to you and me in this household. I can't imagine her betraying us," Mother said.

The door slid open. "Lunch." Sarwon entered carrying a small tray of food.

"Good timing," Mother said. "Come in. We have something to tell you."

The unexpected excitement in Mother's voice filled Na-Young with unease. What would Father do once he found out she was gone? Mother had said that there was nothing he could do to her, yet who knew what he was capable of? A broken engagement would bring Father great grief, shame, and humiliation, not just with the Park family, but with everyone they knew.

"What we're about to tell you is a secret," Mother said.

"It can never get back to Oppa or Father, especially Father," Na-Young said. How could she stress this point? Suddenly, she desperately needed the outhouse and excused herself.

A faint colour of red had spread over Sarwon's face when Na-Young got back. Why was Sarwon blushing? She looked tense, almost afraid. What had she and Mother discussed?

"They're leaving tonight, so you'll have to get everything ready as soon as you possibly can," Mother said to Sarwon. "The gods will understand, don't worry." Mother dismissed her, and she left the room.

"Why do the gods need to understand?" Na-Young wondered aloud.

"Nothing for you to worry about. Eat your lunch and rest up."

Na-Young said nothing in a vain attempt to appear calm. She was getting what she wanted. Why was she so overcome with panic instead of relief?

Na-Young waited for Yeon-Soo by the river. She had just said goodbye to Mother and her heart ached. She thumbed the gold-and-jade lotus-blossom brooch that was pinned inside the knot of her jeogori ribbon.

"Better to hide it and be safe," Mother had said. "This isn't like running off to the closest village over the mountain."

"Yes, of course," Na-Young reassured her. "I wish we were going to the mountains! They're the best places to rejuvenate a person's soul."

"With your spirit of adventure, you should have been born a boy. Pyeongchang is a good choice. My cousin will keep you safe."

Na-Young had said nothing in response because she didn't want their goodbye to end in an argument. Mother's last words were "Don't leave Yeon-Soo's side. No matter what."

Na-Young promised. She patted the side of her chima and felt for the small pouch, stuffed with money, that Mother had sewn into her undergarment. She still didn't know where the money had come from, but the way Sarwon looked absently at her, the lack of her usual gap-toothed smile, told her not to press on. A pain somewhere deep in her throat made it hard to swallow now at the realization that she would probably never see her mother again. Her skin felt hot, as if the night air were just as scorched as day.

Out of the corner of her eye, she spotted someone approaching. When she heard Yeon-Soo's voice, relief coursed through her.

"Ready?"

"Ready," Na-Young said.

Yeon-Soo carried Headless Chicken in a sling, much like one would carry a baby. The bird seemed content enough and didn't put up any fuss. They began to walk. They both had walking sticks and carried bundles filled with food, water, clothing, and blankets. The road was bumpy. Little pebbles poked into Na-Young's light wooden sandals as they made their way along the dirt path.

The eastern mountains that bordered Daegeori became shadows that blended into a larger darkness under the moon's glow, the light that ruled the night. Stars, some brighter than others, overlapped like wildflowers in an open meadow. Small nocturnal animals were everywhere: in tree branches, shrubs, and grass, their movements heard but not seen, like the flow of streams and waterfalls that Na-Young and Yeon-Soo passed as the night grew long.

Sweet Yellow Melon

For three days, they walked through open forests and around mountains rising upon one another. They rarely spoke. Yeon-Soo said it was more important that they listened to the sounds around them than to their voices. So Na-Young listened intently—the sounds of a river faint in the background, the rustle of leaves when squirrels and other small animals passed. Na-Young picked up on the scent of wildflowers, trees, and dry earth. Taking in deep breaths of fresh air, she felt cleansed somehow, despite a lingering fear in the back of her mind. At the rate they were moving, it would take a month to get to Pyeongchang and Cousin Mi-Ra. Na-Young couldn't shake the feeling that Father and a search party were closing in on them. The image of Father's stern face remained in her head.

Sometimes, the trail led them into densely wooded areas. The air was always cooler there; the fear of discovery was diminished, but lingering. The strong earthy smell was pleasant, but because it was difficult to let Headless Chicken loose to run around during their many breaks, they rarely stayed long. After hours in the sling, Headless Chicken seemed happiest when she was let loose to dust-bathe and forage, and that was best done in open spaces.

The paths were sometimes steep and winding. In some areas, they seemed hardly used anymore; they were nearly overgrown with trees and shrubs, so they had to walk single file. Once, when it poured rain, they hid under a tree until the rain turned to a sprinkle. Na-Young passed the time thinking about Mother, wondering what she was doing.

To her surprise, sadness overcame her when she thought about Oppa. She imagined him waking with the sun in the morning, knowing that his only living sister was gone. Did he ever think about Mi-Young? She had been four years his senior, and Oppa had spent more of his childhood with her than he had with Na-Young. And while Na-Young had caused him much grief by getting into all sorts of mischief, Mi-Young, like him, had been sensible. Poor Oppa! She thought back to all the times he had come looking for her. Rather than angry, he'd looked relieved when he'd found her in the neighbouring village and the nearby bamboo forest. He'd even hugged her after he got her out of a deep well. He had laughed when she told him afterwards that she had fallen while trying to catch a frog. Her sorrow at leaving him was magnified by shame. Maybe he was right after all. She wasn't a child anymore. Focusing on this, she summoned all the courage she could. She would stay strong. But then, she wondered whether Sarwon had told Oppa about her plans. How would he have reacted? Would he tell Father? Had Second Mother spotted her absence yet? It was a relief not to know.

Na-Young trusted Yeon-Soo to lead the way, compass in hand, and didn't question her sense of direction as they followed the banks of rivers and small paths, always moving east. Na-Young enjoyed sleeping outdoors and was comfortable falling asleep under the great black shapes that the trees cast, shadows that moved ever so slightly with the wind. The moon, white like the inside of a sweet yellow melon, was their constant companion, and it gave her comfort. Occasionally, the odd animal would poke its head out, startling Na-Young, but Yeon-Soo, who was a light sleeper, always managed to shoo it away. Na-Young was grateful for her bamboo hat, which she used to cover her face from mosquitoes during the night.

They stopped occasionally to collect food and water. Yeon-Soo was particularly adept at spotting edible mushrooms, plants, and roots that grew in the crevices of overlapping rocks. They ate what they could and packed the rest into their containers and handkerchiefs. They were fortunate that the mountains had so many springs gushing up from the rocks that they never worried about refilling their water tins. Yeon-Soo's search for food and water as they walked seemed to calm her sorrow and give her a reason to venture on.

They avoided the main road and instead walked along the little-used side roads that hugged the mountains. Yeon-Soo didn't speak much, and Na-Young stayed clear of any unnecessary talk out of respect for her. Despite Yeon-Soo's slow and steady breathing, Na-Young could not fathom the pain she must be feeling at the loss of her only child.

The bamboo hat that Na-Young was wearing kept sliding to one side, which annoyed her, but it was still better wearing it on her head than carrying it.

"How far do you think we've walked?" Na-Young asked.

"Hard to say."

"Sorry to say, but we'd be farther along if you hadn't brought Headless Chicken."

Yeon-Soo didn't reply. She was careful to keep Headless Chicken out of direct sunlight as much as possible, explaining that, like dogs and cats, chickens were sensitive to heat and cold. Although Na-Young did very little to care for Headless Chicken, it was exhausting her to watch Yeon-Soo manage the bulky sling that forced her to be cautious with every move. They even ended up napping in the afternoons because Yeon-Soo had trouble sleeping. She was worried that the chicken could easily fall prey to nighttime predators, including wild birds, and kept her close at night by tying a piece of string to one leg. Na-Young feared she would continue to slow them down.

Whenever her thoughts turned to home, a wave of apprehension accelerated her heartbeat. How was Mother managing without her? Would Oppa set out to look for her? Would he tell Father? What would they do to her after she was found?

When she shared her concerns, Yeon-Soo rested her hand on Na-Young's shoulder. "At least there's no Second Mother to tell us what to do." She pushed a loose strand of hair off Na-Young's forehead.

Na-Young smiled, grateful for her friend.

After walking for most of the day, they arrived at the base of a small bridge and decided to rest under a nearby tree. Yeon-Soo passed Na-Young some dried dates and dried seaweed. Na-Young ate in silence, studying their surroundings. She noticed a wet white shirt on some rocks by the bridge. Someone must have been doing laundry earlier in the river.

Next to her, Yeon-Soo began feeding Headless Chicken. Using a hollow reed, she gave the bird some water, then a bit of the grain mix of millet and corn she'd packed for the bird. When Headless Chicken had her fill, she strutted around, and Yeon-Soo lit a cigarette.

The day was hot and quiet, and they both had nearly nodded off when they heard footsteps behind them. To Na-Young's surprise, Yeon-Soo whipped out her letter opener. Why had she not brought along a weapon of her own? She chastised herself for being ill-prepared.

A young girl walked out from the trees. She looked just as surprised to see them.

"Don't be afraid," Yeon-Soo said, hiding the letter opener back in her sleeve. "We're just two weary travellers, stopping for a quick rest."

The girl's face relaxed. She smiled, revealing as many missing teeth as Su-Bin had had. "We don't see many travellers around here," she said. She walked over to the wet shirt. Just as she was about to pick it up, Headless Chicken, who had been quiet till then, stretched her wings and began to strut about. The little girl turned quickly to see what caused the noise, but she slipped and fell, bumping her head hard on the wooden bridge.

Yeon-Soo and Na-Young ran to help her up.

"Do you live around here?" Yeon-Soo asked, examining the girl's head.

"Yes," the girl answered between sobs, "just beyond the trees over there."

Her lack of any panic suggested that she hadn't seen Headless Chicken, much to Na-Young's relief. But then Yeon-Soo slipped off the sling she was wearing, passed it to Na-Young, and scooped the child in her arms.

"What're you doing?" Na-Young demanded. "We should keep moving before anyone else sees us."

"We can't leave her like this," Yeon-Soo said. She gestured for Na-Young to gather Headless Chicken. Na-Young stood for a moment in amazement. What if this misfortune were to lead to their own? But Yeon-Soo was already walking. Na-Young secured the bird in the sling and ran to catch up.

Soon, they arrived at a small thatched hut set in the middle of a pine grove, several metres from the dirt path. A woman came rushing out. "What happened?" she asked.

The girl, who had stopped crying, burst into fresh tears upon seeing her mother.

"She was hurt. Now that she's home, we'll be on our way."

The woman looked over her daughter's injuries and, after determining that she was all right, turned back to them.

"Thank you for helping my daughter," she said. "We don't often get visitors." Her eyes looked grey-brown in the sun. Her hanbok was patched together with mismatched, once-white fabric, now the colour of dirt and dust. "May I offer you something to eat to thank you? Please come in."

Na-Young shook her head, but her friend accepted the invitation. Unlike Yeon-Soo, who seemed calm, she wanted to get back on the road. They were still only a few days from home, and the fear of someone coming after them kept her nerves on edge.

Inside, the smell of yams roasting made Na-Young's stomach growl. They sat around a wooden table in the middle of the one-room home. The woman poured water from a cracked clay jug and took a seat across from Na-Young. A fire crackled in the fireplace that served as the stove. Na-Young caught a glimpse of the yams hanging over the fire and her stomach grumbled again. She patted the sling she was wearing, hoping to keep the bird calm long enough for them to eat.

"I can't remember the last time we had anyone with us," the woman said, and apologized for the meager dinner she wanted to prepare for them.

"Nonsense," Yeon-Soo insisted. "We are very thankful for a warm meal." Then, seeing Na-Young with the sling over her shoulder, she said, "We don't mean to startle you, but we have with us a most unusual pet."

"What is it?" the girl asked, her eyes large with curiosity. She was sitting on the floor, little handmade rag dolls scattered around her.

"Don't be scared," Yeon-Soo said. "She used to be my son's favourite pet. She's had an unfortunate accident, however."

Na-Young lowered the sling to show them Headless Chicken. Both the girl and her mother leaped back.

"It's harmless!" Na-Young said, and released Headless Chicken onto the floor. The chicken started moving about.

"She's quite gentle," Yeon-Soo explained patiently. "You just need to handle her carefully—she poops a lot."

The little girl laughed and squatted on the floor to watch Headless Chicken. "She moves like a normal chicken," she said, still smiling.

"She loves to be held," Yeon-Soo said.

Soon, Headless Chicken was sitting on the girl's lap. "Where are you two going?" she asked.

The woman gestured for her daughter to hush.

"It's quite all right," Yeon-Soo said, and explained that they were on their way to visit their mother, a three-night journey away. "Our husbands are both away on business, so we thought it was a good time."

When had she come up with this story? Na-Young realized it was probably wise to protect their identities—just in case anyone from home came looking for them.

"It's good your husbands let you visit your mother," the woman said. She got up, added another log to the fire, and poked at it with a stick. The crackling snaps of the fire and the warmth it radiated made the small room feel hotter.

The woman told them about her husband, who had gone to a nearby town looking for work and had not returned in over a month. "Yes, it's good to have a companion for your journey," she said. "I wish my husband had a friend. One can get lost so easily out there." Her voice was pleasant, and she spoke without hesitation about how poorly the roads were marked and how bears and wolves were known to roam the area from time to time.

Yeon-Soo folded her hands on the table. She looked over at Headless Chicken and was quiet, as if she was letting what the woman was telling them sink in. Na-Young brushed a finger lightly against the edge of the table. It had been crudely made but sanded down, so that it was smooth and even soft to the touch. The promise of a cooked meal helped relax her.

Just then a little boy entered the hut, carrying a limp animal in his hand, and Na-Young heard Yeon-Soo gasp beside her. She saw why. This boy bore a striking resemblance to Su-Bin. They were the same height and their eyes were the same walnut shape, with eyebrows half hidden by long hair. A deep gloom seemed to settle on Yeon-Soo as she stared at the boy.

"What did you catch?" the woman asked.

"A hare," he said, raising his arm to show off the animal. Its head had already been chopped off.

At the sound of his young voice, Yeon-Soo let out a sob, and the woman turned.

"Forgive us," Na-Young explained in a quiet voice. "My sister's son died just last week."

The woman covered her mouth and bowed her head in respect, then grabbed the dead animal.

"Go play outside," she said to both her children. "Until dinner is ready."

"Can we take Headless Chicken with us?" the girl asked. The bird leaped off her lap and kicked the rag dolls around them. The little boy stood wide-eyed.

"She's harmless," Na-Young reassured him. He didn't look

convinced, but the woman nudged her son out the door after his sister.

Turning back to them, the woman asked whether perhaps Yeon-Soo wanted to lie down for a while. She eyed a mat in the corner.

As Yeon-Soo rested, Na-Young watched the woman place the decapitated hare on a cutting board that rested on a stand by the open fire. She made an incision in the animal's stomach and pulled out the bloody guts and entrails. A foul stench filled the air. The blaze of orange fire crackled behind her. She chopped off the feet with two quick blows. Na-Young looked away and wondered where the head was. Whether its eyes were opened or closed. She shuddered. Neither she nor her mother had ever prepared a meal. The task was left to the servant girls who worked in the kitchen.

"Your mother will be happy to see you again," the woman said. "Though she'll be devastated to hear about her grandson." She shook the mess from her hands and wiped them on her apron.

"Yes," Na-Young said absentmindedly. "I miss my mother."

"A good meal might be what you need." She smiled. "Is your mother a very good cook?"

Na-Young nodded yes, although she didn't know the answer.

"Yes, of course," the woman continued. "Perhaps your mother will prepare a feast for you and your sister to welcome you back."

Na-Young wanted to tell this poor woman the truth about what had happened to her mother—that she had once been as beautiful as a queen, but had gradually lost everything after her husband took another wife. Now she was tucked away in a lost corner of her own home, much like this woman, whose house was lost in the middle of nowhere. How had she and her children ended up living in such a remote place? Had she perhaps married for love?

Was this where following love had gotten her? Na-Young looked around. The hut was only slightly larger than the servant's room that she and Mother shared. Under the strong aroma of the roasting yams, it smelled of stale earth, raw animal meat, and rotting straw. One corner of the thatched roof, which had turned a greyish white, was decaying. Still, the woman and children seemed content enough.

"Perhaps you should spend the night," the woman offered. "My husband is away and your sister is quite upset." Then, lowering her voice, she said, "There's been talk about Japanese kidnappers roaming south of us and their military police attacking our people for the smallest infractions. I haven't seen any of them, and I doubt they'll be around here—this place is so remote, even the gods don't know to look for anything living here." There was a hint of anxiety and fear in her eyes.

Na-Young nodded, grateful for the woman's generosity. She was also too tired to summon the strength to think of venturing outdoors with Yeon-Soo in her present state.

Yeon-Soo continued to cry softly into the night. Headless Chicken, though, slept soundly.

"Will she ever stop?" the little boy asked.

Na-Young wanted desperately to offer some words of comfort. Her mother had once advised her not to say anything to a grieving person, because what we said often merely served our needs to quiet the uncomfortable situation. In spite of the hard, earthen floor and the bugs Na-Young kept shooing away, she, too, fell into a deep sleep.

In the morning, Yeon-Soo took a few coins out of her purse to pay their hostess for her hospitality.

"Nonsense," the woman said, and made a dismissive motion

with her hand. "If you run into a man who calls himself Yoon Chun-Heh, tell him not to come home until he has earned enough money to purchase at least three bags of salt." She handed them food wrapped in old handkerchiefs and made sure that they had refilled their water tins.

"Is that your husband?" Na-Young asked.

"Yes." She did not smile, so Na-Young wasn't sure whether she was joking or being serious.

The children bowed to them and petted Headless Chicken.

"Do be safe," the woman said. She laid a hand over Yeon-Soo's and offered a final smile.

Lucky

At one point, the path split. Yeon-Soo turned her head to speak over her shoulder. "Let's rest here," she said. They moved away from the road and settled under some trees. Na-Young dropped her bundles and kicked off her sandals. Her feet had become swollen and badly blistered. Na-Young massaged them gingerly before sprawling on the ground. She was ready to take a nap. When she peeked out from under her bamboo hat, she saw Yeon-Soo smoking a cigarette. She looked older, the wrinkles around her eyes more noticeable.

"My world is slowly disappearing," Yeon-Soo said. She was gazing up at the sky. She was always on the lookout for any changes in the clouds and winds that might indicate rain. Earlier in the morning, the sky looked threatening, with a low patchy fog hanging over the treetops.

"What are you talking about?" Na-Young asked.

Done with her cigarette, she pulled out the letter opener from her sleeve, peeled off the cloth around it, and used it to look at herself in the blade.

"I've lost my husband, my child, my home, and my youth."

"You've got Headless Chicken," Na-Young said. She gestured for the letter opener, and Yeon-Soo passed it to her.

Na-Young looked at herself and, noticing no obvious changes, took a moment to study the blade. It was sharper than she expected.

"Chickens do make ideal companions. They're friendly by

nature, enjoy company, and have their own unique ways. Unlike people, they expect nothing in return except to be treated respectfully. Perhaps we should give her a different name?" Yeon-Soo wondered aloud. There was a hint of sadness in her voice.

Na-Young had always wondered why Su-Bin had continued to call her Headless Chicken instead of giving her a proper name.

"Yes," Yeon-Soo said, answering her own question. "What's a good name?"

"Lucky?"

"Too common."

"How about Dragon King?"

They both burst into laughter at the absurdity of the name.

"The Dragon King lived at the bottom of the ocean and was a hypochondriac!" Yeon-Soo said.

"But he had magical powers and ruled over a kingdom!"

"I suppose," Yeon-Soo conceded. Her laughter released some of the sadness trapped in her eyes. Na-Young, buoyant from seeing her friend's spirit rise, offered to carry the bird and led the way.

Later that afternoon, during the time between sunset and dusk, when the sun started to lose its sharp edge, they came around a small hill and heard male voices. Instinctively, Yeon-Soo and Na-Young stopped. In a clearing about sixty metres away was a group of men around a fire. Yeon-Soo put a finger to her lips and gestured for Na-Young to follow. As quietly as possible, they left the road to hide behind the closest trees. The air buzzed with mosquitoes and beads of sweat dropped from Na-Young's forehead, but she dared not move or even breathe too deeply.

Three Japanese military policemen lounged around a campfire. Two more came up the road, dragging a blindfolded man dressed in rags. It was hard to tell what he looked like or how old he was. Na-Young only knew by his white clothes that he must be Korean. The smallest military policeman issued what sounded like an order, and the two others dropped the man. The Korean man stretched two trembling hands outwards, as if searching for something to hold on to. Another military policeman, who had been crouched by the fire, grabbed several rags that he used to remove what looked like a long metal bar that had been resting in the fire's embers. The small military policeman shouted a command, and the blindfold was removed. The Korean man, seeing the metal bar, started to plead, his arms and hands flailing like the flames of the fire. "No, please!" he shouted in Korean. "Please just let me go. Take all my money! I won't tell anyone!" Two military policemen rushed to hold him down.

Na-Young's stomach dropped. What could this poor man have possibly done to deserve what was about to happen? His cries pierced the air as the small military policeman came towards him with the hot bar and pressed it to the man's chest. His body convulsed in pain as he collapsed, screaming, to his knees. His raised arms pleaded for mercy. Na-Young looked away.

When Headless Chicken started fidgeting in her sling, Na-Young passed her back to Yeon-Soo, who stroked the bird to calm her.

"We need to keep moving," Yeon-Soo whispered. "But we'll stay off the road."

As Na-Young turned to look back, she noticed her bamboo hat sitting in the middle of the road. What if the military policemen saw the hat? Would they start searching around? Yeon-Soo had already gone ahead. The Japanese men seemed preoccupied with the man, who still jerked and cried in pain. Na-Young hesitated, wondering what to do. They had come so far already. They couldn't risk being discovered. She crept onto the road but stumbled. The water tin clanked as it bumped against something in one of her bundles before falling to the ground.

A hand grabbed hers. It was Yeon-Soo. "Stupid girl!" she said in a loud whisper, dragging her friend off the path.

Up until now, she had never even seen a Japanese person, let alone spoken to one. She'd only known to fear them like one would an angry ghost. Out of the corner of her eye, Na-Young caught a glimpse of the small military policeman turning towards them, and she and Yeon-Soo started running, but Yeon-Soo, with her bundles and Headless Chicken, was carrying too much to move quickly.

"Hide behind that tree!" Na-Young told her, hearing the footfalls behind them. She headed in the opposite direction, hoping they would follow her instead.

She didn't get far. A heavy weight fell upon her, causing her legs to jerk and collapse beneath her. A military policeman twisted her wrists behind her back. She craned her neck to see whether Yeon-Soo had gotten away, but she couldn't tell. Na-Young kicked and flailed, barely able to breathe, until something hit her on the back of the head.

When she opened her eyes again, a blur of flickering oranges and reds slowly turned into a campfire in front of her. When she tried to lift her head and turn away from the oppressive heat, she moaned in pain. The air was thick with heat and smoke from the fire. Several empty liquor bottles littered the ground, and the stench of burned flesh hung in the air. It was then that she saw two military policemen holding Yeon-Soo by her arms, trying to keep her from running. She bit one of them, causing him to let go, and for a moment, Na-Young thought she might get away. But then another military policeman intercepted her, raising his rifle and striking her on the head.

Na-Young wanted to run to her but discovered that her hands were tied behind her. The short military policeman, the one Na-Young had thought was in charge, started yelling at the one who had hit Yeon-Soo. He picked Yeon-Soo off the ground and carried her towards the fire. In all the commotion, no one but Na-Young noticed the letter opener slipping out of Yeon-Soo's pocket and disappearing into the long blades of grass only a few metres away.

A military policeman dropped Yeon-Soo on the ground by the fire. Na-Young's eyes burned. She shut them, and wondered whether she was dreaming. Had the past few days finally caught up with her? Had her fears and feelings of homesickness that she had bottled up collected into this one horrific dream? She'd had bad dreams before, like the ones she had leading up to Yeon-Soo's son's death, when she had dreamt of dead chickens falling from the sky.

But Na-Young wasn't asleep. Someone was asking whether she was all right. It was the Korean man. He was lying on the ground, on the other side of her. His chest, where he had been burned with the bar, was red and bloody. She noticed that his hands had since been bound behind his back.

"Don't do anything to provoke them," he said.

She peeked at the small, older military policeman shouting words to his subordinates. Yeon-Soo stirred. What could the military policemen possibly want with her and Yeon-Soo? She thought back to what the woman in the little hut had told them about the Japanese punishing people for the smallest infractions. Her sense of doom deepened.

"What's going to happen to us?" she whispered to the man.

"I don't know about you girls, but I know they'll take me with them. Please, if you get away, you must get word to my wife. She lives down this road, off a wooden bridge, in a pine grove. There's money for her, in a sack that I dropped when they grabbed me. Not far from here." He nodded towards the road he had come down.

Na-Young gasped. This must be the woman's husband who had left his family in search of work! "What's your name?" she asked.

Two military policemen walked towards them and seized the man.

"Yoon Chun-Heh!" he shouted, as the military policemen dragged him away. "My wife has no idea that I've joined a resistance movement. Tell her I'm doing this for our country. For our children."

Your children, Na-Young thought. *Your beautiful children who showed nothing but kindness to a headless chicken.* Smoke and tears stung her eyes. Anti-occupation groups existed, but she knew very little about them or what they did. She had once overheard Oppa and a friend engaged in a heated argument about working for the independence movement. The friend had insisted that the resistance needed people like Oppa: strong, intelligent, and able to speak and write in Japanese to help organize an underground newspaper. Good thing you learned Japanese in school, she had joked when she asked Oppa about it. He demanded to know how much of the conversation she had heard. She pleaded ignorance but he knew better and was upset. He made her promise never to mention it again.

Na-Young wanted to shout some reassurance to the man as they yanked him away, but she was too afraid to say anything. Even the sound of Korean could set them off.

Three military policemen remained behind. Two of them were so young that they looked like boys playing dress-up rather than actual military policemen. One of them had faded bruises on one side of his face, and his lips were chapped and bleeding. Had he fallen? He couldn't be more than five or six years older than Su-Bin, Na-Young thought, and just as clumsy. Or perhaps someone had beaten him. The small military policeman lit a cigarette and started towards some rocks on the other side of the fire. He had a jerky walk, a limp of sorts. He caught her staring and spat on the ground. Once seated, he poked at the empty bottles before grabbing one. He made a brusque gesture to the young military policemen, motioning them to get closer to the girls before raising the bottle to them.

He shouted something and took a swig.

One of the young military policemen fell upon Na-Young, his sudden weight forcing a moan to escape her lips. Despite her efforts, she found it impossible to turn over. For a split second, she caught the older man's eyes. He turned away, spat again on the ground, then kicked at the dirt. Na-Young sank into the ground, her chest crushed as she struggled to breathe. Desperately, she tried to free herself, but the boy was much stronger than she could have imagined. She cursed loudly, realizing what was about to happen. The heat and smoke stung her eyes, despite her shutting them tightly. What a fool she had been. Every decision, big and small, had been the wrong one; and her biggest regret was that she had asked Yeon-Soo to run away with her. Mother and Oppa would have been so ashamed had they known that she had risked not only her life but that of her best friend, trying to retrieve an old battered hat. And now they were about to die at the hands of the Japanese. The Japanese! She couldn't believe her fate.

Suddenly, the weight was gone and her hands freed. Na-Young was flipped over onto her back and she came face-to-face with the small, older man, his stare so intense, she felt he was looking through her rather than at her. Her body was rigid as he traced her face with a finger. The sweat on his forehead threatened to fall on her. But she finally found her voice.

"Please," she begged. "Let me go." Even though he likely didn't understand Korean, she repeated herself, hoping that the desperation in her voice would deliver the message.

As if the pleading had awakened him from whatever trance he was in, his eyes filled with fury. He rose. With one foot, he rolled her over so that she was eyeing the unbearable fire again. She sank back into the dirt as someone—she could no longer tell who—fell on top of her. Fingers dug into her hips. A sudden thrust of weight forced her to gasp for air. Another thrust sent searing pain between her legs and into her chest. A voice moaned uncontrollably in her ears, and pools of sweat felt like hot rain against her neck and shoulders.

Then suddenly, crying voices and shouts of panic filled the air. All three men were suddenly standing, a look of shock on their faces.

"If you destroy it, you'll suffer its wrath for three generations!" Yeon-Soo's voice boomed with authority. Na-Young turned to see her sitting up, her top torn open, exposing her breasts, her red hair matted with dirt and blood. Then, straining to see what everyone was looking at, she spotted Headless Chicken making her way towards them. When she spread her wings, she revealed an impressive wingspan, but without a head, she looked demonic.

The smaller military policeman yelled a command, but both younger men, horror-stricken, did not move. He limped back quickly to the rock where his rifle rested. Yeon-Soo frantically searched through her clothes. The letter opener!

"It's over here!" Na-Young whispered loudly and they both scrambled to retrieve it. The small military policeman raised his rifle and fired, barely missing Headless Chicken. The air around the bird seemed to surge as Headless Chicken flapped her wings and charged onward.

The smaller military policeman fired again, this time hitting Headless Chicken. He lowered his rifle slowly and grinned. Yeon-Soo leaped at him. Suddenly he dropped to his knees, his hand clutching at the handle of the letter opener, which had been plunged deep into his neck. He gasped for air, his breathing ragged and wheezing. Yeon-Soo kicked him hard and he fell back into the fire. The two young men stood paralyzed, watching their burning comrade twist and jerk in the fire as the stench of burning flesh overwhelmed their senses. Then, to Na-Young's amazement, Headless Chicken leaped up, the sun catching the brown and yellow plumes of her wingspan as she raced towards the commotion by the fire. Horrified, the young Japanese men turned and fled up the road where their comrades had gone with Yoon Chun-Heh earlier.

Yeon-Soo scooped Headless Chicken into her chima. They ran back towards the path they had come from. When they got to the same place where they had rested before, they stopped. A thick grove of trees stood on one side of the path, and large rocks and boulders on the other side.

"We'll hide there," Yeon-Soo whispered, pointing at the rocks.

They crawled painfully on their hands and knees, keeping low as they made their way farther and farther away from the path. In the darkness, they heard only the usual sounds of night animals. Na-Young's heart had stopped racing, but her body ached everywhere. Frightened and confused, she wondered whether perhaps she might wake up at any moment to discover everything had been a nightmare.

Pale Moon

When Na-Young woke up early the next morning, the aching pain everywhere in her body was the only thing that let her know she was still alive. A pale moon hid behind grey clouds, and all around her the darkness of night was beginning to lift. She imagined a series of low mountains, worn with time, in the not-so-far distance. And beyond that, home. A thin layer of dew rested against her flesh and on the leaves around her. She drew a leaf to her lips and drank from it. But where was Yeon-Soo? She looked up to see her friend approaching.

"There's a river nearby," Yeon-Soo said. "Let's go wash up." As she extended a hand to help her up, she appeared to notice something and pointed towards the sky. "Did you see that?"

Na-Young gasped in wonder at an enormous spiderweb that hung high in the branches between two trees. Silver-coloured, it was beautiful, with intricate silky spiral patterns. She squinted to see whether she could get a glimpse of the spider, perhaps hanging by a thread underneath it. The sight of the web up close, its only function to serve as a trap, suddenly chilled her. She quickly turned to see whether anyone was watching them and was relieved to find no one.

The water felt good. She surrendered herself to its coldness, not moving as it slowly washed away the layers of sweat, dirt, and blood from her body. She closed her eyes, took a deep breath, and went under, and for a moment it felt no different from swimming back in the river in Daegeori, where they did their laundry and swam on hot summer days. When she came back up, the first rays of the sun were shining, and she was filled with a strange sense of optimism. Yeon-Soo had already climbed out of the water and was getting dressed in her tattered hanbok. The right sleeve of her jeogori had torn off at the seams, so that her shoulder, cut and bruised, was exposed. Na-Young wanted to stay in the water, to let it cleanse her, heal her. It eased the pain in ways she couldn't understand. But Yeon-Soo was waving her back.

"I need to bury Headless Chicken," Yeon-Soo said.

In all the confusion, it hadn't dawned on Na-Young that Headless Chicken had died. Once hailed as her little village's miracle, she had survived a beheading, been made a public spectacle that drew visitors from as far as Jeju Island off the southern coast, and survived her master, a ten-year-old boy.

Although it was obvious now to Na-Young that Headless Chicken had died, she was startled at the realization. Had she died from that one gunshot wound? Or had the Japanese military policemen shot her again? Had she died as they fled? Na-Young felt a sadness deeper than she could have imagined. She looked over at Yeon-Soo and a new fear overcame her: Her best friend would now have no reason to go on—the one thing she valued, because it had been loved by her boy, had been destroyed.

"Wait here," Yeon-Soo said, and disappeared into the darkness.

Na-Young was left alone. The one thing she had promised Mother was never to leave Yeon-Soo's side. Without thinking, she touched her brooch. It was gone! Frantically, she patted down her clothes and searched her surroundings. Na-Young struggled to breathe. Her legs were shaking violently. The ceaseless moaning of the Japanese military policeman rang in her ears. She sucked blood from a cut on her lip. On the verge of tears, she rocked herself, trying to escape into happy thoughts. Images of home, Mother sleeping peacefully, and their little room where no one bothered them strangely calmed her. Then she remembered her impending marriage. How could life force her to choose between two such horrible outcomes? Inevitable death out here, or marriage to a man who would likely be no different from Father? Either way, it would be a life away from Mother. Na-Young thought of Sarwon, happily in love with Oppa. He'd never be able to marry her, lowly servant that she was. But at least she was happy, even if temporarily. And warm and comfortable, in the safety of her home. Their home. Suddenly, she ached for it.

When Yeon-Soo returned, Na-Young told her that she wanted to go back.

"Selfish girl," Yeon-Soo chided, and sat down. "I just buried the only thing I had left of my son. If we just give up and go home, what was that even for?"

Their bundles gone, they no longer had blankets or their water tins or food. They stacked some branches alongside a fallen tree and made a makeshift shelter. In spite of Na-Young's exhaustion, her mind would not stop racing. She could see that Yeon-Soo's face had drained of all colour. What could she say or do to keep her going? Then she remembered the Korean man the Japanese had dragged away.

"The man," Na-Young said. "Yoon Chun-Heh . . ."

"Yes." Yeon-Soo repeated the name.

"We have to let his wife know, don't we?" Na-Young remembered what he had said about the money. "We can't fetch it, but surely we've got to go tell his wife there's money . . ."

"We can take that money and keep running," she said.

"How could you even suggest that?" Na-Young asked. She couldn't believe that her friend was suggesting that they steal from someone even worse off than them.

"Na-Young, we killed a man. A Japanese man of the law. And you're worried about petty theft?" She wiped her tears with the back of her hand. "I can't go back."

"We've got to go back," Na-Young insisted. "There's no other way. Like you said, they won't stop looking for us."

"I know you're afraid," Yeon-Soo said. She took a deep breath. "But listen. Look around. What do you hear?"

Na-Young glanced at the treetops and watched a bird fly into the air above their heads. Her eyes fell back down to a nearby tree, whose trunk displayed patches of white, brown, and grey colours, and a litter of dark needles and leaves that had dropped from it. She listened intently but could only hear the usual comforting sounds of the outdoors.

"We're safe right now," Yeon-Soo said.

Na-Young nodded.

"I need to think. I'll figure something out."

Although Na-Young didn't completely believe her, she felt reassured.

Without having to stop and constantly care for Headless Chicken, they found themselves back at the wooden bridge by the river within two days.

"This is a bad idea," Yeon-Soo said again. "We should just keep going."

Still, she had agreed to come. They had decided not to look for the man's money—it was too risky. Instead—Na-Young had decided without telling her friend—she would give the woman part of the money she still carried in her secret pouch. Then they would be back on the road to Pyeongchang.

"We've been making good time," Na-Young said. "We're doing the right thing. Besides, I promised Mr. Yoon I would tell his wife we saw him." It was a lie; she hadn't had the courage to promise, but Yeon-Soo could not have known this. Unlike her, Yeon-Soo hadn't spoken to him at all. Perhaps that's why Na-Young felt such a great need to deliver his message. Something told her his family would never see him again, and they had to know the truth.

The little boy and the girl came darting from the woods, their faces lit with anticipation as they asked whether they could play with Headless Chicken.

"She's gone," Na-Young answered flatly. "Is your mother home?"

"Gone?" they asked in unison, but Yeon-Soo and Na-Young ignored them and stepped inside.

The woman's smile faded as soon as she saw their bloodstained and torn clothing, and she shooed the children back outdoors.

"Yoon Chun-Heh," Na-Young said. "We have a message from him."

The woman's mouth opened, then closed again. She nodded, fear in her eyes. She gestured for them to sit at the table and, after fetching cups of water, gave Yeon-Soo one of her jeogoris to wear. She said nothing, as if she knew that they could only have bad news. Na-Young gulped her water as Yeon-Soo thanked her and changed clothes.

"The Japanese have taken him away," Na-Young blurted out, no longer able to contain the news.

Yeon-Soo reached across the table and cupped the woman's trembling hands.

"Maybe it wasn't him. Perhaps you're mistaken," the woman said, pulling her hands away. "There's no reason why the Japanese would be interested in my husband. Look around. We've got nothing they could possibly want."

Na-Young wondered how to tell her that he was involved with a resistance group. But just then, the door flew open and the children rushed in.

"There are three Japanese soldiers by the river," the boy said.

Everyone jumped to their feet.

"Are you sure?"

"They're in brown uniforms."

"The military police!" Yeon-Soo said, and surveyed the room. There was no place to hide. She grabbed Na-Young's hand and started for the door. "Please don't say a word about us," she said, turning to the children, then to the woman. "Your husband wanted you to know he was on his way home with money he had earned."

The woman's eyes popped open, her lips parted slightly, but before she could say anything, Yeon-Soo was out the door.

"You dropped this the last time you were here!" The woman grabbed something out of a pot and ran to put it into Na-Young's hand. The gold-and-jade lotus-blossom brooch! How had she lost it here? Overcome with gratitude and relief, Na-Young quickly pinned it inside her sleeve. Then, remembering the money she still had, she pulled hard at the pouch sewn into her chima's underskirt. It wasn't until she was holding it that she saw the familiar embroidery pattern of a pink lotus flower. Where had Mother gotten this money? A flashback came to her: Sarwon's sickly face, her mother telling them that the gods would understand, and even her own feelings of unease.

"Go quickly!" the woman said, and snapped Na-Young back to the present.

"Your husband wanted you to have this," Na-Young said, and placed the money pouch in the woman's hands before running to catch up with Yeon-Soo.

Na-Young and Yeon-Soo made their way into the pine forest, away from the path. Pine needles lashed against their arms, faces, and hands, and bit as badly as mosquitoes. Yeon-Soo pulled Na-Young behind a giant tree, and they dropped to the ground.

"I don't think they're following us," Yeon-Soo whispered.

Then, gunshots, three in a row, blasted in the distance, sending a rush of birds from the treetops. The noise startled Na-Young so much that she threw her arms around Yeon-Soo, terrified. Could the unspeakable have just happened? Eyes shut tight, Yeon-Soo sank against the tree.

Everything froze in time, like a painting. Nothing moved, not even the air.

Finally, Yeon-Soo tugged Na-Young's arm to release her grip. She looked up at the sky, saw that the sun was to their right, and determined that they needed to keep running in that direction.

They stopped at a river. Na-Young dipped her hands into it to splash water on her face. She looked up and was startled to see how much Yeon-Soo's appearance had changed now that she was dressed in an old, patched-up jeogori, with dirt and dust in the creases of her face. The dark circles and swelling under her eyes made her look like a sad common raccoon dog instead of the dignified and strong woman Na-Young knew.

Yeon-Soo sighed heavily. "I'll walk back to our village with you, but I won't stay, and I can't be seen by anyone there. And I need you to make me three promises."

Night

Night had fallen again. Na-Young listened in the darkness for any foreign sounds, for the sound of men. Nocturnal animals were surprisingly noisy, scurrying about, snapping branches here and there. Owls hooted, and the occasional wolf howled in the distance. Danger seemed to lurk all around them, every shadow now a possible threat to their lives.

Nine nights had passed since they first set off, yet it felt like a lifetime. She unpinned the gold-and-jade lotus-blossom brooch from her inner sleeve and held it. Finding it had filled her with a renewed hope and now an intense yearning to see her mother again. She focused on the memory of combing Mother's hair and felt her nerves calm.

"A family is dead. A Japanese man is dead. For that, we'll lose our lives. They won't stop looking for us, and when they catch us, they will kill us," Yeon-Soo said.

Silence fell between them, and again Na-Young became unnerved by the night sounds.

"I'm so sorry that you've been part of all this," Yeon-Soo said, and wrapped her arms around Na-Young. "But you still have your whole life ahead of you. A marriage. Who's to say it won't be a good one? And children of your own."

"I don't want any of that." Why was everyone, including Yeon-Soo, so determined that she needed to spend her life serving a man and bearing his children?

"I have nothing to return to, unlike you," Yeon-Soo said. "And it's safer if we part ways. The Japanese authorities will come looking."

"Safer for who? Surely not you if you're on the run." It was a staggering thought—the idea of Yeon-Soo not staying with her, knowing that she would be out here with no one. *I shouldn't have given the woman all my money*, Na-Young thought with regret; she had nothing to give to her friend. "But what will you do, all alone?"

Yeon-Soo smiled at the thought. "I've never been physically alone, yet I've been alone most of my life," she said. "The only time I thought I'd feel truly connected to anyone was with my son, but even he never wanted to be held, not even as a baby."

Na-Young thought of Su-Bin and the short life that fate had destined for him. A pang of guilt swept through her yet again as she remembered that even she had called him Chicken Boy, a cruel nickname for a little boy with such odd, uncontrollable behaviours. But he had cared for and protected Headless Chicken, who in turn had fearlessly saved her and Yeon-Soo's lives.

"I hate feeling so scared," Na-Young said. She fought to contain the swirl of emotions: anger, fear, and, worst of all, the daunting feeling of helplessness that was closing in at the realization of what her life had become and how hard things could only be from now on.

"It's a feeling. Don't ignore it," Yeon-Soo said. "My mother used to tell me that our feelings were no different from cloud formations that predict the weather. They let us know what our inner weather is like. What do people do during a storm?"

"They wait for it to pass."

"Your negative feelings are no different. We must let them pass."

How could she be so naive? Na-Young wondered, but couldn't bring herself to say it out loud. Or perhaps Yeon-Soo was merely telling her what she thought Na-Young needed to hear to protect her.

"I suppose my mother was preparing me for the inevitable," Yeon-Soo said. "She was a wise woman, in her own way. She told me, before she sent me away, that I must never refuse two things in this world: food and my husband."

Na-Young's stomach groaned miserably. The heavy scent of pine and earth surrounded them.

"But Na-Young, you don't have to eat everything someone gives you," Yeon-Soo said. "Some things will make you sick. Others will just make you fat. I can't keep eating everything life tries to feed me. I'm too full to eat any more!"

Na-Young's stomach groaned again, and then, realizing just how hungry they both were, she laughed, and Yeon-Soo did, too. The two held each other so closely, Na-Young could feel her friend's heart beating.

"Who knows," Yeon-Soo said softly, "maybe I can still make something of my life."

"Like join a resistance group?" Na-Young joked.

"Man-se! Long live our nation!" Yeon-Soo raised her arms, palms upturned, and reached for the clouds.

Na-Young smiled, but her heart was full of fear and uncertainty.

It was still dark when they arrived in Daegeori. The mountains that connected the village to the sky and the stars welcomed them back without judgement. Na-Young took comfort in the familiar scents and shadows of trees and fields in the distance. Days had passed, and although she was standing right where she had started, she knew things would never be the same—that a line had been drawn between the life that she had once known and the huge, harsher world that she had been forced into. Even the air around them had changed, from luminous blues and greys to a thickening darkness that descended upon them, layer by layer.

"Will I ever see you again?" she asked Yeon-Soo, desperate for her friend to lie and tell her what she needed to hear.

Yeon-Soo forced a smile and reached out to touch Na-Young's face. Na-Young's heart fell, and she burst into tears. Everything Yeon-Soo had done left her unable to express her gratitude and affection. She hugged Yeon-Soo, and when she felt the other woman's body trembling, Na-Young embraced her even tighter. It would be useless, Na-Young knew, to ask her to change her mind. Yeon-Soo's decision to keep running was her way of protecting Na-Young.

"Remember your three promises?" Yeon-Soo gazed softly at her friend's face.

Na-Young nodded. "One, let you go. Two, visit Su-Bin's grave and tell him you said goodbye." She swallowed hard, wiped her tears, and forced herself to keep going. "And three, don't look for you under any circumstances."

As they hugged, Na-Young discreetly pinned the gold-and-jade lotus-blossom brooch to the inside hemline of Yeon-Soo's jeogori.

Na-Young stood for a long time, watching Yeon-Soo as she became a shadow and then darkness. When would Yeon-Soo discover the brooch? Na-Young knew that she would never have accepted the gift, but she wanted Yeon-Soo to have it. She thought of Mother's words: "Jade is a living stone. It will protect you on your journey."

Alone, in the early-morning light, Na-Young quietly entered her home. She felt whole again as her lungs filled with familiar air and the lingering scent of ginseng, bark, and chrysanthemum from Mother's many medicinal teas. She shed her torn, filthy clothes. The room's warmth released her from any need to be brave.

Wedding

No one had dared to tell Father that Na-Young had run off. The story was that she had taken ill and had to rest before the wedding. Even Second Mother had played along to avoid Father's wrath, hoping Na-Young would return. When Yeon-Soo's relatives came, asking whether the family had seen her, everyone agreed that Na-Young had been too ill to receive visitors, so Yeon-Soo hadn't been by. Na-Young shuddered at the thought of Mother having to conspire with Second Mother.

"What would have happened when I didn't show up for my own wedding?" Na-Young asked.

Mother sighed deeply. "I was going to deal with that when the time came. In the meanwhile, Sarwon and I did our best to maintain a sense of normalcy. What else could we do?"

When the dressmaker had arrived to take the measurements to make the wedding hanbok and several other outfits for Na-Young to take to her new home, Sarwon had stepped in. Unfortunately, she was a good five inches taller than Na-Young. Realizing this, Second Mother had one of the servants cut blocks of wood, which she then had nailed to the bottom of Na-Young's wedding shoes.

"What happened to you out there?" Mother had repeatedly asked. "Did you fall? Is that what caused all your bruises?"

"Yes, we ran into some trouble, but everything worked out. Yeon-Soo decided to go on and I chose to come home." Na-Young was trying to reassure both Mother and herself. She felt faintly sick about lying, but it was all she could do to manage the recurring images of Headless Chicken running frantically towards her and Yeon-Soo, or to escape the smell of the sweat of the Japanese military policeman who attacked her.

When Mother asked about the brooch and the money, Na-Young lied and told her she had lost them, much to her mother's disappointment. Thankfully, Mother did not press. Na-Young did her best to keep their conversation about the wedding, which would happen as planned, two days later. Mother, who had looked sickly before Na-Young left, seemed a bit better. All the more reason not to ask about where the money pouch had come from, Na-Young reasoned. After all, few things made her feel closer to her mother than their secrets.

"As long as you're safe and back home, we'll be all right," Mother said. She finally looked relaxed.

Na-Young woke on her wedding day before the sun was up and realized that, for the first time in days, she hadn't been startled awake by a bad dream. *A good omen*, she thought. A cooling drift of air came sweeping through the room when she slid the door open a crack. For a happy moment, she remembered playing five-stones with Mi-Young in the courtyard as a child. Her older sister had also taught her tricks to spin her wooden top faster and longer than Oppa could, which irritated him to no end. When Na-Young once teased Oppa for being a sore loser, it was Mi-Young who told her that she needed to be a good winner, that unless one accepted victory with dignity and humility, the win was hollow.

The memory of her sister soothed her. Mi-Young had been right, of course, Na-Young thought. Despite her aching body and blistered feet, she would move through the day with dignity and grace, for Yeon-Soo, Mother, and the memory of Mi-Young.

By midmorning, the entire household was busy preparing for the celebration and the arrival of the bridegroom and his entourage.

In the main room, the two women who had been recommended by a matchmaker and hired by Second Mother for the wedding day insisted that Mother and Sarwon stay back and remain quiet. Wordlessly, they powdered the bride's face white to conceal her fading bruises and oiled and braided her hair into an updo, crowned with an elaborate gold headdress of precious stones and ribbons.

"We can help her get dressed now that you're done," Mother said finally. "It's my turn to insist: You must have something proper to eat and drink after doing such an exceptional job with my daughter." The two women had scarcely a moment to say goodbye before Mother closed the door and, taking Sarwon's arm, laughed gently.

"I can't believe they told me to breathe more quietly!" Sarwon said.

"If they weren't doing such a good job, we wouldn't have put up with their nonsense!" Mother laughed; then, turning her attention to the wedding hanbok, she said, "At least the concubine has good fashion sense. I give her that."

Mother and Sarwon helped Na-Young slip into her wedding hanbok. The dress, though soft and silky, reminded Na-Young of the consequences of the day: Her home and identity would dramatically change forever.

"Ah! It's like a whole new world up here," Na-Young said, nervously slipping into her wooden platform shoes. "Sarwon, you must surely see a lot more dust than I do." She eyed the top of the framed photos and the broken folding-screen panel in the room.

Sarwon laughed. "Not if I keep my eyes low."

Suddenly, three Japanese military policemen rushed into the room, one of them shouting words they could not understand.

Alarmed, the women froze.

The Japanese military policemen then pointed their rifles at the door and gestured for them to leave. Shaken, Mother and Sarwon helped Na-Young manage as she stumbled on the elevated shoes.

Outside, Japanese military police stood like a formidable wall around the courtyard. Na-Young stood next to Mother, towering over her. Kitchen staff, smelling of hot peppers, ginger, and roasted sesame seeds, wiped their hands on their aprons as they rushed to line up next to them.

"What's going on?" someone whispered. Then, as if knowing to be afraid, the female servants huddled together, seizing each other's arms in fright as their eyes stayed locked on the brown uniforms. This was the first time any of them had seen Japanese military policemen.

"There's obviously been a mistake," Second Mother said. She scanned around and, upon spotting Father and Oppa rushing into the courtyard, let out a small sigh of relief. "They'll straighten this out," she said confidently. "Thank goodness the guests haven't arrived yet."

Na-Young turned and, to her horror, recognized the two young Japanese military policemen who had witnessed their superior officer attack her before Yeon-Soo had kicked him into the fire. One Japanese military policeman's face still showed traces of blue-and-purple bruising on his forehead and cheek. Accompanied by another Japanese military policeman, who had a permanent stern look, they started walking along the line, gazing into the face of each woman.

When Second Mother, who stood near the front, protested

that this was highly inappropriate, given that it was a wedding day, a fourth Japanese military policeman pulled her out of line, causing her to fall. He struck her on the head with his baton so that she collapsed face down. Her pinned hair unravelled, covering her face. For a moment she did not move. Then slowly she stirred, groaning in pain as her hand reached for the bloody spot where she had been hit. Father moved to help her regain her feet, but he was restrained by the firm grasp of two other Japanese military policemen. No one else dared to move.

A Japanese military policeman shouted a string of harsh words in Japanese.

"Treason?" Oppa said, translating. He exchanged some words in Japanese with the policeman, then told his family, "They're looking for people accused of killing a Japanese military policeman. If we let them do their job, they'll be on their way." He assured the household that they had nothing to worry about.

Na-Young clapped her hands to her chest. Yeon-Soo was in grave danger, but she was still free.

As three Japanese military policemen inched closer to her, Na-Young felt so paralyzed with fear that she thought she would surely pass out. What would Yeon-Soo have done? She was so much braver than Na-Young. Then, a voice inside her whispered, *Don't make eye contact with either of the two boys.* She steadied her breathing and held her body and head as rigid as possible, helped by the stiff collar of her wedding jeogori, which was made of heavy satin. But when the Japanese military policemen reached her, they simply glanced at her and moved on. She exhaled in relief. But one of them, the one with the bruises, stopped and looked back. The stern one said something, but the other shook his head. He brought a hand to his eyes. He was indicating the height of the person they were looking for. Na-Young's heart swelled in gratitude to Second Mother for the elevated shoes, and to fate for granting her this reprieve. Satisfied that the person they were looking for was not there, the Japanese military police left. Father rushed angrily to help Second Mother up.

"My hair!" she cried. "They've ruined everything." A servant girl helped her inside.

"Don't just stand there!" Father barked at the servants. He slapped the nape of a houseboy's neck. "We have a wedding to prepare for!"

Na-Young returned to the main room to continue getting ready. Mother shooed the maidservants out, telling them to bring back some cold tea.

"Speak the truth—do you and Yeon-Soo have anything to do with what just happened?"

"What do you mean?" Na-Young asked, trying to sound casual.

"They were talking about treason—the highest crime imaginable."

"I didn't do anything," Na-Young said firmly. In her mind's eye, she saw Yeon-Soo, struggling against the military policeman before he fell into the fire. Again, the stench of burning hair and flesh assaulted all her senses at once, and she almost gagged.

"The Japanese have been punishing us for the smallest things. I can't imagine what would happen if . . ."

"I didn't do anything," Na-Young repeated. She was desperate to tell Mother the truth, to unload some of the burden that haunted her, even if it felt like betraying Yeon-Soo. But she wanted, above all, to protect Mother. Ignorance would serve her the best. If the Japanese military police ever came back, Mother would truly know nothing.

"Yeon-Soo is still out there," Mother whispered. "Who knows what her mother-in-law will say about her disappearance."

"Yes, but no one knows that I was with her. For all they know, she left alone with Headless Chicken."

"Yes, her actions certainly sound mad."

Na-Young pictured Yeon-Soo far from the village, eyeing the sky, using the sun, the moon, and the stars to guide her out in the wilderness. Where was she now? She looked down at her wedding hanbok, its material luxurious against her skin, and blinked back tears.

"It's a good thing that you'll be leaving here." Mother exhaled deeply. "You'll be far away if the Japanese military police ever come back."

Less than an hour later, the groom, his father, and a manservant arrived, followed by the same guests who had attended Su-Bin's funeral weeks earlier. When the time came, Na-Young was led to the centre of the courtyard, where she saw her fiancé, Min-Ho, for the first time. He was a handsome young man, despite his intense expression. His eyes reminded her of black onyx. For a moment, her preoccupation with all that had gone wrong subsided, and she wondered whether perhaps her luck had changed. Had fate gifted her a good marriage? Healthy children to come? A pang of guilt coursed through her as she thought about Yeon-Soo on the run, but she took a deep breath. Her friend had taught her to focus on seeking calm or even pleasure in the moment.

After a Buddhist monk chanted prayers and the bride and groom bowed several times to each other, they were husband and wife. But before she had a chance to speak with her husband, Na-Young's new father-in-law congratulated her.

"Welcome to our family," he said. He was slightly taller than his son. His warm voice and smile put her at ease right away. "I regret our home is without a mother-in-law to receive you. I promise I'll do everything I can to make up for it."

Na-Young bowed deeply to him. Out of the corner of her eye, she saw Oppa and her husband together. *What are they talking about?* she wondered. Were they talking about her?

"Anyang will feel like a big lake compared to the quiet pond that is this village," Father-in-Law said. "Still, the same moon will glow upon you and your new family." He continued to describe her new home.

But Na-Young was distracted. Why hadn't her husband joined his father to speak with her? She grew annoyed at Oppa for failing to anticipate that she might want to get to know her new husband, too. If she could exchange words with her husband for the first time while they were surrounded by others, perhaps they would feel less awkward with each other later that night.

"Let us feast!" Father announced loudly. Soon, the sound of men's voices faded as they left for the outer quarters to take their meal. The opportunity to speak with her husband lost, she retreated to the main room, where the women celebrated.

Pink, green, and white rice cakes, chestnuts, and fruit were laid out on a table. The women drank barley tea and rice wine as they laughed and gossiped.

"Are you excited for your wedding night?" Lady Cho teased.

"I'm sure she's more afraid than excited," Lady Shim said. "We've all endured it. You'll get over it."

"Wait until she's pushed out her sixth baby," Lady Ko said. "By then, she won't even feel anything."

"Stop being vulgar!" Yeon-Soo's mother-in-law said.

"Aye, you're just upset that your good-for-nothing daughter-in-law took off with your golden goose!" Lady Shim stuffed a pink rice cake in her mouth.

Lady Cho hushed her. "Yeon-Soo just lost her son. I can't imagine. No wonder she ran away. For all we know, she could have taken her own life. I might have done the same if I had no child or husband left."

Na-Young held her breath and fought to stay composed. As much as she was afraid for her friend, she was just as fearful of her wedding night. Her body still ached everywhere. How would she endure the pain of being with her new husband?

"Stop being melodramatic!" Lady Shim said. "It's Na-Young's wedding. Speaking of, where is your Second Mother? I'd assume she'd be here strutting her peacock feathers."

"She's hurt," Lady Ko said. "Leave her alone. Besides, only male peacocks have colourful tails."

"She's certainly tall enough to be a man," Lady Shim said. "And who knows, with those sharp features . . ." She laughed, directing a sly glance at Na-Young. "She's probably in her room, happy to be away from the likes of us. If you ask me, I think she enjoys being pretentious. It likely helps her forget who she really is."

Although Na-Young regretted that the Japanese military policeman had attacked her, she was relieved that Second Mother had retired to her room and had stayed away for the rest of the celebration, giving her mother the space to shine. Mother directed the maidservants to take more food out to the men, and looked more animated than she had been in years. *This is where she should be,* Na-Young thought, *amongst her old friends, dressed in silks and not rags.*

After spending tonight with her new husband, Na-Young and Min-Ho would join the wedding procession back to Anyang, a journey that involved an eighteen-kilometre walk and a train ride.

She thought back to what Oppa had said to her: "Don't be sad. Your real life is out there, waiting for you." He'd reminded her that, as a young child, she had always sought adventure—she was the risk-taker who had climbed the highest tree branch and swallowed a caterpillar whole on a dare.

Like him, she had a duty and obligation to her family. Focusing on this, she summoned her courage. She would stay strong. For Oppa. For Mother. Who was to say that fate would lead her to a married life of hardship? Maybe, like stars, there were infinite possibilities in life.

A room had been prepared next to Second Mother's. The bedding Second Mother had made for the bride and groom included a thick floor mat with a light cotton blanket. Na-Young had been under the blanket, dressed in her undergarments, when she heard her husband at the door. Thanks to the strong sedative powers of valerian root tea, of which, thanks to Mother, she'd had several cups, her heart was no longer pounding. Even her shortness of breath subsided as she lay waiting.

Eyes closed, she braced herself for the inevitable. But to her surprise, Min-Ho ignored her. Perhaps he thought she was asleep? He undressed, then turned off the lamp. He fell asleep, his back to her, a welcome barrier between them. Her body, still sore from the attack, finally relaxed, and she lapsed into a deep sleep.

PART II

town

Mosquito Netting

Anyang, 1924

Two weeks had passed since the wedding. As she had done every morning, Na-Young stared at the ceiling through the white mosquito net, feeling trapped in a cloud. But this was hardly a prison. Her head sank into the soft silk pillow, which was filled with goose down. It didn't support her head and neck nearly as well as her old one, which had been stuffed with wheat husks. *This room is too large for one person,* Na-Young thought, recalling the tiny space she'd shared with her mother.

The room had once belonged to her late mother-in-law, who had inherited the furniture from her own mother-in-law. It was furnished with an elegant, black-lacquered table inlaid with a mother-of-pearl mountain landscape, matching two-level and three-level chests that held the new clothes Second Mother had prepared for Na-Young, and an oversized chest made of dark persimmon wood that housed her sleeping mat, blankets, and pillow. Each time she saw it, she was reminded of Yeon-Soo, who had had a similar chest in her room, but this one had elaborate brass handles that were shaped like butterflies. Where was Yeon-Soo now? The possibilities darted through her mind, like small animals running wild in a field.

Now that she was a proper married woman, she was expected to dress and look the role. From her sleeping mat, she eyed an elegant red lacquer accessory box filled with combs and hairpins, and a matching box with a mirror hinged to the top panel. Its drawers contained used cosmetics and brushes. Beyond that, there was a folding screen by the window depicting grapes, persimmons, dates, and other fruits that symbolized fertility, which added a bright splash of colour and blocked cold drafts.

Na-Young clutched the blanket tighter around her neck. She had never spent so much time alone before. The silence was unnerving.

Boksun, Na-Young's maidservant, asked permission to enter from outside the door and, as usual, before Na-Young could reply, the door slid open. The girl, dressed in a freshly pressed white hanbok, carried a breakfast tray, which she set on the table. The smell of bone soup quickly filled the air.

"Are you feeling better today?" Boksun inquired, sweeping the canopy to one side. She passed Na-Young some warm jasmine tea.

"Yes, getting better by the day," Na-Young responded. When Boksun had remarked on the many faint bruises on her arms and back, Na-Young lied and said that she had fallen off a horse. Had Boksun perhaps told her husband? Could he be kind enough to wait for her to completely heal? The thought warmed her.

Boksun smiled. Na-Young thought: *She looks about my age. How is it that the universe has determined that Boksun be born into a family with no means, leaving her to lead a life of servitude, and I into one that entitles me to be served by her?* Still, she couldn't help but envy her maidservant a little. Unlike her, Boksun was at home here, her mother having served the Park family before she passed away.

Na-Young was grateful for Boksun's company. Mother had told

her that it was the mother-in-law's job to welcome a new bride into the family, but since her husband's mother had passed away and there was no lady of the house, she had been left to her own devices. A forgotten visitor.

"It's a beautiful day," Boksun said. She folded the quilt and rolled up the sleeping mat to put them away. "You should go into the courtyard. The open air will be good for you." As always, she kneeled, watching Na-Young sip her soup.

"I wasn't expecting it to be so quiet here," Na-Young said.

Boksun, who usually answered her questions without hesitation, explained that at one time, four generations of the Park family had resided in the house, each room filled with screaming children. Today, the inhabitants had been reduced to just Na-Young's father-in-law, his only son, Min-Ho, and the household servants who tended to them.

Na-Young imagined the noise that had once occupied the house and, to her surprise, found herself missing the noisy commotion of Second Mother's little boys, who'd storm in with bare feet, tracking the dust and dirt from their outdoor play into the main room, where she used to sit to do her needlework. Their constant roughhousing and the way Second Mother doted on them used to annoy her, but now she missed them.

"Why hasn't Father-in-Law remarried?" Na-Young asked. It felt strange that a man would pass up the opportunity to have more children.

"It isn't as if there haven't been any inquiries," Boksun said with a faint smile. "Many prominent ladies have tried to gain his affection. But my mother used to say that his heart died the day his wife passed away." She collected the tray. "Are you finished with all your sewing?" she asked.

"Yes," Na-Young said, unhappy that she was almost finished

taking in the new clothes that her family had made using Sarwon's measurements. It had given her something to do. "I'd be grateful if you could fetch me some more thread," she said, "to match the colours of the fabrics." She wanted to keep herself busy so as not to lapse into dark thoughts.

Unlike in her own home, where she regularly sneaked around the property, she dared not be so forward here; she didn't want to take the chance that she would run into her husband, his father, or any other men who might be visiting.

Very quickly, the charm of having her own things—a room she didn't share, new furniture, and clothes—wore off. While she had thought plenty about what married life would demand of her during the night, she hadn't anticipated that her new life would be filled with such boredom during the day. When her mother told her to accept her new role with grace and dignity, as it was the easiest way to win over her in-laws, she had expected her father-in-law to be just like Father. Although they had interacted only during the wedding, he appeared to be kind and gentle. Na-Young could only imagine his wife to have been the same and lamented that she did not have a mother-in-law to teach her how to please her husband and new family.

But with each passing day, she started to lose interest in needlework and sewing. Her lower back had begun to ache; the panic that seized her whenever she had flashbacks of the Japanese military policemen's attack left her chest so constricted that she thought she was dying. She tried to follow all of Yeon-Soo's suggestions for staying calm: *Breathe deeply. Pay attention to the things around you. What do you see? Hear? Smell?* Stretching, she gently massaged her back and legs and felt increasingly more disoriented. *If my heart doesn't kill me, my mind will,* she thought.

While it was tempting to share her thoughts with Boksun, Na-Young was hesitant—social customs prevented her from getting too friendly with the servants. Nevertheless, as their comfort with each other grew, Na-Young noticed that Boksun lingered longer each time she came to Na-Young's room.

"You can ask me anything," Boksun said, her eyes wide. "Or tell me anything."

"I've never been so bored," Na-Young said. "Tell me about this neighbourhood."

"It's pretty quiet around here. We're a bit far from the main section of town and the family printing press where your husband works. There's some nice shops and outdoor markets, but of course nothing like the capital, which is just over twenty kilometres north of us."

Na-Young had trouble imagining the rest of the town. She'd have to go exploring. But then a voice reminded her to remember her new role. Her duty was to the household and the space inside.

"What about this family?" Na-Young asked. "Is there anything you can tell me about them? Anything." Then, realizing the desperation in her voice, she added, "Sorry if I've crossed any lines. It's one of my many faults."

"My mother used to say curiosity is the best medicine for boredom and that's why women so often get into trouble!" Boksun laughed as she swept the room.

Na-Young thought about home and the dusty paths that led to creeks and hilltops where she spent her early mornings, often climbing the highest branches she could to gaze at the sun perched on the horizon. The upwards-moving sun was different from the one that sank in the evening. The reds and oranges were more intense against the washed-out sunsets of the same colours. Even the sounds were more animated in the early hours, from wild birds to the rooster. Despite being alone, Na-Young had never truly felt lonely until now.

"My mother served your father-in-law's wife," Boksun said. "I was told that she was the most beautiful woman he'd ever seen. She cast a spell on him, no doubt, and no woman can replace her. She was only twenty-two years old when she passed."

"That's a shame," Na-Young said. "He's a handsome man; I wish he'd remarried." It didn't seem fair that he didn't have a wife when Father had two.

"Yes," Boksun agreed.

Na-Young wondered about Min-Ho, and debated whether she could trust Boksun enough to ask any questions about him. She massaged her clammy hands. "Is there a river nearby?" she asked, changing the subject.

"Yes, there's a river that feeds into a small lake where the men fish," Boksun said. She threw Na-Young a puzzled look.

"It's been so hot," Na-Young said. "I'd love to go for a swim."

"Ahh," Boksun said, nodding. "I can show you sometime, if you'd like, but it'll have to be after I complete my afternoon chores."

Na-Young accepted the offer, but as soon as Boksun left, she realized that she couldn't spend another moment in her room. Determined to find the river on her own, she left the women's quarters and slipped into the outer quarters.

Like her old home in Daegeori, this one had separate quarters for men, women, and servants. However, with its polished wooden verandas and elegant curved roofs that appeared to hold up the sky, everything here felt grander. The men's quarters consisted of rooms for Father-in-Law, Min-Ho, and guests; a main receiving room; and a study that also served as a library. A small wooden structure set off to the side housed the male servants. A gated stone wall separated the men from the women.

The women's inner quarters included a main receiving room, Na-Young's room, and some smaller rooms for her future children and daughter-in-law. A kitchen and sleeping quarters for female servants were in a separate structure near the back of the property. Two ancient juniper trees stood like guards in the courtyard outside Na-Young's room.

Clouds moved slowly across the sun. It was hard to believe that it was the same sun that she and Yeon-Soo had looked up at so many times while on the road. Na-Young slipped past the gate and into the outer male quarters.

When she heard male voices, she slid the nearest door open ever so slightly, saw the room was empty, and dashed inside. Books lined each wall, neatly arranged on shelves, from ceiling to floor. The smell of dust and stale tobacco was heavy in the air. *This must be Father-in-Law's study*, she realized. Boksun had told her that since leaving his business affairs to his son, he spent most of his hours writing.

A low pinewood desk designed in the classic Confucian style, with a wing top and drawers for paper and writing implements, was in the middle of the room. A large cushion with a backrest and armrests sat on the floor behind the desk. An elegant, six-panel folding screen stood behind it. Each gold-leaf screen depicted stunning images of colourful flowers and peacocks.

A long mirror that reflected her whole body hung between the columns of books. Na-Young had never seen a reflection of her entire body before. Amused, she traced a finger along her new jeogori and chima. They were made of fine, light grey silk. She thought that the colour made her look older, more mature. Gone was the long braid she used to wear, a sign of her youth. Instead, Boksun had tied her hair into a tight bun each morning and used a long, golden hairpin to decorate it. She straightened her back, pleased with how ladylike she appeared.

A charcoal sketch of a woman's face, pinned just above the mirror, caught her eye. Startled, Na-Young thought, *She looks just like me.* She looked back at her reflection. They had the same large eyes and full lips. Their pinned-back hair revealed the same long neck.

The door slid open. Father-in-Law tossed his hat into the room before entering.

"Well, hello," he said.

Red-faced, Na-Young bowed deeply and apologized.

"Nonsense," he said. He hung his hat and sat behind his desk, gesturing for her to sit across from him on the floor.

"I've never seen so many books," she said shyly, looking around the room again. Her eyes stopped at the drawing. He followed her gaze.

"That's a sketch of my late wife," he said, lighting his pipe. The rich, aromatic scent of tobacco filled the air. Then, as if he had read her mind, he added, "Yes, there is a remarkable resemblance. The first time I saw you, at your father's home, I thought I was seeing a ghost. Your eyes . . ." His voice trailed off for a moment, but he smiled when he looked at her.

When had he seen her? Was he referring to her wedding day, or had he seen her somewhere before? It didn't feel proper to inquire. Instead, she asked him how he knew Father.

"We met when we were both students in university, studying medicine in the capital."

"Father studied medicine? Then why was he so opposed to Oppa doing the same?" Her voice trailed off. Questions raced through her head. Why hadn't Father chosen to practise himself? Father was also the first son; perhaps he'd had no choice but to take over the family business. He had always stressed the need for everyone to fulfill their roles and duties, especially within the family. The possibility that her father had sacrificed his own ambitions caught her off guard.

Father-in-Law pulled at his beard. "When tasked with the choice of responsibility, we both walked the same path."

What did that mean? Na-Young wondered, but it seemed impudent to ask. A red ribbon poking out of the golden pages of a black leather-bound book that sat on the table caught her eye.

"That's the Holy Bible," he said when he noticed Na-Young staring. "The most sacred book for Christians."

"Are you a Christian?" she asked, intrigued. The only Christian she had met was a missionary who had visited Daegeori and asked the villagers about their religious practices.

Father-in-Law raised an eyebrow and laughed. "Yes. I even know the English language so that I may read it."

"You know English?"

"Yes, I learned the language from a missionary whom I befriended at medical school."

The information about her father fascinated her. "Does Father know that you're a Christian?" She imagined Father's reaction to his friend practising what he considered a white man's faith. Her family rarely talked about religion or faith. She assumed that the Buddhist temples and monks her mother referred to were just part of everyday life in Korea and did not hold any sacred significance beyond the traditions they practised.

"I'm sure he suspects. We were amongst the first medical school students to practise Western medicine. The hospital associated with the university was founded by American Protestant missionaries," he explained. He took a few shallow puffs on his pipe. "But enough about us old men. How are you?"

Na-Young found herself curiously wanting to know more about her father and what his life had been like before he became the man she knew. Since she was a child, she had assumed that he was difficult and selfish, and used to getting his way. Her throat tightened unexpectedly at the realization that she had judged him without ever truly knowing anything about him. The thought saddened her. "I miss my mother," she said, wanting to change topics.

"Have you written to her yet?" he asked.

"I don't know how," Na-Young said, embarrassed.

"Surely your father insisted that you learn?"

"He didn't believe any girl should go to school." She recalled that once, when she told Father that she wanted to go to school like Oppa, he had said, "A girl need only look to her father, then her husband, for instruction." Even Mother believed that her greatest duty was to produce a son.

"Nonsense! I can teach you. If a white man can teach me a foreign language, surely I can teach another Korean how to read Hangul, our own language."

Na-Young gazed around at all the books. Could it be possible that one day she would be able to pick up any book and read it? She imagined her fingers flipping through the pages. Could she learn history? The geography of places far, far away? She felt smarter already. Knowledge is a powerful weapon, Oppa had once said, when she asked him why school had been so important to him. Maybe for a man. Could it be different for a woman? Could knowledge make her feel more fulfilled?

"Yes, I would like to learn," she said, her heart feeling light. It thrilled her that she would be able to write a letter to Mother, even though her mother wouldn't be able to read it. Oppa would have to help her.

"That settles it. We'll meet here every morning after breakfast, and you shall learn our Korean alphabet, Hangul, and who knows, perhaps English after that."

He put his pipe down and unrolled a sheet of rice paper, dipped a brush into an inkpot, and made several brushstrokes on the page.

"What does it say?" she asked, admiring the black strokes and lines that graced the white paper.

"This, Na-Young, is how you write your name. In Korean, Japanese, Chinese, and English. I shall teach you how in all four languages."

She was amazed at how a single word could look so different, yet sound exactly the same. Chinese looked the most complex, followed by Japanese, then English. Thankfully, Korean looked the simplest. She might be able to learn to read and write after all.

His unexpected kindness flooded her heart. He reminded her of Old Man Yang with his generosity and easygoing nature. She only wished that he had not mentioned the number four, jinxing the moment. It was such an unlucky number, according to Mother, but she doubted, with his education, that he was superstitious. But it would have been rude to say anything. Instead, she stood, bowed deeply, thanked him for the paper with her name on it, and left the study, careful not to overstay her welcome. It wasn't until she was back in her room that she wondered what her new husband would think if he found out about his father's invitation.

Inkstone

"Good morning," Father-in-Law said, looking up from his desk.

"Sorry, I meant to visit earlier," Na-Young said. Her original plan had been to schedule a lesson around the time that Min-Ho left for work, but today, for reasons unknown to her, he had been delayed in leaving.

"How have you been?" He gestured for her to sit on the cushion across from him.

"Very well."

Father-in-Law studied her face for a moment. Could he tell she was lying? That she was filled with boredom and loneliness? But he didn't say anything. Instead, he placed a gift, wrapped in a beautiful green silk cloth, on the table. "This is for you," he said. His face was radiant.

"This is very generous," Na-Young said as she unwrapped an elegant calligraphy set consisting of a bamboo brush, ink stick, and inkstone. Somehow it didn't feel proper for him to be giving her such lavish gifts. But how could she refuse?

"I thought perhaps you would like to learn the traditional method of writing, which is highly elegant and artistic," he said. "Do you know what the ink stick is made from?" He gently removed the black stick from its little paper box.

She shook her head.

"The soot of pine trees. It takes a good craftsman about two months to make this, and another five years for the properly designed stick to dry. And this"—he picked up the inkstone—"is made out of solid rock, but look how smooth the surface is." Lastly, he picked up the brush. "The best brushes are made of bamboo and human hair. Feel how soft it is."

Na-Young was happy to receive such fine gifts but couldn't understand why her heart was suddenly racing.

"To make ink, add a few drops of water to your inkstone and then rub the ink stick until the water becomes dark." He did this.

"This paper is made from the inner bark of mulberry trees." He ran his fingertips along a large sheet and gestured for her to do the same. It was coarse, the fibres interwoven tightly—a sharp contrast to the delicate bamboo brush hairs.

Then, picking up the brush, he showed her how to hold it, so that her thumb gripped it from one side, her fingers on the other. It felt awkward at first, and when she dipped the brush into the ink, her hand trembled slightly.

"We'll begin with some straight lines," he said. He picked up his own brush and, with confident control, drew five vertical lines. The thickness of each line and the speed with which he painted were consistent.

Na-Young tried to do the same, keeping the tip of the brush high on the paper. It was much harder than she expected. Embarrassed, she wanted to cry at her clumsy attempts.

"Try to hold the brush like this," he said. "It takes time to learn to control it, to master it." He swung around the desk and held his brush next to her so she could study his grip more easily. They continued to draw vertical, and then horizontal, lines until she began to develop a consistency and evenness of her own.

"You learn very quickly," Father-in-Law said with a wide smile.

A wonderful warmth filled her. *I will continue to work hard,* she promised herself, *to be a good student—and to keep pleasing him*. Her thoughts were interrupted when, to her dismay, she heard Min-Ho speaking with a servant outside the door.

Father-in-Law gestured for her to stay seated, but she dashed behind the folding screen.

The sliding door opened.

"Father, this places me in an awkward position," Min-Ho said. "Imagine what my friends would think if they thought that my own father was sympathetic to the Japanese!"

Stunned by his belligerence, Na-Young wondered how he could raise his voice to his father or, even worse, challenge him so openly. If he spoke to his father this way, how would he treat her?

"Nonsense!" Father-in-Law exclaimed. "It's a business proposal. Your youth blinds you, son. You must trust me."

"A periodical on modern medical practices and the modern diet? What does that even mean? Can you not see that from a certain vantage point it looks like we're promoting Western and Japanese propaganda?"

"By writing about good eating habits and staying healthy?"

"Who would even read such nonsense? It may end up losing money. Still, people would know and talk. And now all our permits are taken out in my name. *My* name will be the one on the tips of their tongues."

"Yes, I understand. The permit may not even be granted."

"You're missing the point. It's *my* reputation!"

"No!" Father-in-Law raised his voice sharply. "Your reputation is but a twig on the tree that is our family. Our honour should be your foremost concern, and I would never compromise it."

"You're the one who left me in charge," Min-Ho said.

The agitation in his voice caused Na-Young to tense up even

more. The door slid open and shut. What had happened? Had Min-Ho left the room? She hesitated about what to do next for fear of being discovered. Finally, she peeked out from behind the screen.

Seeing her, Father-in-Law perked up. He invited her to sit back down with him. "My apologies for the interruption."

Na-Young blushed. Her mind spun trying to figure out what to say. She apologized, and, although intrigued, she assured him that she had no interest in their business affairs.

"No need," he said, shaking his head. "I'm sorry that you overheard our exchange. I'm afraid my son doesn't share my philosophy when it comes to dealing with the Japanese." He picked up his calligraphy brush as if to examine it. "I suppose it makes sense that the boy is furious with me. I did leave him in charge. All he sees is my meddling. But now that the Japanese are easing their tight control and allowing for some freedom in what is being published again, we need to seize this opportunity to grow our printing press." He gently placed the brush down and reached for some candy on a tray.

"I've always thought the Japanese were dangerous people," Na-Young said tentatively. "Your son sounds very upset. I think my father and brother would agree with him."

"My son is still young and does not yet realize that business is business. Japan's had their hooks in this country since the beginning of time."

Na-Young's ignorance kept her from asking him to continue, but he must have sensed this. He added, "Why, I was alive the last time Japan tried to take over Korea. They assassinated our queen and then burned her corpse. It took two years after that for the country to regain independence. And here we are again."

Na-Young had heard of Queen Min, but had not realized that her death had been so recent. How long ago had this happened if Father-in-Law was there?

He leaned into the table, his back slouched. "It was selfish of me to leave my affairs to my son. But neither of us are getting any younger. It's time that he took over the business, and now I can spend my days writing my book."

He placed a candy in his mouth and then offered Na-Young some. "It's chocolate," he said.

She slipped a piece into her mouth, not sure whether she should suck or chew it. When she saw him bite into his, she did the same. It was sticky and sweet, and dissolved slowly on her tongue. Delighted, she closed her eyes. He wasn't upset with her; he was upset with his son.

"You've never had chocolate before?" He laughed. All the muscles in his face relaxed. "What a secluded life you've lived. This particular chocolate is from Belgium. It should be eaten slowly, so one can appreciate its refined taste."

She nodded but said nothing, partly annoyed by his mention of her living a secluded life—although in truth she had never heard of Belgium or chocolate—and partly overcome by the marvel of the sweetness in her mouth.

"Do you like it?" he asked. "Would you like another?"

In spite of herself, she smiled. He laughed again. "If you take little breaths through your mouth, you'll taste all the flavours."

He was right. The subtle airflow around her tongue as the chocolate melted captivated her.

Suddenly, the door slid open again.

"What is she doing here?" Min-Ho demanded. "She has no place here."

Na-Young jumped to her feet, almost choking on the chocolate, which made it hard to swallow. She bowed deeply.

"Relax, Min-Ho," his father said. "She's new to our household and our family."

"It's good to see you again," she said, keeping her head low.

"You have no business here," he repeated. "Leave us."

She bowed again and retreated to her room. *How foolish!* she thought, angry with herself for having antagonized her husband. But part of her was disappointed that Father-in-Law hadn't stepped in. After all, he had allowed her to stay, had invited her to study with him. What was to become of her lessons now?

Waves

Na-Young was dressed in only her undergarments when Boksun rushed in. She had woken up with a queasy feeling in her stomach, her breasts tender and heavy.

"You have company!" Boksun exclaimed. "Ladies from the neighbourhood." Then, seeing Na-Young's obvious discomfort, she added, "Are you ill? Should I send them away?"

Na-Young shook her head. The idea of finally meeting other women lightened her mood.

"I'm coming to that phase of the moon," she said. Her monthly cycle was off, but that had happened before. "Quick, help me get ready."

Boksun selected a pink porcelain hair stick in the shape of a butterfly and looped it through Na-Young's bun. "The short, plump woman is Lady Ahn, a horrible gossip. Watch what you say to her. She's married to a doctor. Her sister, with the rotten teeth, is almost as bad. She's married to an accountant. The third woman, Lady Oh, is a widow, so don't mention any husband." Na-Young slipped her arms through the jeogori that Boksun held out for her, then watched as Boksun wrapped the long sash of her chima before smoothing it out.

The ladies looked as old as her mother. They sat on cushions around the table in the main room, holding paper fans with the same old-fashioned pink-peony-blossom design. Na-Young's heart sank; she had mistakenly assumed they were her age.

"What pretty fans," she said, concealing her disappointment. She sniffed the air. Someone had strong body odour.

"It's so wonderful to have a lady of the house again," said the woman to her right. "We wanted to make sure you were settled in before calling on you."

Na-Young saw that her teeth were the same colour as seaweed and determined that she was Lady Ahn's sister, the one married to an accountant.

"We understand you're from Daegeori. I've never heard of it before," the plump woman said.

"It's a very small village—so small that we don't even have a doctor."

"My husband is a doctor," she said, straightening her back. "A very good one."

"The town of Anyang is truly lucky, then," Na-Young said, and offered another smile.

"Ay! Anyang has many doctors!" her sister shot back. Na-Young tried to avoid looking at her teeth. What could have caused them to turn such a vile colour? If her brother-in-law was such a good doctor, why hadn't he prescribed some sort of medication to help her?

The plump woman asked, "Have you had a chance to visit any of the shops in town or perhaps the new gallery?"

Na-Young shook her head.

"*Aigoo!* What have you been doing all this time?" She looked around the room, which was empty except for the small table they sat around and the five large silk cushions on the floor.

"Leave her alone!" the widow said. "She's only been here for a month." Lady Oh was a very thin woman and looked younger than the sisters.

A month? Time was passing, leaving Na-Young in its shadow. She thought of all the clothes she had laboured to alter to her size and the needlework she was working on. Boksun entered, carrying a tray of teacups and rice cakes. If only she could stay and save Na-Young from these old ladies! Between the foul smell that hung in the air and the oppressive heat, she was sure she'd soon pass out. To her relief, Boksun handed her a fan, its design identical to the one on the ladies' fans. Na-Young thanked her, but Boksun kept her head down and avoided her eyes.

"We should take you shopping," the widow said, "make this house a home for you."

Na-Young agreed; it was sparsely decorated. She wondered how it might have once looked when Father-in-Law's wife occupied this space. Or perhaps it had looked the same. She hadn't yet considered it her duty to redecorate any of the rooms within the inner quarters.

"I'm afraid I know very little about my new family," Na-Young said, confessing more than perhaps she should have. She shrugged, trying to hide her embarrassment. She thought back to how Second Mother ruled the household. She was now the lady of the house, a role she felt ill-prepared to assume. She made a mental note to inquire further—but whom would she ask? Boksun, who was likely her age, wouldn't have been around when Father-in-Law's wife was alive. Did she dare ask Father-in-Law himself? She recalled the sketch of his wife in the study. He had clearly been in love with her if he kept the picture displayed for so many years. Unlike these ladies, she would never age. Father-in-Law would be spared the sight of her grey, thinning hair, brown spots, and sagging neck.

"I remember when this house used to be full," the sister said. A fly caught her attention, and she poked the air with her fan. "How many maidservants live here now?"

It's her, Na-Young realized, *with the bad body odour.* She wanted to cover her nose, baffled at what the woman could have done in her past life to be cursed with such bad teeth and pungent body odour.

"I'm not entirely sure," Na-Young said. To restore some dignity, she added, "I spend most of my time reading." But the lie made her sweat. She was about to wipe her forehead with the back of her sleeve but caught herself, and instead used her fan.

"Wonderful!" the widow said. "I love reading, too, unlike these ladies, who dismiss it as a male pastime. I'm reading Lady Hyegyeong's last memoir. A classic, yes? But before that, I read Yi Gwangsu's *The Heartless,* which, as you may know, is considered revolutionary in its form, inspired by the Russian writer Tolstoy. What are you reading now, may I ask?"

Na-Young's head spun. The only book that came to mind was the one sitting on Father-in-Law's desk in his study. "The Holy Bible," she said.

"You're a Christian!" the plump woman said, and gave a little laugh. "I suppose it shouldn't surprise us. So many young people today are abandoning the ways of their parents. My son is obsessed with some national Christian council. A national council just for Christians, in Korea! Can you imagine?"

"Oh, leave her be," said the widow. "She's a Christian. Who are we to judge?"

"Lady Oh, you baffle us," the sister said. "Did we not visit a Buddhist temple just last week? Now you defend Christianity?"

"Buddhism is a state of mind; Christianity is a way of life. They can coexist," the widow said.

The sisters shook their heads before Na-Young had a chance to think about what the widow had said. Could they coexist? Her ignorance of the Christian faith and Buddhist ways outside of what Mother had told her kept her from saying anything.

"Why Christianity?" the plump woman pressed. "Isn't it dangerous? Christians have long been persecuted in Korea."

The widow put her teacup down, causing Na-Young to do the same. "Because in Christianity, unlike the ideals spouted by so many neo-Confucian men today, women are equal to men. Our dear hostess, you may be too young to know, but it wasn't that long ago, and hundreds of years before that, that women were treated even worse than they are today. For centuries, men played us like stones on a Go board. These so-called wise men happily made all the game rules, too, controlling how women should act and think by writing it into their laws and social mores. They made it so that all the doors made for women opened into the same dark room. You asked if religion was dangerous. Would you rather seek truth and enlightenment or shackles and security?"

Na-Young wanted to listen, to understand, but the heat persisted. She heard the faint crowing of a rooster. If only she had the courage to open the door and let the air circulate.

"*Ah-hee!* You're only being political to show off!" the plump sister said. "She's even given her cats fancy Russian names."

"Anna from *Anna Karenina* was Russian, yes, but Nora, from *A Doll's House*, was by a Norwegian," the widow explained.

Na-Young repeated the names to herself. She was intrigued and listened intently, but the plump sister interjected, "Surely our dear hostess won't be impressed by such airs! What does it matter anyway? Soon, all we'll have are shrines to worship the Shinto gods. As much as I hate the damn Japanese, I have to admit that they're a clever people. There's no better way to slaughter an entire population than to kill them spiritually first."

Na-Young had never heard women speak like this. Expressing bold ideas and opinions was what men did. She was intrigued by what the widow had said about Christianity and wanted to know more, but was distracted by the combination of the heat, body odour, and the lies she was telling. A dizzying sensation seized her, followed by a wave of nausea. All three ladies noticed Na-Young wrap her arms around her stomach. She hoped that they would see it as a cue to leave.

"Have you been feeling this way a lot lately?" the widow asked. Did Na-Young notice a faint smile?

"No," she said. "I rarely get sick." She was desperate to end the conversation.

"It only takes one time." The sister giggled and popped a rice cake in her mouth. "Then you'll know nine months of nausea and pain."

"Hush! Children can be a woman's greatest blessing," the widow said. She started to get up off her cushion. Na-Young leaped to join her, hoping that they were leaving.

"Yes, even if they do nothing but worry you constantly," the plump woman said. The others nodded.

"At least your Sung-Min's a scholar," the sister with the bad teeth said between bites of rice cake. Each time she reached across the table for more food, the stench got worse. Na-Young pushed down the bile rising in her throat. How could the others not notice?

"A scholar! All he does is read foreign books and lecture about how Korea needs political reform. What's the point of building a great medical practice if you have no son to follow in his father's footsteps?"

"We'll visit again," the widow said. "If you haven't read any of Lady Hyegyeong's memoirs, I'd be happy to loan you a book." A fly buzzed around her forehead and settled on her hair. Na-Young nodded, sincerely wanting to know more about the royal family and Korean history.

As soon as the ladies were gone, Na-Young hurried back to her room, afraid that another wave of sickness might seize her. The sister's words stayed with her: "It only takes one time . . . Then you'll know nine months of nausea and pain." Two full moons had passed since she left Yeon-Soo.

She stopped herself from falling into dark thoughts. Instead, she wondered: How could she ever give her husband a legitimate son when he refused to visit her? The last time they had seen each other was in his father's study. How pointless it felt now that she had rehearsed what she would say to him later, in explanation—that she had gotten lost in her new home. When Min-Ho had told her that she had no place here, she had thought he'd meant his father's study, but perhaps he meant the Park household.

Eyes closed, she considered the possibility that he had a mistress. Somehow it was better to imagine another woman than to accept his lack of attraction to her. Not that she had any desire to be with him, but she had a duty that she could only fulfill with his help. She thumbed through Mother-in-Law's box of used cosmetics. The pink blush added a soft glow to her cheeks, so she applied several more layers. If only she had a larger mirror, she thought. But when she looked back at her reflection, her face looked as if it had been slapped and beaten. Horrified, she threw the blush and mirror back into the box and placed it outside her room for the servants to discard.

Sticks and Dirt

Having grown fond of her servant, Na-Young confessed to Boksun that she didn't know how to read or write and was learning to do so from Father-in-Law, and she promised to share her new knowledge with Boksun. Under the shade of the juniper trees in the courtyard, they practised, using a stick as a brush and dirt for paper. Luckily for both of them, they had good memories and quickly memorized the alphabet, after which it became easy to sound out basic words. Boksun was overjoyed. Na-Young worked diligently, too, practising her brushstrokes and improving her reading skills.

One day, when Na-Young was feeling especially bored, she asked Boksun to show her the rest of the inner quarters. They walked past a gate and into a much smaller courtyard, where wet clothes hung on two clothing lines. The sweet smell of plums and berries mingled with the strong, pungent smell of chili peppers as the fruits and vegetables dried on mats in the sun. Rows of green peppers, onions, lettuce, and other vegetables lined the perimeter. The nearby rattling of pots and pans and the familiar sound of rice being pounded into flour reminded Na-Young of home. In the kitchen, an old woman laboured to stir a giant pot of boiling oxtail soup. As she wiped pools of sweat from her forehead, Na-Young realized she was missing two fingers from her hand. She grunted when Na-Young greeted her, using the formal tense to show respect. The other two women barely acknowledged her as they chopped vegetables and shaped the rice flour into little cakes.

Na-Young stopped, intending to make some small talk, but Boksun pulled her away and led her through a back door and into a narrow walkway, which, in turn, led out to a road adjacent to the one by the main gate. No wonder Na-Young never saw any of the house servants enter or leave the premises.

"They're not very friendly," Na-Young said.

Boksun nodded her head in agreement and looked down the road.

"Where exactly are we in Anyang?"

"We're on the outskirts. There's nothing around here."

They soon arrived at a river that ran north to south, with mountains on the east side.

"It's very quiet," she said. "Back home, we'd all be doing laundry here or bathing."

Boksun laughed. Women in Anyang, she explained, had stopped washing their clothes in the river ever since each household had a water pump installed and public bathhouses became popular.

At Na-Young's request, they started taking long walks together, often in silence, stopping occasionally to scribble words on whatever they could. It delighted them that they could write "dirt" on the dirt road, or carve the word "tree" into its trunk.

"Who knew how smart I could feel just by learning to write?" Boksun said. "I never realized how much power words have."

She was right. Na-Young felt smarter, more confident. Did Oppa feel this way all the time? Was this why Father hadn't sent her to school? So she'd never feel as smart as a man?

"How many words do you think it takes to write a book? Would you ever want to write one?" Boksun wondered aloud.

Na-Young looked at her, hunched at the foot of the tree, scratching letters into its root with a stick.

"Me?" Na-Young asked, surprised. What could she possibly write about? Unlike Lady Hyegyeong, who had an entire palace, complete with fascinating characters, including an insane husband, she'd barely left the inner quarters of her home. "I'd have nothing to say," she said.

"You could make up stories," Boksun suggested, "if there's nothing too terribly interesting to write about in your own life. Make your hero a woman. Make her liberate Korea from the Japanese."

Na-Young's heart skipped at the notion of writing a story about a woman liberating the country. She'd rise from her ordinary, mundane existence and be driven to do extraordinary things in the face of danger and unwavering commitment to freedom. In her mind's eye, she saw her heroine—who bore a striking resemblance to Yeon-Soo—standing amid the smoke of battle, everyday people celebrating their final victory. Ordinary people had become heroes.

She laughed at the foolishness of her impossible dream. "Do you know if my husband's mother owned any books?" she asked.

Boksun yawned. "Yes, I suppose she would have. There's an old chest in one of the closets with some of her personal belongings that were considered too precious to throw away."

How exciting! Na-Young couldn't wait to get back so she could look through Mother-in-Law's possessions. She turned to face Boksun, who was now lying under the tree. Watching her stomach rise and fall with each breath, she realized that Boksun had fallen asleep. Sighing, she lay next to her and was lulled into a sleep of her own.

Suddenly, out of nowhere, she and Yeon-Soo were running frantically through the forest. Images, fast and fierce, came to her: her straw hat on the road, Headless Chicken shot dead, and the Japanese military policeman's neck gushing blood. Her throat tightened at the smell of the Japanese military policeman's burning flesh, and she heard, yet again, the three horrific gunshots that had sent birds fleeing from the treetops.

She bolted upright. For a second, she didn't recognize where she was. A quick flashback of her dream came to her: She saw her gold-and-jade lotus-blossom brooch, with its metal pin, shockingly the size of the letter opener, lodged in the Japanese military policeman's bloody neck.

An alarmed Boksun tugged at her arm, causing her to jump. Na-Young drew in several deep breaths and focused on the cloudless sky. Although she knew she was safe, she was unsettled at how confusingly real something imaginary could appear.

"I'm okay," Na-Young said, "just a bad dream."

The sun had already gone down, with only a glimmer of light hanging amongst the trees. Realizing the time, they had to run back to the house. Because she was the youngest and most able-bodied servant, Boksun was expected to carry the heavy trays that took the men's meals back and forth from the kitchen to the rooms in the outer quarters.

"Tell them it's my fault you're late," Na-Young told Boksun.

She nodded, but the look of concern on her face worried Na-Young. She was foolish, she realized, for taking so much of Boksun's time and keeping her from her work.

"Don't worry," Boksun said as she slipped through the back door, and told Na-Young to rush back to her own room. "I'll be fine."

"Are they cruel to you?" Na-Young wanted to know. Second Mother used to beat all her maidservants.

"I'll be fine," Boksun repeated. "Will you?"

"What do you mean?" Na-Young asked.

"It's not the first time you've woken up screaming," Boksun said, her voice tentative and low.

"I'm fine," Na-Young snapped. "Go!"

She felt ill and embarrassed to know that Boksun not only knew she had had nightmares but had now disclosed that to her. Who else in the household knew? Did they tell Father-in-Law? The visiting ladies? Na-Young felt shaken thinking about their judgement and gossip. Was this why her husband stayed away at night? To avoid a mad or troubled wife? For a moment, she thought of calling Boksun back, but the old woman who had grunted at Na-Young earlier was yelling and cursing at Boksun to get into the kitchen. Feeling helpless, Na-Young turned and retreated to her room.

Requiem

A few days had passed since Boksun revealed she knew about Na-Young's nightmares. It seemed awkward to ask after the lapsed time. Instead, Na-Young asked about Mother-in-Law's chest. She was surprised at how excited she felt thinking about finding the woman's personal belongings. Could she have kept a diary? What glimpses into Mother-in-Law's life as lady of the house could Na-Young discover and learn from? What other insights about this family could she glean?

Na-Young and Boksun spent back-to-back afternoons searching everywhere in the inner quarters. A few of the servants noticed them poking around in the corners of rooms and in storage baskets and bins and asked whether they could be of any assistance.

"Just playing a game," they said, to avoid suspicion.

"Perhaps they were thrown away when she died?" Na-Young finally said, disappointed.

"Maybe your father-in-law knows?" Boksun asked. "Could you ask him?"

Na-Young paused, then sighed. Her fascination with finding a diary suddenly embarrassed her. Finding Mother-in-Law's diary would be a breach of trust, and whatever information she stumbled across, regardless of how it might help her connect with her mother-in-law, would be tainted. She was certain that Father-in-Law would believe the same thing and perhaps even judge her harshly.

Maybe we should keep things in fate's hands, Na-Young thought. So they stopped looking for Mother-in-Law's chest. Something—maybe it was the way the older women servants looked at her from the corners of their eyes, or the ongoing mystery of her husband's absence during the nights—told her it was best to refrain from disturbing the household's natural rhythm.

★

Na-Young took comfort in her studies with Father-in-Law; they were the distraction she needed to mute her rattled nerves. Like a diligent student, Na-Young practised her reading eagerly. After she'd studied and memorized two vocabulary picture books, he gave her another. She even enjoyed his gaze on her, which she perceived as warm and protective, and took great care to present herself properly in freshly pressed hanboks, always ensuring that the decorative hairpins that held her bun in place complemented the outfit.

As time passed, she found that she particularly enjoyed listening to foreign poetry.

"One of my professors was fond of English poets," Father-in-Law said. "He told us that we could not heal a man's body if we didn't feed his soul, so, strangely enough, in the middle of biology or chemistry, he'd recite Byron, Keats, and Kipling, some of the best English writers."

Na-Young, who was trying her best to impress him, asked, "Do you have a favourite?"

"Yes. Kipling was English but he spent some time in India." He flipped through his book. "This poem is one of his most famous because it talks about a man's need to be rational, humble, and truthful in the face of adversity." As he read, she listened intently and did her best to follow the continuous stream of sounds that, despite her best efforts, left her feeling lost. What power there must be in knowing how to speak so many languages and being able to learn about different cultures.

Oftentimes, he even read from the Holy Bible, which he had to translate, since his only copy was in English. Na-Young enjoyed the stories about Adam and Eve and Noah's Ark, although she couldn't understand how people could believe that a single god had created the entire world. It seemed far too simple, but she didn't say anything for fear of offending him. She was thankful that he didn't make any attempts to convert her, so there was no need to ask any questions for clarification or guidance. Instead, she found happiness listening to Father-in-Law, thoroughly entertained and amused by stories about a coat of many colours and people turning into salt. Not only were the stories violent, they were dominated by men and a vengeful god. It appeared that the fate of women in the West wasn't so different from what the women in Korea knew.

"Surely only a handful of people can actually believe this to be true," she mused. How this could be regarded as a religion thoroughly baffled her.

"Christianity is the most practised religion in the world!" Father-in-Law grabbed a large book off his shelf. "This map shows the different countries and the many faiths that people follow."

She had never seen a world map before. It was filled with odd shapes and complicated lines that ran in all directions. Father-in-Law told her to think of the map as showing how one might see the world from the moon—except of course Earth was just as round as the moon.

"This is where you are right now. Korea. And this is Japan. Here is China."

Why, Japan was just as small as Korea! And China, compared to both of them, was huge! How was it, then, that the Japanese had become so powerful?

"This is east, where the sun rises, and this is west, where it sets. North and south."

"Why is north at the top of the map?" she asked. "Has anyone seen all of the world to be able to draw it? How accurate is it? What do the lines running up and down mean?" She looked up from the map to see that Father-in-Law was smiling. She apologized for all the questions.

"Nonsense! Your insatiable curiosity delights me."

"Mother used to get annoyed whenever I asked too many questions," she said. "And the only thing I ever asked Father was for permission."

"We're shaped by the questions we ask. It leads to greater self-awareness and helps us understand the world we live in."

"Is that what Christianity has taught you? I think you're the wisest man I've ever known."

He chuckled. "I'm far from wise, I assure you. And I find the older I get, the more courage I need to ask the questions that truly matter. That's why, in your youth, you should ask as many questions as possible."

Na-Young looked down at the map. She asked, "If you could visit a foreign land, where would you go?"

He thought about it for a moment, and then tapped a spot on the paper. "One of the missionaries told me about Kilimanjaro in Africa. It's a snow-covered mountain on the equator." He pointed to a line that divided the map. "Climbing Kilimanjaro takes several days. It's like walking from the equator to the Arctic—you experience every type of climate, from the extreme heat to the bitter cold." His finger moved to the top. "In the beginning, it will be very hot in the rainforest. Then will come grasslands and bogs. Then will come land without trees, until finally, at the summit, sheets of ice. The mountain is higher than any we have in Korea. The air is so thin on top, few things can survive there." His finger tapped a different location. "But this, this is the highest mountain in the world, Everest. Unlike Kilimanjaro, no man has ever reached its summit."

A mountain so tall it created its own weather? A mountain without air to breathe? It sounded mad. What would Mother think if she heard about a mountain that sounded like the reincarnation of a thousand angry spirits? For her, mountains were sacred.

Father-in-Law closed the book.

"Keep asking questions, yes?" He smiled.

"Yes," Na-Young agreed.

"Yak-sok?" He offered his pinky finger, which interlocked with hers as acceptance of their agreement. *Such a childish gesture*, she thought. *Is that how he sees me?* When she was younger, Oppa would constantly remind her that this act was binding. If one broke a vow, the pinky finger had to be cut off to make things right again. She'd always been a little scared then, but now she accepted, determined to prove her worth to her new father-in-law.

A couple of weeks had passed since she'd received the calligraphy set when Father-in-Law said, "I have another gift for you." As he handed it to her, his fingers brushed against hers. The present was wrapped in the same green silk cloth. Speechless, Na-Young found a brush with her name engraved on a small silver plate, which was glued to the bamboo.

"Having such a diligent student has restored me in ways I cannot describe," he said to fill the silence.

"You've given me too much already."

"I'm your father-in-law. It's only natural that I would want to take care of you."

Seeing the letters so neatly etched in the silver made them look elegant to her. For the first time, Na-Young felt an unexpected pride in her name.

"I also treated myself," he said, and lifted a large piece of cloth to reveal something next to him. "Is it not the most beautiful thing you've ever seen?" He traced a finger along the golden flaring horn of a new gramophone. "Let me show you how it works," he said, and placed a record on the turntable. Carefully, he started winding the box.

Na-Young laughed when he dramatically released the brake lever. Much to her delight, the turntable started spinning and playing music.

"That's wonderful," she said, but he hushed her by putting a finger to his lips.

"It's Mozart," he said. "Probably the most brilliant musician ever. Did you know he started writing symphonies when he was just eight years old? Can you imagine? This is one of his most famous pieces. He died before he could finish it. It's appropriately titled *Requiem*—a hymn for the dead." He raised the volume.

Na-Young was unfamiliar with the style of Western music, and the sombre tone of the different instruments left her feeling suddenly out of sorts and anxious. Nevertheless, she maintained a smile for Father-in-Law's sake.

The door slid open. Breathless, Boksun pressed against the doorframe. "Your husband and his friend have just entered the main gate." She left, closing the door behind her.

Wide-eyed, Na-Young turned to Father-in-Law, who stopped the music and grabbed her hand in his, pulling her behind the folding panel screen. She was so startled, she didn't know how to react, but seeing Father-in-Law's big smile made her panic. *He's enjoying this,* she thought, *like a child playing a hiding game with another child.* She gave him a stern look and warned him to be quiet by putting a finger to her mouth. Thank goodness she was still holding the brush with her name on it. What would her husband think if he found it? The brush was dangerous. It was proof that she had disobeyed his orders to stay away from the outer quarters.

"He's not here. Where could he be?" Na-Young recognized Min-Ho's voice.

"Out to lunch, perhaps?"

"No, the old man's become quite the recluse as of late."

They heard the shuffling of paper and the soft, sharp sounds of stone against stone as one of them used the abacus on the desk.

"Don't touch that!" Min-Ho snapped.

"It's just a candy. Relax."

"It's white man's chocolate. Don't touch it."

"A music box!"

"It's white man's music."

"Yes, I know—don't listen."

Seeing Father-in-Law's amusement, Na-Young gave him a sharp stare. Did he not realize how much trouble she'd be in if her husband found her? Father-in-Law might be older, but maybe he wasn't necessarily wiser after all.

Someone banged a fist on the table. "These numbers don't lie!" Min-Ho said. "He insists that the Japanese keep advertising in all our publications! It's driving business away! Old bastard."

"Ay! The old man is your father, don't forget. Besides, like you always say, it's his money."

"Which will one day be my money, if there's any left. The old man puts on too many airs to try to impress everyone. Both the Koreans and Japanese will denounce him as a traitor at this rate."

"That's absurd. Your father is no Japanese sympathizer. Let's go. I'm hungry, and you won't let me have a single candy," the other man whined, giggling like a child.

"Quit being such a bastard," Min-Ho said, but his voice had softened.

Silence followed. Na-Young listened intently. What could they be doing? She turned to Father-in-Law. His head was lowered; the excitement at their predicament seemed to have passed.

"Let's get out of here before the old man returns," Min-Ho said. "I know where I can feed you." The anger and gloom in his voice were gone. Na-Young heard the men's footsteps recede as they left the room.

"That was close," Na-Young said. "Should I go?"

Father-in-Law waved a dismissive hand. "They're not going to be interrupting us anytime soon," he said.

Na-Young cocked her head. What could he know? Before she could say anything, Father-in-Law took his usual seat and apologized for their interruption.

"My son—he's too stubborn. He doesn't see that unless we do business with the Japanese, our company will go under. We live in an occupied country; it benefits us to cooperate."

"He's young and proud." She couldn't believe she was defending her husband when she hardly knew anything about him.

"My existence is a nuisance to him. That's his perception, and perception is his reality."

"At least he has a good friend he can talk to," she answered. She thought of Yeon-Soo and felt a gust of sadness, but tried to hide the shift in her mood. How much time had passed since they had parted? Almost three months? She thought of Boksun and how close they had become. A shadow of guilt further darkened what she was feeling, first at the thought that befriending someone else might be betraying Yeon-Soo somehow, and second, knowing that her mother would strongly disapprove of her friendship with a house servant, which was unbecoming of a proper lady of the house.

"Good friend? Sung-Min!" Father-in-Law burst into laughter. "He's an opium addict and a good-for-nothing. It's easy for him to advise my son when he has no job and no prospects of his own."

Na-Young sat back down at the desk and fingered the abacus beads, which were made of black stone. She thought back to Yeon-Soo's advice for calming one's nerves. *Pay attention to something and focus on that.* How perfectly round and smooth the beads were to the touch.

"What does his father do?" she asked.

"The man's a doctor."

"Doctor?" Could this Sung-Min be the plump woman's son? She recalled Lady Ahn boasting about her doctor husband.

Father-in-Law nodded, and Na-Young explained how Sung-Min's mother, her sister, and another woman had come calling the week before.

"Of course," he said. "Gossips. You must stay away from them. As a proper, married woman, you must understand what to make public and what to hold private. I regret that you have no mother-in-law to teach you these things, but if you trust me, I will do my best to teach you."

Na-Young nodded dutifully, but she was distracted. She wanted so much in that moment to ask him whether he knew about his dead wife's missing chest, or whether he knew of any women writers. She quickly dismissed the idea; it certainly wouldn't be appropriate. Instead, she asked him to teach her how to use the abacus. Sometimes it did take too much courage to ask the questions to which you truly wanted answers.

Later that night, Na-Young woke up suddenly and, unable to fall back asleep, walked outside into the dark. The moon and the star-filled sky seemed to call to her. Under the larger juniper tree, where for the first few nights she had cried, she closed her eyes and imagined that it was the tree outside the room she had shared with Mother. If she opened her eyes, she would see the room dimly lit and, beyond that, her mother sitting on her sleeping mat, setting her grey hair in a high, loose bun to sleep in. Every muscle relaxed.

The October nights were beginning to feel colder. She welcomed the night breezes that stirred her spirit and moved like creek water from her head, down her neck, chest, stomach, legs, and gently flowing to her feet, back out into the universe. Na-Young wandered into the servants' quarters, past the little courtyard and the little lane that led to the back road. The darkness made the sounds more noticeable, and she found comfort in them: crickets and grasshoppers, an owl in the distance. Yeon-Soo had taught her how to listen intently, as they always had to stay alert in the wild. She learned to focus on the different sounds around them: birds pecking at trees, the whooshing of birds in flight. She had joked that the black-crowned night heron, with its barking squawk and hoarse clucks, sounded like Second Mother, making Father the fish she preyed on.

"But she's a woman." Yeon-Soo had laughed, reminding her that in mythology, it was the men who were birds; women were fish.

"But she's as tall as a tree. She's almost a man," Na-Young quipped back. Recalling a story Mother had told her about Yuhwa, a water nymph turned into a goddess, she had been happy that women were associated with water. She had always been drawn to water and found the greatest comfort whenever she and Yeon-Soo were near a river. The flowing sounds were calming, much like the gentle fall of rain or the soft breathing of the wind in her ears.

Na-Young looked up to see a nighthawk plummet out of the sky and disappear just as quickly in search of prey. If only she had the power to fly. The places she could go! She drew in a deep breath and imagined soaring above the great wall that she'd heard about in China, and far beyond that the Sea of Galilee, Bethlehem, and the Jordan River—places that Father-in-Law made sound exotic while reading from the Bible, though she was assured they were real. She tried to remember where these places were on the world map.

How unfair it was that in the ancient stories, men were the ones able to transform into birds, enabling them to take flight and travel freely, while women were kept hidden beneath water, sometimes as food for the birds. She imagined an eagle, its talons ready to grab the poor fish who swam too close to the surface. In her mind's eye, she saw its dramatic dive towards the water and its ascent with its prey. She cringed at the thought of the poor fish, torn apart by the eagle's strong beak.

She would be happiest if she could be left on an island in the middle of the Pacific Ocean—which she now knew was the largest body of water anywhere—with her mother, Yeon-Soo, and Bok-sun. She had never before thought of leaving Korea. Could it be the only way for her to find true peace?

The sound of the river in the near distance led her to it. Suddenly, she heard a muted cry. Terrified, she stopped and looked around. As quietly as possible, she climbed a big branch of the nearest tree and strained in the darkness to see whether anyone was there. The moonlight created a beautiful cascade over the river.

Then she saw them. Something in the sharp breeze told her to look away, but she continued to watch in spite of herself. At one point, one of the men lifted his head, as if to sense something, but seeing no one, he continued to thrust until both men were lying sprawled on the ground, their bodies still. A match was struck to light their cigarettes, and in the few seconds that followed, she saw her husband's face and the face of his companion: the doctor's son, Sung-Min. She gasped. Was this why her husband had refused her? One of the men was up now; she couldn't tell whom. He extended a hand and helped the other up. They were headed back her way! She felt the urge to run but it was too late. She remained frozen in the tree as the two passed her.

"There's more money to be made in the newspaper business," Sung-Min said. "Think about it. Ads bring in money on a daily basis, not monthly."

"Father would never go for that," Min-Ho said.

"But it's your company now."

"But the business itself is still in his name."

"A technicality. We both know you're right. The company needs your vision if it's going to survive."

Min-Ho stopped in front of Sung-Min and pulled his arms

around him. "You always see the best in me. You're the only one who does."

Na-Young thought back to Oppa and Sarwon. The same intimacy she'd seen between her brother and Sarwon was unfolding before her. She waited awhile, too stunned to move, before making her way home. Were Min-Ho and Sung-Min in love? Same-sex relations were considered immoral and deviant. She had thought she understood why: They violated the rules that governed the roles that husbands, wives, and children had within the family. But for the first time ever, she had witnessed tenderness in her husband.

Back in the courtyard, she sat under the larger juniper tree and waited for daylight. So, it seemed that she was not the only person with secrets.

Punishment

Na-Young hovered between sleeping and waking, and her dream threatened to become lost if she opened her eyes. She was with Father-in-Law, practising brushstrokes as usual, but instead of sitting in his study, they were outside, by the river, under the big tree she had climbed a couple of nights ago when she saw Min-Ho with his companion. Across the water, the brown mountains were silhouetted against an orange sky. When a breeze sent the mulberry paper she was writing on into the air, they both chased after it. Just when she feared it would fall into the river, Father-in-Law leaped high into the air, snatching the paper from the breeze, and yelled, "I've got it!"

He smiled proudly as he waved the paper in the air. *He's very handsome*, she thought, despite his age. Then, to her surprise, he held the paper above her head and said, "You must give me a kiss if you want it back."

She opened her eyes, feeling flushed. She had never dreamt of a man before, not in that way. Her body ached as she dressed, her breasts swollen and tender to the touch. A cold swim later in the afternoon would help refresh her body and relax her mind. But thinking about the river brought back her dream, which both intrigued and embarrassed her. How could wanting to spend time with Father-in-Law make her feel so happy and anxious at the same time? *You're being silly*, she told herself as she swept her hair into a bun. She was too young and inexperienced in the ways of the world to attract a man of his intelligence and maturity. He likely pitied her, and that was why he was spending his time teaching an illiterate to read and write: so she could be worthy of her status as lady of the house and his daughter-in-law. Hopefully soon, she would have the skills to write down her dreams, although this last one had to be kept secret.

Why did she feel anxious despite knowing that things were finally settling down around her? Could feelings, like sunsets, be layered in shades of wildfire and darkness? *Mixed feelings are a sign*, she thought, *but of what?*

Na-Young grew impatient waiting for Boksun. She didn't want to be late for her writing lesson because her servant hadn't arrived. Finally, annoyed, she walked out into the courtyard, where she saw that nine house servants had gathered along the perimeter. A long wooden bench had been placed between the two juniper trees. The women who worked in the kitchen, still wearing their food-stained aprons, looked over at Na-Young and quietly whispered amongst themselves. The old woman with the missing fingers waved her hand to hush everyone. What was going on?

Na-Young watched with growing unease as Boksun was escorted in by two manservants, who led her to the bench and ordered her to lie face down on it. Boksun kept her head low and offered no resistance. Na-Young's chest tightened as she sensed what was about to happen.

Min-Ho entered through the main gate on the other side and stopped, his eyes scanning everyone present. Na-Young dropped her head and looked back up only when she was sure he wasn't looking her way. His personal attendant, whose short stature, flat nose, and brown skin had earned him the nickname "Mongolia" amongst the servants, stood next to him, holding a large, wooden paddle. Na-Young shuddered. Where was Father-in-Law? Only he'd have the power to intervene.

For a brief moment, she thought she was dreaming again. She looked up at the morning sky, blue and cloudless, expecting to see birds flying. How wonderful it would feel, she thought, to dive into the river and surrender completely to the cold water. She took a deep breath and a wave of relief washed over her. If only she could breathe underwater like a fish and stay below the surface as long as she wanted. *Perhaps fish are better off than birds, after all.* Water ebbed and flowed like energy, and possessed the power to heal.

The crack of the paddle and the muted gasps of the women servants broke the silence. When Na-Young looked at Boksun again, she saw that her chima had been raised to her waist, exposing her bare buttocks. With every blow Mongolia delivered, Boksun cried out, her body jerking on impact. Her backside quickly reddened. Na-Young's heart pounded and her thoughts swirled. Was Boksun being punished because of her? Because Na-Young had kept her from her work? Servants were regularly punished back home, but privately, and never this cruelly. She wanted to protest but did not dare.

Na-Young glanced over at the old woman, who, as she wiped her nose with a sleeve, met Na-Young's shocked gaze. In that instant, Na-Young realized who had complained to her husband about Boksun. She shot the old woman a raised eyebrow to indicate that she'd figured this out, but the old woman had already turned away.

With the punishment over, the courtyard emptied quickly.

Min-Ho looked around and, upon seeing Na-Young watching him, lowered his head and walked away.

Na-Young slouched against the doorway. Eyes closed, she fell into the silence and fog that grew long and wide around her.

Leaves

Almost a month had passed. Autumn, with its lush orange, yellow, and red hues, was Na-Young's favourite season, but it arrived quietly this year. The courtyard where Na-Young had spent her nights sitting under the juniper trees was no longer a happy place. Boksun's punishment was still vivid in her memory; the girl's cries of pain rang in her ears each time she glanced at the two trees.

She missed Boksun, who had been sent away immediately after her punishment. Na-Young had desperately hoped to apologize. It was, after all, her fault; she had kept Boksun from her work and, worse, had caused problems between her and the other house servants.

Although she couldn't understand why she felt intimidated by the old woman—someone who possessed no power—Na-Young grew frustrated by her own weak attempts to assert her authority with the household staff. But how did one become an efficient lady of the house? Second Mother thrived on fear. No one felt safe in her presence, and everyone did just as she demanded. Unfortunately, Na-Young was too young to remember just how Mother ran the house, although Na-Young recalled house servants happily sneaking sweets to her and covering for her whenever she wanted to slip out to play by the river.

Hari, Boksun's replacement, was a meek girl who was too

afraid to say anything beyond muttering the polite salutations of hello and goodbye. When she entered Na-Young's room for the first time and Na-Young asked her whether she knew where Bok-sun was, her hands trembled so much, Na-Young thought she'd drop the dinner tray she was holding. She shook her head, and Na-Young dismissed any thoughts of getting help from her.

One early morning, Na-Young heard a boy's voice in the courtyard. It was a servant boy, no older than Su-Bin had been when he died, looking up at something in the trees. She paused in the doorway, spotting the squirrel he was trying to coax down, and smiled.

"Good morning," she said.

Seeing her, the boy fled, an object falling out of his pocket as he ran. The squirrel made its way down the tree and drank from the rain puddle by the gate.

"You dropped something," Na-Young called, but the boy was already gone. She stepped outside and felt welcomed by the chilly air. It was a crudely made slingshot, much like the one Su-Bin used to play with. When she reached down to pick it up, she was struck by a sharp, debilitating pain in her abdomen. She staggered to the trees, leaning against one for balance, and threw up. Eyes tightly closed, she drew several deep breaths. But when she opened them, she was on her back, gazing up at the blue sky. Had she fainted? She saw the little boy was watching her from several feet away, and she realized that his slingshot was still in her hand. *He looks just like Su-Bin*, she thought, and her heart ached with missing him. She gestured for the boy to come fetch his toy, but he ran away again.

"I was sick for most of my pregnancy," she recalled Yeon-Soo once telling her. "Maybe that's why he turned out to be the way he is." Her friend's words echoed deep in her memory, forcing her to confront a truth she had tricked herself into denying: She was indeed pregnant. Her assault had not been punishment enough for running away and wanting to lead her own life. A child would serve as a constant reminder of her pain and struggle. Fate had been merciless.

She had lost all interest in learning to write and read. Her disappointment with Father-in-Law for not intervening on Boksun's behalf prevented her from visiting him again. She was also terrified of running into Min-Ho. But her biggest fear was the baby she now knew was growing inside her. What could she do? No one would understand how she had come to carry a Japanese bastard. She would have to destroy it. But how? Boksun was the one person she might have trusted enough to ask for help in finding the right herbs and medicinal plants to end a pregnancy.

The silence in the courtyard magnified Na-Young's fear.

The widow, Lady Oh, returned twice, each time bringing several books and magazines with her. But the visits were cut short as bouts of nausea caused Na-Young to excuse herself. When the widow tried to visit again, Na-Young sent her away, anticipating the widow's questions about her condition.

One dreary afternoon, Na-Young ventured out to the courtyard, and although she couldn't bring herself to enter the servants' quarters, she could hear how busy it was. She heard the banging of pots and the crackling of an open fire, where she imagined sweet potatoes—she could almost smell them—roasting. Despite the wonderful scent of cinnamon and sesame seeds, her stomach was unsettled. She circled back and found herself at Father-in-Law's study.

He wasn't there. Na-Young took a deep breath, and the usual scent of pipe tobacco in the air unexpectedly improved her mood. Her eyes wandered to the sketch of Father-in-Law's late wife. Such a tragedy to die so young! Mother-in-Law's gaze was lowered slightly, and Na-Young saw a sadness in her eyes that she hadn't noticed before. Father-in-Law had commented that Na-Young's eyes looked the same.

For a moment, she wondered whether his wife, too, could have been as miserable as she was, but she quickly dismissed the idea. Father-in-Law had clearly been in love with her—after all, he'd kept the sketch all these years. They'd had a child together. His wife had been adored and happy in her marriage.

Her own situation made Na-Young's heart ache. Her husband had betrayed their marriage, but so had she by wandering back to Father-in-Law's study. She patted her stomach. What was she doing here? Perhaps, hidden deep in her subconscious, she wanted to trust Father-in-Law and seek his assistance. He might help her, she reasoned. He seemed genuinely fond of her. Initially, his attention had made her uneasy, but quickly, she'd found herself enjoying it. In fact, the way he looked at her when he thought she was distracted with her brush and paint had led her to pay closer attention to ensure her hair and makeup were set perfectly. She bit her lip and chastised herself for her lapse in judgement—the man was her father-in-law, and he had failed her already by not helping Boksun.

The autumn leaves would soon all fall, and winter would come. Her belly would continue to swell. She thought of Yeon-Soo. Was she living in the mountains? What might have happened if their roles had been reversed? What if she had been the one who'd needed to flee? What would she do, knowing that she was wanted for treason, a crime punishable by death?

She suddenly pictured the little hut in the middle of nowhere. She thought of the little boy and girl, shot dead along with their mother. As horrific as it sounded, their home would be abandoned and, for a little while anyway, would be a good place to stay. The woman had kept a good vegetable garden. Could she somehow flee there? What would life be like on her own? She would have to learn to trap rabbits and catch fish in the nearby river. She leaned her head back, closed her eyes, and imagined herself standing in the pine forest. As dangerous as it was there, she would be free from the prying eyes of gossiping servants who would soon discover her condition, and a husband whom she feared and loathed. For a moment, she entertained the possibility of having the child. She wouldn't be alone. Should she attempt to go back to the hut and try to make a life for herself and her child? Could she ever forget the pain and violence that had caused its life? Or ignore its tainted blood? The thought left her instantly panicked. She could not have this baby under these circumstances. Time was passing with doomed certainty. Quick action would be needed to protect the names of both houses: her husband's and her father's. She left the study, brushing past Father-in-Law outside.

"Why don't you join me in my study?" he asked. "We can talk."

She kept walking.

He followed her into the courtyard of the inner quarters.

"Please don't be angry with me," he said. "I know that you cared about Boksun. She told me how lonely you are. She was grateful to you for everything."

Na-Young wanted to call him a liar—Boksun wouldn't betray her confidence by telling him how she'd been feeling.

"She told me you were teaching her how to read and write," Father-in-Law said, "because you cared deeply about her."

Na-Young closed her eyes. So Boksun had told him everything!

"It was very kind to teach her what you knew. It confirmed what I believed about you. You have a generous nature." He paused. "But I've arranged new employment for her. She'll be fine."

She turned to face Father-in-Law. "Where is she?"

"The Ewha Girls School in the capital. She'll be able to study and work to earn her keep."

"Why didn't you tell me?"

"You didn't give me the opportunity. I knew you'd be worried about Boksun. You, my dear, must not violate the natural order of things in our household. Remember your place as the lady of the house."

Did she dare tell him anything about her marriage? Did he have any idea what kind of husband his son was? That he not only refused to take her as his wife in bed, but acted as if he truly hated her. And she now knew why. But surely whatever feelings he had for Sung-Min, his male lover, would pass? They would never be able to marry and have children, so what would be the point of their union? Did his father suspect anything? As much as she wanted answers, she was too embarrassed to broach the subject. Maybe Mother was right in saying that marriage and love were separate, and that love was a choice. Maybe Min-Ho's family knew about him. Maybe his marriage to her, as much as it was an illusion, allowed the Park family to maintain an imagined reality and social acceptance. He had already chosen to love someone else, even if it meant having to do so in secret.

Where did this leave her? She had no choice but to take charge of her own life. She rested a hand on her belly, and the heaviness that continued to weigh her down distressed her even more.

"Are you not well?" Father-in-Law asked. "It's from being cooped up indoors day after day. Tomorrow, you will escort me to the capital. I have some papers to drop off and sign. You can shop while I tend to business. We'll leave early in the morning on the train and be back by nightfall."

She nodded in agreement. Finally, she could search for someone, possibly an apothecary or a doctor, who would know how to end her pregnancy. And maybe she could find Boksun! Perhaps she would know someone in the capital who could help. Maybe hope, often the cruelest of emotions, didn't have to merely live in her imagination. But she would have to act carefully and quickly.

Apples and Plums

As they settled into their seats in first class, Father-in-Law said, "I'm famished." He gestured for the train attendant to bring over a snack.

"And will your wife care for anything?" the attendant asked.

Father-in-Law broke into a grin.

"Yes," he answered. "I'm sure she's hungry, too. We rushed to catch the train and didn't have breakfast." Then, turning to face Na-Young, he asked, "Yeobo, would you like some fruit?"

She was beside herself. How could he let a stranger believe they were married? How could he call her his darling wife?

"Still hungover?" he said, then, turning back to the attendant, lowered his voice to add, "Too much drinking at last night's party. She'll have what I'm having."

Na-Young turned to face the window, stunned. Yet she couldn't help but also feel a little thrilled that he had called her his wife. She shook off the feeling. They were in a public place. What could happen?

"Aye! Don't be mad at me," he said. He poked at her arm. "I didn't want things to be awkward between us." He let her stare out the window without saying anything for several minutes. Finally, he said, "I'm sorry about Boksun, but you need to let that go. Surely you can't hate me forever. You do like me, even just a little?" His voice was low but soft. A part of her wanted to reassure him.

"If you're going to be this stubborn, blink once for 'yes' and twice for 'no' if you understand what I'm saying." A playfulness had crept into his voice.

She desperately wanted for him to think she was still angry, but couldn't help herself; no man had ever made her want to laugh so freely.

She blinked once.

"Do you like apples?"

She blinked once again.

"Do you like plums?"

She blinked twice.

"Do you like me?"

A smile came to her lips, unbidden. She swallowed and chose to be honest. When she blinked "yes," she felt his hand fall on her thigh—a gesture that sent butterflies fluttering. Then the unthinkable came to her. Did she dare flirt with him? Could she eventually make him believe the child was his?

They both looked up when the attendant cleared his throat and accepted the trays he held.

"I'll eat your plum slices," Father-in-Law said, "now that I know you don't like them."

She looked down at the thin plum slices, their red juice like blood, and passed him the small plate.

I'm finally in the big city, thought Na-Young. One of her favourite childhood stories was about the giant wall that once surrounded the capital city, standing for hundreds of years. Her mother had stood, arms stretched high over her head, as she explained how the ancient wall had kept out tigers and bears and protected the city from invading barbarians. In her young mind, Na-Young had envisioned a wall so high, it touched the clouds. But much of the wall, worn with time, was gone now, torn down by the Japanese. The gate entrances, however, were left standing.

Father-in-Law, like a knowledgeable guide, pointed out landmarks and spoke about them with energy and confidence. "And that's the South Gate," he said, looking off into the distance. "You'll find almost anything you need in the market there."

Na-Young eyed the clouds—grey patches that dotted the sky over Namdaemun, the South Gate. A giant pagoda with two tiers rested above the stone arch that allowed people and vehicles to move in and out of the capital. Traffic congestion brought together horses, carts, rickshaws, and the rare automobile. Men cursed each other for right of way. People were everywhere: men with their white robes and wide-brimmed hats, missionaries, businessmen in suits, female house servants with straw baskets full of groceries balanced on their heads, and children playing near the trolley tracks. A farmer with a wooden backpack loaded with straw and wood, his hair in a topknot, caught Na-Young's attention. He easily could have been one of the men who worked in the fields back in Daegeori. Her heart swelled as she thought of home. She took a deep breath and did her best to ignore the feeling.

At a glance, it appeared as if the vendors at the outdoor market, who were mostly Korean, with some Japanese and Chinese merchants, were struggling for spaces, but Na-Young quickly realized that each had his own spot. Goods for sale included everything from straw sandals to paperback novels.

Father-in-Law explained that despite rumours that the Japanese would close the market, it continued to flourish, largely because of shrewd pro-Japanese politicians who negotiated deals in their own interests. "The Joseon Farming Company that oversees the market is managed by pro-Japanese Koreans and Japanese entrepreneurs," he said. "They benefit by charging high rent and seizing part of the vendors' profits."

His business acumen impressed Na-Young, who, despite not fully understanding what she heard, felt reassured that Father-in-Law knew what was good for the family business.

A crisp cold hovered over the market. An old woman sat rocking back and forth on a thin straw mat. Her hanbok was layered with dirt and her greying hair, pinned back in a bun, threatened to come undone. Her husband was scooping soybean sprouts into a sack for a waiting customer. The woman reminded Na-Young of her mother, who, after losing Mi-Young, rocked for hours when she felt overwhelmed. She claimed it soothed her soul. Na-Young kept her emotions in check and focused on the moment.

"I need to tend to business now. You shop and get anything you want," Father-in-Law said. He had already given her enough money to mean what he said. "I won't be long." He looked up at the sky. "We'll meet back here when the sun is at its highest point."

He was gone. Na-Young turned to the old woman and her husband. "How might I get to the girls' school?" she asked.

"Ewha? You can take that bus," the old man said, pointing off into the distance.

A bus? Na-Young thought. Suddenly, finding Boksun felt daunting. She'd look for a medicine shop on her own.

The crowd seemed to grow. A few metres away, a toddler stumbled and fell, crashing into a stack of clay kimchi pots for sale. His cry cut through the noise of the people. A young mother ran to fetch him, hushing him as she frantically tried to stop the bleeding from his arm. The merchant, assessing the damage to his property, demanded the woman pay for her son's clumsiness.

Na-Young took a few steps and, distracted by the scene, collided with a Japanese policeman who was heading towards the shouting merchant, causing them both to almost lose their balance. Stunned, Na-Young bowed, avoiding eye contact, and moved towards the shops.

"Tomare!" he shouted. He continued to shout at her in Japanese, but she couldn't understand him.

He switched to Korean. "Stupid and clumsy!" Shaking his head, he said something else in Japanese. Na-Young could tell by his mocking tone that she was in trouble. Her knees threatened to buckle, but then the merchant, whose property had been damaged, shouted so loudly, the policeman's head turned. Seizing the opportunity, Na-Young dashed into the crowd. When she finally stopped, she saw an old man heaving a bag larger than himself onto a pull-cart. A horse that reminded her of Oppa's stallion was tethered a few metres away. Without thinking, she walked towards it. Just as she was about to stroke the horse, she came face-to-face with Old Man Yang. He gasped when he recognized her and became his usual amicable and charming self. She was so happy to see him, she fought the urge to cry.

"Why, you're all grown up!" he said. "I was hoping to bump into you again one day. I run into the most unexpected friends in the city!"

He fumbled through one of the bags on the pull-cart and placed a fistful of her favourite candy into her hand. The gesture touched her, and she burst into tears.

"Am I so hideous you cry for me?" he joked. He handed her a handkerchief.

"Have you been to Daegeori recently?" she asked, blowing her nose.

"Yes, yes," he said.

Na-Young's body tensed. "Omma? Oppa? How are they?"

Old Man Yang looked away and tied the candy bag closed. "They didn't want you to worry," he said, "and I don't think I should be the one to tell you, but your oppa volunteered to help the Japanese military police as an aide."

Na-Young was dumbfounded. "What does that mean?"

"Korean men who speak Japanese are sometimes recruited to work with the military police, you know, to translate and get their messages across to everyone. Regrettably, the job places your brother in the cruel position of becoming a mouthpiece for the bastards." He spat on the ground, then, noticing Na-Young's hands, added softly, "You're shaking." He gently placed a hand over hers. "He did it for your family. The Japanese have stopped harassing your family ever since."

Na-Young imagined Oppa working alongside the Japanese military police. He was meant to be a doctor, a healer, she thought. Not a traitor, helping their country's oppressors.

"Those Japanese military police came back to your father's home with more questions. Someone drew a picture of Yeon-Soo, whose identity was confirmed by her brother-in-law—the idiot! Apparently, the Japanese military police didn't believe Yeon-Soo's mother-in-law and thought she was hiding her. They tore her estate apart and had a man camped out there for over a month to spy on everyone."

"What about me?" Na-Young had to ask.

"You don't need to worry. Everyone swore that you were always there preparing for the wedding. Even your second mother swore that she was with you resizing your bridal hanbok on the actual day the Japanese military policeman was killed."

Na-Young's chest tightened at the thought of Second Mother lying to protect her. The last thing she wanted was to owe her anything. But she'd only lied, Na-Young reasoned, because, for all she knew, Na-Young had been home the entire time. Would Second Mother have checked in on her anyway?

"But since your brother started helping the military police, they've left your family alone. I suppose that made them see that your family was loyal after all. They even gave him a black uniform to wear."

"I still don't understand why he'd offer to work with them! Didn't he realize how humiliating that would be for Father?"

"Everyone refused to believe that you could have killed anyone, let alone a Japanese military police officer. Still, your oppa felt this was the best way to avoid any suspicion." Old Man Yang hesitated. "The last I heard your second mother was . . ." With one hand, he spun small circles by his temple. "In the head, I mean. I don't mean to worry you, but your father has also been unwell since your brother left. Maybe I shouldn't be telling you any of this."

"No, I want to know," she said, stopping him, although she wondered whether not knowing was better. She was hit by a pang of guilt but resisted the impulse to succumb to it. She needed to think. Danger seemed to be everywhere—and it had all started with her. Was it even possible to make things right again?

"I need your help," Na-Young said. "I have no one else who can help me. But you must promise me that you'll guard my secret." Unlike her father, who owned the second-largest land in their village, Old Man Yang had only his pull-cart and everything on it.

Yet he was strong and generous. He always laughed with her, and her heart had always felt warm and safe in his presence.

"I've known you all your life. Of course I will keep your secret. Yak-sok," Old Man Yang said, and offered his pinky to show his commitment.

As she told him about her pregnancy, his face grew long and his downcast eyes brought Na-Young close to tears. But he didn't disappoint her.

"I know just where to go," Old Man Yang said.

The shop was called The Peacock with Its Tail of One Hundred Eyes. Peacock feathers hung in its doorway—green, blue, and bronze plumes displayed like ornaments. The most pungent blend of smells she'd ever encountered washed over her. Where had Old Man Yang brought her?

Na-Young slipped her shoes off in the small foyer and stepped into the shop. It was tiny, and two of its walls had shelves lined with big glass jars, containing everything from herbs to animal parts. She marvelled at how much could be crammed into the small space. A dog barked, and she was startled when she saw his disfigured face. The poor thing was missing his nose!

"How can I help you?" an old woman—the proprietor—asked. She was filling a cloth sack with dried mushrooms from a jar on the counter.

Old Man Yang whispered something to her.

The dog barked again.

"What happened to your nose?" Na-Young asked gently. She'd never seen a dog without a nose before. "I'm sorry to say, but don't you scare away customers?"

"That's part of her job," the proprietor said, looking up at her. "To discourage anyone I don't want in my shop from lingering. But Old Nosey loves people." Na-Young somehow felt more at ease, knowing the dog was female. That, and the dog's friendly demeanour. The proprietor came out from behind her counter and looked at Na-Young, as if assessing her physical appearance.

"May I see your tongue?" she asked.

"What would that reveal?"

"The tongue is the beginning of one's digestive tract, so it reveals the health of one's digestive system."

Na-Young hesitated a moment, but seeing Old Man Yang nod his head, she let the woman inspect her tongue.

"Your tongue is slightly purple," she said. "I don't want to give you anything stronger than you need for your condition." She patted Na-Young's arm.

"Thank you." Na-Young paid and exhaled slowly. She was relieved that the shopkeeper was a woman and appeared to understand her vulnerability and need for secrecy.

The proprietor moved with a surprising nimbleness as she mixed liquids from different jars and handed her a small vial.

"What is it?" Na-Young asked. She sniffed it and gagged.

"It'll do its job."

Na-Young became distracted again by Old Nosey, who was licking her hand. She squatted down and scratched the dog's back, and the dog's tail wagged. A feeling of calm came over Na-Young once more.

"You should get a dog," the proprietor observed.

"To help me relax?"

"Yes. Dogs have a natural ability to protect their masters."

I can use all the help I can get, Na-Young thought as she slipped back into her shoes and stepped outside. She drew a deep breath, only to smell wilting cabbages on a cart and fried mandu from a nearby noodle shop.

"Aye, Na-Young," Old Man Yang said. "Don't be sad. Life is better when you keep a positive outlook. Look at me! I may be just a poor man forced to peddle my wares everywhere, but I'm happy because my travels allow me to bump into old friends like you."

Na-Young felt lighter, grateful that his attitude had impacted hers in a good way.

"Do you believe in fate?" she asked. She was certain that he would say yes, believing just as Mother had in fortune tellers and shamans who knew someone's future because it was predetermined.

"Aye, but not like most people. I love my fate! I'm my own boss, and, like I said, I get around, which makes me happy."

Na-Young pondered this. Another man might argue Old Man Yang's fate was filled with hardship and loneliness on the road.

"I admire how you've chosen to be happy," she said. "I'll try to do the same."

"Promise?"

"I swear," she said, and bowed.

After leaving Old Man Yang, Na-Young tried to blend in with the crowd to avoid running into the same policeman, and she soon found herself back at the meeting place. The old woman she had seen earlier, sitting on the straw mat, was still rocking back and forth. Na-Young headed towards her. The woman's husband called her over. He flashed a smile as he placed a fistful of soybean sprouts into her free hand to examine. He didn't seem to notice the beetles scuttling amongst the sprouts he was selling. Na-Young looked over at his wife.

"Is she my Minja?" the old woman asked the man. "Has she come back?"

"No, it's not her," he said gently, patting her shoulder. "She's a customer."

"Is that my Minja on the bus?" the woman asked, pointing to a prison bus filled with women, which was making its way down the road. "Help me find my daughter, please!"

The bus was headed west towards Seodaemun, having just entered the city through Namdaemun Gate.

Na-Young turned to look. But how could she help when she didn't even know what the daughter looked like? For a split second, she was seized by a possibility: Could Yeon-Soo be on the bus, or one like it? Had she been captured? If so, what truths had she told? In a panic, she squinted, straining to catch a glimpse of red highlights amongst the dark-haired women on the bus. But she recognized no one, and the bus drove away. *Don't give in to complete fear just yet,* Na-Young thought. Then, remembering the promises she had made to her friend, she heard Yeon-Soo's voice in her mind: *Don't look for me—under any circumstances.*

Back on the train, Father-in-Law fell asleep after eating, his head heavy against her shoulder. What would become of them now? she wondered. She thought about the vial of potion in her money pouch. The sooner she took it, the better. But what if she got sick? What if it killed her? Mother had always said that they could not control fate. It was a predetermined force that controlled events to come. But what about destiny? Couldn't an individual's disposition, efforts, and actions shape the course of one's life? After all, what would be the point of trying to rise above any hardships if they were set up to inevitably fail? Who could accept such irrationality?

The sun was falling fast through the dust of the windows. Sloping grasslands rimmed by enormous camphor, oak, and zelkova trees blurred into different shades of autumn. Then the view changed dramatically, as if all of the country lay before her. Lakes, mountains, and villages dotted the distance. Above, birds circled the sky. Na-Young closed her eyes, but the image of the countryside stayed with her. Couldn't she be the creator of her own destiny?

Sitting so close to Father-in-Law reminded her of the times they sat side by side at the table in his study. The same strange, yet wonderful, physical sensations ran through her. The thought returned: If she couldn't get rid of this baby, could she seduce him and pass the child off as his? She shook her head; the thought was ridiculous. But then at least the baby would be a Park and, while illegitimate, it might be able to pass as a Korean child. Lies upon lies. Could one sin be worse than another? Na-Young wondered what Father-in-Law's Bible had to say about that.

Waiting

"Please bring me some tea," Na-Young said to Hari. "Then let me rest." The vial of potion felt cool and hard in her hand. What would happen if she drank the entire potion at once? Would it kill the baby and her? She felt a tinge of regret for all the bad decisions she had made that had brought her here. Regret was as useful to her as shame and guilt. A luxury. Though it wasn't her fault that she was pregnant. She poured the entire vial into the tea that Hari had brought her, waited for it to cool, and drank it quickly. The dull cramp in her stomach escalated into a tight knot. The women in her village enjoyed talking about how pregnancies were riddled with pain and discomfort. It was proof that they were stronger than men after all. Or, was it the potion doing what it was supposed to do? She couldn't tell, and it added to her anxiety. Then to her dismay, she threw up. Her vision blurred with tears as she understood the harsh reality that any possibility of the poison working was now lost.

Later that night, Na-Young climbed high up her favourite tree, an ancient sycamore that guarded the river. Without the heavy, leafy canopy of summer, she felt oddly exposed under the starry night sky. Nearby, brown leaves clung to the oak trees, refusing to take their leap to death. Wedged between the trunk and a sturdy branch, she recalled a legend that Oppa had once told her about a young man who, despite being in love with his wife, abandoned her because she could not have children. The wife, who had no parents to return to, begged him to stay. When he refused, she chopped him to pieces and secretly buried him. She remarried and gave birth to twenty-two children—which, incidentally, was the number of her dead husband's severed body parts—and died giving birth to her twenty-third child. The gods, amused by her plight, turned her into an oak tree with leaves that would not fall, even in winter, to protect the birds and animals seeking shelter. The first husband, who had put unborn children before his wife's love for him, became a pine tree, Korea's eventual national tree.

Na-Young's finger absentmindedly traced along the bark of the branch. If only her own husband had refused her openly and forced her to return home. Then the river in front of her would be the one back in Daegeori. Despair and loneliness sank deep into her heart. Movement in the distance caught her eye. Although he was a mere silhouette in the pale light, she recognized Min-Ho. He stopped, no more than a hundred metres away. Startled, she watched as he gazed at the quarter moon. He stood tall, the same height as Oppa. In a different lifetime, he and Oppa might have even been friends. She shook the thought away—her brother would never have befriended someone with such a cruel, malevolent nature.

As Min-Ho paced back and forth, likely to stay warm, a sinking feeling of dread settled in Na-Young's chest: He was waiting for his Sung-Min. Now, not only did she have to wait for his lover as well, she had to witness them together again. She shook her head; she had been wrong to believe that the cold December weather would force them to find a warmer place to meet.

As the night grew longer and colder, she fought through the

pins and needles that ran through her legs and feet. To fight boredom and fatigue, she twisted her hemline, her hair, and even bit into her interlaced fingers. The chill and the smell of earth and the river made her nose and eyes ache. She repositioned her shawl so that it wrapped tightly over her head, exposing only her eyes. Whom did she feel more sorry for? she wondered. Min-Ho, the jilted lover who chose to freeze rather than believe his partner had forsaken him; or herself, stuck high up in a tree, forced to witness their sad unravelling? Was it patience or ego keeping him there? Either way, her mind did flips trying to coax itself from feeling even just a bit sorry for him. The moon, which had been high above them when Min-Ho first arrived, had since dipped westward. Her eyes grew heavy and finally she surrendered to sleep, telling herself she would rest for just a moment. Suddenly, in what felt like a lucid dream, Na-Young had a sharp sensation of falling, and she cried out. But she had really fallen, and she landed with a thump.

Min-Ho came running. "What are you doing here?" he demanded.

"What are *you* doing here?" she asked in return, somewhat dazed.

"Do you make it a habit of sleeping in trees? What are you doing out here?" His mouth hung open in surprise.

"I went for a walk," she said, then added, "just like you."

Perhaps he sensed that she was trying to protect his reputation. His eyes softened. She tried to sit up but winced in pain.

"You're hurt," he said. He wrapped an arm around her waist to lift her up. It was the first time he had touched her. Instinctively, she pulled away.

He shifted uncomfortably.

"Can you blame me?" she blurted out. "You've been nothing but cruel to me." To her surprise, the pain she felt overrode any fear.

"I can't just leave you here," he said.

"I like sleeping outdoors."

"You'll get cold." Min-Ho's eyes flickered between her and the river. "A bear might eat you."

She laughed in spite of herself.

"It could happen," he said, a little smile now on his face. He lifted her, careful to avoid the broken branches and vines around her.

"It's good that I was out, then, and found you," he said. "Otherwise, who would have been around to save you?"

She shook her head. "I would have managed on my own. I always do." She kept her tone firm.

Perhaps it was the outdoors, a neutral space away from the inner and outer quarters of their home, or the night sky that protected them both, but Na-Young had a strange feeling that tonight could change the course of their relationship.

Min-Ho slowed as they reached the back gate. They crossed into the servants' quarters. Just as they were about to enter Na-Young's courtyard, a light flickered behind them. Had she imagined it? They ducked into her room. He lowered her gently onto the sleeping mat before dashing to close the door. When he turned on the lantern, she noticed blood on his coat.

"Are you hurt?" she asked.

He gasped at the sight of her blood-soaked chima. "No, it's coming from you. How badly did you fall?"

Na-Young's first thought was that she'd lost the baby, but before she could react, she saw the gash on her lower leg. Min-Ho examined the wound, which was red and raw, and wrapped his handkerchief around it. He did this without asking, which to her surprise pleased rather than offended her.

They exchanged glances when they heard movement outside. She hadn't imagined the flickering light after all. Min-Ho turned off the lantern, plunging them into darkness.

"What should we do?" he whispered.

"Wait for them to leave."

"How long will that take?"

"I don't know," she said.

"I hate waiting."

"Me too."

"I get too impatient."

"Me too."

They both sighed. To fight the pain and aches she felt, Na-Young imagined the moon above the horizon. Had Min-Ho turned to the moon just as she had because it was his only constant companion? He seemed too pragmatic and angry to worship the moon as some of the villagers back home did. Still, there was something in the way he had looked up into the night sky that suggested he, too, might be as alone as she was.

Ghosts

Na-Young woke with a start, bathed in sweat and trembling. Her injury was just a dream, she reassured herself, but the pain in her leg told her otherwise. She was alone. Abandoned. Her belly turned and she feared throwing up. Feverish, lying somewhere between waking and sleeping, she continued to have the most startling dreams. In one, she followed Father-in-Law across a river, up a walnut tree, and over the wall of a royal palace. Sweat running down her forehead, she struggled to keep up with him. Bees, wasps, and small stinging insects trailed behind her as the rushing of the wind urged her on. In another dream, Yeon-Soo was kneeling in front of a fire, raking out the cinders, while the sun, red in the sky, transformed into the Japanese flag.

Na-Young drifted in and out of consciousness. When her fever broke, she woke to see Min-Ho's anguished face. A sour taste in her mouth caused her to gag, and she threw up. But rather than be repulsed, Min-Ho patted her back and gave her a fresh handkerchief.

"You're going to be just fine," he said. "I'll call the doctor back."

He hadn't abandoned her after all. When she woke up again, Min-Ho and Dr. Lee stood in the doorway, looking like ghosts in the greyish light. What were they whispering about? Did Dr. Lee know that Na-Young's husband was his son's secret lover? How did Min-Ho feel talking to the father of his secret lover?

"She needs rest," the doctor finally said, turning to her. "Give her this medicine later, after she's eaten something." A stale smell of decaying leaves, earth, and dark spices cut through the air as he transferred several scoops of medicine from his bag into a small pouch he set aside for Na-Young.

"Meanwhile, this will help her regain the energy and nutrients she needs." He put something into the teapot that was on the table next to her sleeping mat. "Thankfully, the baby seems fine."

Min-Ho froze, as did Na-Young. The doctor barely looked up as he gathered his things and bid them farewell. Without a word, Min-Ho followed him out.

The desire to explain her baby to Min-Ho overwhelmed her, but just as quickly, she was grateful to be alone. Na-Young listened for a while. Sensing no movement outside, she reached for the teapot. A few dark drops splashed, and she thought it a shame to spoil the fine white linen that lined the tray. She let out a slow breath and rested a hand on her belly. Of course she was still pregnant—the Japanese bastard refused to die. She struck her stomach and suddenly felt great shame for having raised her hand at something even more helpless than she. Despite the pungent odour of the medicine, she thought she smelled flowers. She closed her eyes. Dark blue gentians hung in the air against a backdrop of fog, thin and fragmented like ice crystals. Something happens to your senses when you feel yourself losing your mind, Mother had once said. But in her case, there was no loss. Or was there? Surely, she had lost parts of herself, her dreams for a good marriage, a good future. And now that Min-Ho knew about the baby, would he tell his father? The unknowability of just about everything left her feeling as if she was sitting on the edge of an abyss, the separation of light and dark, apart and together, alone and yet not alone—her child was still with her.

Proposal

A week later, she was back at the river. Back in the tree. In the distance, the treetops were crowned by clouds, the forest beyond them deepening into the dark.

The night was exceptionally cold with only the faintest glimmers of starlight. She blew on her hands, which were already numb. Unlike the last time she was out, she'd only be able to wait a short time despite her many layers of clothing. Then, just as she was about to give up, she spotted a shadowy figure. Her heart skipped, but she stayed still; her leg ached whenever she put pressure on it. It troubled her that Min-Ho knew about the baby but not the cause of her pregnancy.

Min-Ho stopped under the tree, as if he knew she was there. "What are you doing here?" he said. "I was sure the bitter cold would keep you away."

"You never gave me a chance to explain." She waited for him to say something. The cold air pinched her flesh. She tugged on the scarf that was wrapped around her head. "You must have questions for me."

He said nothing, causing her to ask, "Are you mad at me?"

"How I feel has nothing to do with you."

Then something clicked in her mind. "Sung-Min," she said. "I know you care deeply for him."

When he didn't reply, Na-Young looked at him and saw his body tense. He threw himself down at the foot of the tree. She cautiously descended and sat next to him.

"His father sent him away. He's never coming back," Min-Ho said.

"How do you know?"

"I asked his father—the doctor who treated you. He said Sung-Min joined an electrical engineering apprenticeship program and left."

"He'll be back after training though, yes?"

"The whole thing's a lie. Sung-Min never mentioned any such program, and he'd certainly never leave without saying anything."

"Then why do you keep coming here?" she asked tentatively.

"What else can I do? My life feels empty now."

Na-Young, who had never heard a man talk like this, was speechless. She peered at the darkness that was the river in front of them. If one didn't know it was there, one would walk right into it, realizing its existence too late.

"Why do you come here?" Min-Ho asked.

Before she answered, she warmed her hands with her breath again. Her mind raced, her eyes focused on her breathing. Her thoughts took her down the path beyond the hills of Anyang, to the worn paths where generations of her grandmothers had walked.

"I was attacked and raped by a Japanese military policeman."

He whipped around. She caught a glimpse of his dropped jaw before she gazed back out at the darkness.

"Does my father know?"

"No."

Min-Ho's head fell back on the tree with a soft thud. "Why? Why haven't you told him?"

"I've been trying to get rid of it. Nothing's worked so far." Then, knowing how much her husband despised the Japanese, she added, "More than anything, I hate that it's Japanese."

"Yes," Min-Ho said. A curse escaped him. "And here I was convinced it was my father's child." He got up and walked restlessly back and forth along the edge of the river. She could barely see him. Then, to her surprise, she heard him yell more curses against the Japanese, then against his father. There was a note in his cry that shook something deep within her.

"You always seem so angry," she said, only to realize that she had seen him happy—when he was with Sung-Min. Na-Young brushed back a strand of hair. He dropped down next to her again.

"I'm sorry," she said. "You must miss him terribly."

To her surprise, he leaned into her. Was he crying? She'd never seen a man cry—a boy, yes, but never a man. What was she to do? She thought back to Oppa and how he treated her whenever she was upset.

"You need to stop whining and move on," she said firmly. She pretended to hit his head. How absurdly funny to tell a man what to do! She leaned into him and was happy to see how his body helped warm her.

"What am I going to do?" he asked.

She sensed an opportunity. Although no one was near, in a low, hushed voice, she said, "What if we passed the baby off as yours?"

"But it's a Japanese bastard." He paused. "If only the baby was my father's child . . . we could keep the bloodline going. Are you sure it can't be my father's child?"

"I would never do such a despicable thing. Why would you attack my character in such a vile manner?"

"I could have helped you get rid of it. Why didn't you come see me sooner?"

Na-Young broke out into spontaneous laughter. Men were so stupid.

"After the way you treated me?" Quickly, she realized that if she were to get what she wanted, she would have to coax him to agree. She repeated her suggestion again, this time in a stern voice. She added, "You have nothing to lose and everything to gain. You'll get a son, and the marriage will appear intact. You'll continue to have the freedom to love whomever you want in the future."

"It sounds so ludicrous." He half laughed, but the way his voice trailed off signalled some hope. "It would surely shock the old man," he said. "He's in love with you, you know. You shouldn't have led him on the way you did."

Stunned at his accusation, she had the instinct to scream at him, but she controlled it.

"I'm sorry if that's how you perceived it. You're wrong, of course. Think about my proposal," she said, and got up. "It benefits us both." She left before he could say anything else.

Onions

In the days that followed, Na-Young sat in her room, so bored she started to take notice of the mundane: the different ways kitchen workers cut the vegetables that Hari brought to her like clockwork every morning and evening. She wondered which cook chopped the onions and carrots into thick chunks. On other days, the same dish would have vegetables diced into tiny, pebble-like pieces. Did the old woman who despised her so much ever spit into her food? Without Boksun around to amuse and entertain her, Na-Young felt even more cut off from her own staff. She sensed they were talking about her but couldn't know for sure.

She imagined their whispers:

"Had he visited her all this time without us knowing? She's pregnant."

"How far along?"

"The doctor thinks four months, which is how long they've been married."

"Could we have been wrong about the young master all this time?"

"What were we to think? He never visits her."

"And what about his father . . ."

She shuddered at the thought. If only Min-Ho hadn't planted the idea of Father-in-Law in her head. How naive she'd been to spend so much time with him.

One early morning, before her breakfast was even served, she ventured out to the servants' quarters. She was eyeing the cracked clay pots resting against a railing and wondering whose job it was to replace them when she overheard talking in the kitchen. Someone spoke her name. She hadn't been imagining their gossip after all. She was trying so intently to listen that she jumped when the old woman slipped a quilted blanket around her.

"It's far too cold to be out here in your condition," the old woman scolded.

"You're talking about me," Na-Young said.

"Our talk should not interest you." She walked into the kitchen. Na-Young followed her. The smell of roasting garlic, lotus roots, and tree bark, though not unpleasant, overwhelmed her. She scooped a handful of dried mint and ginger on the table and sniffed deeply. It did little to settle the queasiness in her stomach.

"You need to stop bad-mouthing me," she said. Two other women who were peeling onions stopped their work and quietly slipped out. When the old woman refused to acknowledge Na-Young, she raised her voice and repeated herself. "I'm talking to you."

The old woman was in a sudden, flaring rage. "Did I say I didn't hear you?"

Na-Young's chest constricted, but rather than surrender to the old woman's wrath, Na-Young kept her head high. For a moment, she debated whether to threaten the old woman with a punishment similar to Boksun's.

Impatiently, the old woman flapped her hands in the air, causing Na-Young to wonder whether it had been disease or injury that caused the lost fingers. Regardless, it must have been painful, she thought, and felt a strange physical sensation in her own hand. She pulled the quilt closer to her, and feeling the warmth of it wrapped around her, she realized it was better to try to repair their relationship.

"I can't control how you feel about me. All I ask is for your courtesy, nothing more or less. And I offer you the same." She was about to remind the old woman she was the lady of the house, after all, but stopped. They both knew this already. She folded the quilt in two and handed it back. "Thank you for your kindness."

The old woman said nothing. The women who had been peeling onions passed her as Na-Young stepped outside. She overheard the old woman tell one of them, "Prepare some tea and take it to the lady. Foolish woman, she'll likely catch cold walking about as she is."

Na-Young sighed. Her small victory at having stood up to the old woman felt crushed. How could she ever fulfill her role as a mother, wife, and lady of the house if each step forward meant testing the limits of the edge of a cliff? *This house*, she lamented, *will never be my home.*

Birds

Na-Young tried carefully to pay attention to the things around her, choosing to be outdoors as much as possible. The two juniper trees in her courtyard were good companions, and she marvelled at how patiently they watched time unfold with no alarm, no panic, no emotions. She wondered whether the two trees ever talked to each other, and imagined their roots intertwined, a hundred pairs of holding hands, buried deep beneath the winter soil.

One afternoon, when her eyes were closed after gazing high above at the grey sky, someone tapped her shoulder. For a split second, she thought it was one of the trees and cried out, but it was only Father-in-Law. When she told him she'd thought he was a tree, he broke out into spontaneous laughter. "You have a wonderful imagination," he said. He was immaculately clad in his fine silk hanbok. They stood without talking, observing the trees.

"You haven't attended your lessons," he said finally. "In fact, I haven't seen you since the season changed."

"I was injured."

"Are you well now?"

"Yes."

"I see. Perhaps you will return to your studies with me. A few more lessons and you'll be able to write to your mother."

How could he not see that she was pregnant? she wondered. Even under the many layers of winter clothing and her winter shawl, surely he would notice her swollen belly and wonder how she had gotten pregnant. And hadn't he heard, since the whole household was talking about it? After all, he knew his son liked men and would never accept her as his wife. She recalled the drawing of her dead mother-in-law and their close resemblance. She finally acknowledged the truth she'd been avoiding: Father-in-Law had been planning to take her for himself. She felt foolish at how devoted to him she had been. Drawing a deep breath, she looked up at the darkening clouds. Snow would fall soon and the juniper branches would sag ever so slightly under its weight.

Without learning to read and write, part of her mind would always be locked away. Then another frightening thought came to her: What if the child was a girl? Would the child's fate be any different from her own? Or her mother's?

Then, unexpectedly, Min-Ho entered the courtyard. In spite of herself, Na-Young smiled at seeing him. She observed, for the first time, a remarkable resemblance between her husband and his father. For a second, she wondered whether her half-Korean son would have the same wide-open eyes or the same pouty lips when he was angry or sad. She shook the thought away—she didn't want to know.

"Why is everyone standing in the cold?" Min-Ho said. Then, sensing the tension around them, he added, "She should be resting and taking care of our child."

Na-Young caught the confusion in Father-in-Law's eyes. A wounded look on his face, he stared ahead, his focus on the juniper branches.

"Yes, we have good news," Na-Young said. Her world was quickly filled with a strange possibility. In her mind's eye, she saw the news skip from servant to servant in the kitchen:

"We were wrong! It's the young master's child after all."

"Better get indoors," Father-in-Law said. Fatigue had settled into his eyes, and his hollowed cheeks made him appear as old as her father.

Na-Young bowed deeply to him, a gesture that seemed to catch him off guard. The men, in return, bowed to her before leaving.

Later that night, despite feeling freed from her father-in-law's expectations of her, she was struck thinking about the possibility of having a girl. She thought back to the grey clouds. The expanse of the sky took her beyond the courtyard wall, to the river, unmarked by any gossip or stringent household rules, beyond the town, and farther past to Daegeori, and somewhere beyond that. Then, to her surprise, as she held her belly, for the first time she felt concerned for the child's destiny.

When her swollen belly would no longer let her see her own feet, Na-Young felt a new level of panic and fear, as if she'd been cornered into something she couldn't fully grasp. Like a child, she longed for her mother, for her best friend, Yeon-Soo, and even her sister, Mi-Young, whom—she acknowledged with a twinge of shame—she rarely thought about.

Her panic rose and fell depending on which thoughts invaded her mind. How could she possibly deliver the baby without ripping in half? There would be a midwife who knew what to do. But what if she couldn't bear the pain? What if she bled and died? "My child would be without a mother," she said aloud. *The child would be even more alone than I've ever been.*

"You should always stay out of your head," she recalled her mother saying. "It's like a dark part of the woods—leave it as quickly as possible." If only it were that easy. The dark woods were really a swamp. They looked calm, even tranquil, but the closer she stood along their murky boundary, the easier it was to slip and fall.

Na-Young sat on her room floor and dipped her writing brush into her water basin. She wrote her name on the floor, delighted that she could write it out anywhere she pleased. Yet the name disappeared, like a mirage, as the water dried. She felt a sense of disappointment: It was yet another reminder that whatever she valued, she could lose. That this was the way of the world, especially for women who appeared and disappeared in the presence of men, depending on their whims and desires. Then the idea returned to her: What if the baby was a girl? She heard her mother chastise her: If only you had learned how to invoke the proper deity to confirm a baby's sex.

Na-Young accidentally bumped the basin, and water ran out, seeping between the legs of the chest that housed her bedding during the day. When the cloth she used to mop up the spill snagged on something under the chest, she yanked it in frustration. To her surprise, a piece of wood popped out. Attached to the wood with a length of string was a book. A photo was wedged between the pages. Na-Young recognized Father-in-Law's wife, dressed as a bride. Though the image was faded, she could easily imagine the bright red roses and yellow jasmine in the background. Again, she was struck by her resemblance to Mother-in-Law, and her face flushed.

Mother-in-Law's diary! The pages were filled with writing and sketches: the junipers as two small trees in the courtyard, a self-portrait, and a bird in flight. She turned the pages, looking for pictures, and observed that the penmanship started to become more hurried about halfway through the book. Then, to her shock, she saw a sketch of a woman and a child in midair. If Mother-in-Law hadn't also drawn the jutting edge of a cliff and depicted the woman's long, loose hair and chima flowing upwards, the woman could have been swimming on her back, arms extended towards the sky, legs kicking. Had she imagined water below? But Mother-in-Law hadn't drawn any ground beneath the woman, and Na-Young couldn't tell. Her stomach lurched. As a child, she had often dreamt of falling. Although she usually forgot details, she always remembered being swept by euphoria as she fell until the thought that the falling might not end woke her in a panic.

Why had Mother-in-Law drawn this picture? Most disturbing of all was the child, so much smaller than she, in a similar free-falling pose. Yet she was making no attempt to reach for him.

Na-Young flipped back to the previous page. Another drawing. A woman and a child were walking along a winding path, but their backs were to her so that she couldn't see their expressions and had no clue about what they might be thinking or feeling.

She continued to flip between pages. Mother-in-Law's hair was usually tied in a bun, but in the last drawing, the one in which she was falling, it had come undone. In another picture, a woman with one eye stared back at her. Had Mother-in-Law merely been superstitious, or could she have gone mad? Why? And what would possess her to draw a picture of a woman who allowed her child—her son—to die? *Nothing can harm you as much as your own unguarded thoughts,* Na-Young reflected. Her own mother had feared that there might be a pin's head of truth to the superstitious beliefs around pregnancy. Worried that dead souls could pass curses onto her unborn child, she had chosen not to attend her own mother's funeral because she was carrying Mi-Young.

But her sister got sick and died anyway. Maybe mothers went mad or, rather, lost all hope because they could no longer cope with the chaos. Losing one's mind was a relief.

The thought of Mother-in-Law, only a few years older than she, sitting in this room and possibly going insane, filled her with unease. What had become of Mother-in-Law? How had she died?

"This house has more secrets than the sky has stars!" Na-Young said, slamming the book closed and slipping it back under the chest.

★

When she realized how consumed she was by Mother-in-Law's diary, Na-Young tried hard to distract herself with other things. Her thoughts returned to the possibility of having a girl. She looked for signs, any clues to confirm what she was thinking.

The sign came in the most unexpected way. Early one morning, Na-Young stood in the courtyard, entranced. The trees that had already produced new leaves and the flowers had a light dusting of snow. By midmorning, it was gone, but all things white called for her attention from then on: the rice in her bowl, the clothes that servants wore. Birds perched in trees chirped loudly as if to tell Na-Young to look around: Even the tiny red, yellow, and purple wildflowers that grew along the river bowed their heads so that only the white ones stood up. A blackbird, in flight, soared amongst the white, fleecy clouds.

Then, finally, the ghost of her dead mother-in-law came to her. Crouched low next to Na-Young's sleeping mat, she said, "What but a girl could survive the multiple attempts to harm her?"

Before Na-Young could say anything, the ghost was gone. It was settled. She was going to have a girl. Then a new fear came to her: What if the girl had already begun to absorb her mother's disturbing moods? Could an unborn child do that?

Someday this child will ask me why my mind is so disturbed, she thought. Just as dawn came slowly, followed by the promise of a new morning, the realization came to her that she and her daughter had to leave this household to have any chance of a better life.

Flight

The sounds of spring moved through air, water, and stone. Animals barked at night in search of mates, and birds settled over eggs in their nests. The courtyard smelled of sweet earth that lured patches of grass to grow back. To Na-Young's surprise, Min-Ho paid her a visit one afternoon. The skies were overcast and the sun nowhere to be seen as they stood by the junipers.

"I have a gift for you." He kept a respectable distance and bowed ever so slightly as he offered her a small plate of decorated rice cakes.

She accepted them, yet her growing trepidation prevented any joy or peace that might have come now that their sham of a marriage was no longer a barrier between them.

"What happened to your mother?" She hadn't planned on asking the question, and for a moment she feared she had crossed some line that zigzagged between them. They were neither friends, lovers, nor acquaintances. Yet she found herself compelled to break from the secrets that surrounded them.

He looked up at the sky as if he was searching for something. A bird in flight? The sun poking out from behind layers of clouds?

"I was only four years old when she killed herself. I can still remember how blinding the sun was, and what a relief it was to go into the woods and get away from the direct heat. We were walking—she was holding my hand."

Na-Young walked by his side, careful to stay slightly out of view, hoping that would encourage him to speak freely.

"We stopped at a waterfall. I remember being scared because the rush of falling water was so loud and we were so close to the rocky ledge. She got on her knees, so that we were eye to eye. 'I want you to be brave,' she said. 'It'll only be scary for a moment.'"

Suddenly, Na-Young was afraid. She had already suspected that her mother-in-law had died by suicide but was unprepared to handle the actual truth. She glanced around, concerned that nosy servants might be nearby trying their best to eavesdrop.

"I had no idea what my mother was talking about," Min-Ho said finally. "But she was smiling and holding my hand, so I wasn't afraid. I remember what happened next because it was almost in slow motion. Our attention was suddenly caught by the cries, high above us, of a blackbird captured by a giant eagle in midair. My hand was suddenly free as Mother lost her balance and struggled to get her footing again. As she fell over the edge, her hands clutched the air." He stopped. "I always wondered if she had hoped to grab my hands instead and pull me down with her."

A quiet settled over them.

"I could have jumped after her, but I was too afraid. It was an accident, I told Father. I told him about the eagle, but I don't know if he heard me. He blamed me." He bit his lower lip so hard it bled.

"It wasn't your fault. This was about your mother, not you." She had never met the woman and yet, she had grown to realize that appearances were often deceptive. Her mother-in-law hadn't been the happy bride depicted in the drawing that hung in Father-in-Law's study. As for Na-Young, everyone around her assumed she was carrying a full-Korean-blooded son, and yet, she knew deep inside that her mixed-blood baby was a girl and a traitor.

She gestured for Min-Ho to eat a rice cake. "You should talk to your father again and make him understand," she said.

He leaned back against a juniper and slid down. "My father? He thinks I'm a monster. A deviant. Can you imagine, he once tried to save my soul? Begged me to pray to his Christian god. He was so desperate to keep his bloodline alive that when he found out about me and Sung-Min, he brought you here for himself. He's no different from the Japanese who see sex purely as a means to create more people to serve them on hands and knees."

He crumpled into himself. Na-Young's head spun. Should she tell him that her baby was a girl? Or should she flee secretly with this knowledge? Women could not survive here. That was the fate of this house.

The visit had grown long, and she needed him to leave so she could plan her next steps. "Think of everything that life has to offer you," Na-Young finally said.

He rose and dusted off his pants. He laughed mockingly. "You have no idea how lucky you are to be a woman, and an ignorant woman at that." The sound of his voice was playful, yet his words pricked Na-Young's feelings like thorny locusts. "What else but ignorance would let you believe that life is worth living? Knowledge is dangerous. I hope you never change." He bowed his head, his usual way of saying goodbye.

"I can't stay," Na-Young said. "Here, with you . . . in this house . . . in Anyang. I need to leave." Despite succumbing to the temptation of speaking her mind, she composed herself and rested the plate of rice cakes above her amongst the low branches. "I'm sorry." She said nothing else despite sensing his indignation, his silence demanding an explanation.

Finally, her resolve got through to him, and he blurted out, "I always thought your presence in this house was an evil sign."

She gasped aloud, his accusation feeling like a striking hand.

"You can go, but the boy stays," he said.

She silenced her first instinct, which was to say no. Instead, she said, "And if it's a girl, she's coming with me."

"Fine."

"Fine," she repeated. She retrieved the plate and headed inside.

Alone, she wondered whether she had just imagined their whole conversation. Then, absorbing the extraordinary conversation that had just happened, she imagined the servants' whispers spreading across the estate. Although she was weary, she was surprised at how little she cared.

Before retiring for bed, she took a small knife and carefully etched her name into one of the juniper trees. It took much longer than she expected, but she was filled with a lovely sense of having completed something. Her initial indignation over what Min-Ho had said ebbed away as she realized she could be free from this house that had never been her home. Where would she and her daughter go? How did one go about changing a life? Did it happen suddenly, like a violent thunderstorm, or was it more like a summer monsoon, a shifting of the winds that caused heavy rains, followed by dry spells?

The more one learned, the more one questioned. It was like getting lost in a loop. Was learning a circle, like the seasons? Could a woman ever rise above a man with her knowledge? Even in nature, the gentle moon was able to block the entire sun and cast darkness on Earth.

Maybe I'll go to the capital, she thought, but just as quickly, she brushed the thought away. But the idea had ignited something. *I can already write my name in four languages,* she reminded herself, and thought about Boksun at the girls' school. Perhaps she could go there, too. And Yeon-Soo. What if she, somehow, had made her way to the capital, too?

She cradled her full belly. Life had already thrown her enough setbacks and disappointments. What else could a woman who refused fate have to lose?

PART III

city

The Bluebird Sings Here

The Capital, 1927
Two Years Later

The Bluebird Sings Here Teahouse was tucked away on a side street off Jongno, a major street that ran east to west in the centre of the capital. With its classic tile and wood details, there was nothing remarkable about its exterior. It wasn't until patrons passed through the main entrance, where they slipped off their shoes before entering through the flower-decorated doors, that they felt a sense of arriving somewhere. Five seascape brush paintings hung side by side on the east wall, and if patrons glanced quickly from left to right, the waves moved in a circular motion. Large silk cushions, the colour of lapis lazuli, made for comfortable seating on the floor around the twelve rectangular wooden tables spread throughout the room. Most of the patrons were men who worked in the area. They came during their morning, midday, or afternoon breaks for a cup of tea and light refreshments to relieve their stress and sate their hunger.

Na-Young glanced up at the clock that hung over the kitchen entrance. Fifteen minutes to closing. Now that she knew how to tell time using a clock, it ruled her days. She woke up at 7:30 a.m., left for work at 8:20 a.m., ate lunch at 11:30 a.m., ate dinner at 4:00 p.m., and went home at 7:00 p.m. The clock even determined how long she spent on any one activity. Everyone from Nearby Tree, the cook who prepared all the meals for Lady Boss, to her staff—

Matchstick, Flower Petal, and Twilight—was expected to move from task to task in an orderly fashion.

The only person who came and went as she pleased was the shopkeeper's wife, Lady Song, whom the staff called "Lady Boss." She dressed in silk hanboks, usually in shades of dark grey and black with green or dark blue accents—colours associated with mastery and energy. While she was fond of the colour red because it evoked fire, Lady Boss believed it was socially unacceptable for married, middle-aged women to don the colour. She settled on maroon accents instead. Her makeup was impeccable. She preferred neutral tones so that her face appeared natural, with a hint of blush on her cheeks and soft pink rose tones on her lips. Her hair was divided into two braids and then rolled into a bun that was decorated with a gold-and-sapphire bluebird hairpin that she wore every day.

The teahouse offered twenty-seven varieties of teas, including its own fusion teas and imported specialty teas. Lady Boss was generous with her staff and allowed each of the workers to drink two cups per day, so Na-Young was able to sample all the different varieties. Her favourite was maesil-cha, a plum tea that was richly sweet and sour, and delicious hot or cold.

Na-Young worked six days a week and had Sundays off, as the shop was closed. When she'd arrived at the capital two years ago, she'd stayed at an inn for a month, and then settled into a boardinghouse a ten-minute walk from the shop.

When Na-Young asked Twilight how she had acquired such an unusual nickname, she'd replied, "Master Lee, when he was around, could never remember our names, so he gave us nicknames that just stuck."

"What was he like?"

"He and Lady Boss fought over everything. And she always won, because in the end, they both knew she was right." It had been Lady Boss's idea, for example, to transform the teahouse, once run by a doctor specializing in medicinal teas, into a modern teahouse. The couple had argued about that and she'd won, but to appease her husband, she still served six teas that were medicinal, including ssanghwa-cha and yuja-cha, drinks Na-Young's mother often consumed.

A few weeks before Na-Young had started working at the teahouse, the shopkeeper and his wife had had their biggest fight. Twilight was convinced he had left for good. He had discovered, quite by accident, that his wife had been secretly teaching the girls who worked in the teahouse how to read and write.

"How else would they know if they were being cheated at the market or by a customer?" Twilight said, mimicking Lady Boss. The lessons hadn't been a difficult thing to do, since Lady Boss's husband had never entered the kitchen or the adjacent back room where the girls ate their meals—he considered those spaces to be the women's quarters.

Every day for half an hour, the four young women who worked there—two who served customers and two who worked in the kitchen—took turns sitting in pairs with Lady Boss during their meal breaks. Na-Young soon joined in, practising Hangul and conversational Japanese with Lady Boss in the back room.

Lady Boss was clever enough to realize that it would look improper for her to run a business on her own, so she took great care to create the illusion that her husband was still an active part of her life and the teahouse. Lady Boss even scheduled her husband into her agenda book, recording his imaginary whereabouts.

"Mr. Yang, so good to see you after so much time has passed.

I'm so sorry that you missed my husband," she told a customer. "He's away in Busan on business. The poor man, he simply works too hard."

Na-Young wondered how she managed to keep up with all the details of her lies—she was so adept at maintaining her illusion.

"I suppose it's easier to give a false impression than lie," Twilight said. "Technically, she could be right. Her husband is away. For all we know, he could be in Busan on business."

"And he could be working very hard—somewhere else and *with* someone else," Flower Petal said. Twilight bit her lower lip and stifled a laugh.

It was then that Na-Young understood that the staff believed that Lady Boss's husband was with another woman, perhaps with a secret family in a distant village. No one dared to suggest this to the lady. Instead, they played along, partly to preserve her dignity, and also because conspiring to hide the truth had become a source of entertainment for them.

For Lady Boss, the trick was to avoid follow-up questions. When another customer asked Lady Boss where in Busan her husband was visiting, she smiled and said, "Mr. Han, is it just me or are you also working too hard? You appear somewhat weary. Please allow me the pleasure of serving you directly." Mr. Han burst into an appreciative smile.

But in reality, Lady Boss never served customers. Instead, she would motion one of the girls over to the table, where she would end up pouring tea for both the customer and Lady Boss, who sat inquiring about the man's activities and interests.

"It's all in the details," Twilight observed. "Then our stories are consistent." When the landlord came by at the beginning of the month, Twilight told him, "The master is visiting his uncle in Daegu." Lady Boss, who conveniently arrived at the teahouse after the landlord's visit, said within earshot of several patrons, "If Daegu wasn't so far, I, too, would have enjoyed a short time away."

What intrigued Na-Young most about Lady Boss was just how easy it was for her to spin her stories. Her facial expressions, voice, and demeanour never betrayed a trace of guilt or remorse as she misled or obscured the truth from others.

In confidence, she told Na-Young, "The art to getting what you want from others is to please instead of disappoint."

At what cost? Na-Young wondered, but didn't ask aloud.

Transitions

Na-Young had arrived in the city unprepared for how dramatic the transition would be. The village she was born in—or even the town of Anyang—was a seed compared to the capital, a vast meadow of wildflowers. Situated north of the Han River, the area was surrounded by eight mountains, with four main mountains marking the city boundaries. A stone fortress wall had once surrounded the city, its eight gates opened and closed daily.

The main street, Jongno, featured a large bell that had once marked the times of the day and the opening and closing of the city gates. Trolley cars ran along the street, which was lined with government and business offices, markets and shops, and theatres and galleries. Buddhist temples and Confucian shrines and monuments were scattered throughout the city along with Myeongdong Cathedral and Protestant churches, which were growing in popularity. Ewha Girls School, where Boksun was studying, was located in the west end.

Upon first arriving in the capital, Na-Young had stood outside the train station, overwhelmed by the noise and the number of people and the stark realization that she was truly on her own. Luckily, the people she encountered were kind and made sure she was never truly lost. A railway worker recommended a nearby inn. The innkeeper, in turn, helped her get to Ewha Girls School, where Boksun was supposed to be living, but not before serving Na-Young a hot lunch of porridge and kimchi. The headmistress at Ewha greeted Na-Young warmly and quickly summoned Boksun.

Boksun smiled but then bowed her head deeply.

"You're no longer my maidservant," Na-Young reminded her. "It's great to see you again." She hugged her, unable to hide how pleased she was to see a familiar face in the big city.

That night, Na-Young treated Boksun to dinner at a nearby restaurant as they caught up on each other's affairs.

"I've been studying English and Japanese," Boksun announced. "I'm planning to become a translator."

Na-Young laid her spoon down, intrigued. Father-in-Law had kept his word. Not only was she able to study and earn her keep at the same time—Boksun would one day become a professional woman. As she sipped her tea, Na-Young wondered whether her former maidservant, the one she had taught to write her own name, knew that Na-Young was still reading and writing at an elementary-school level. Immediately, she blushed and redirected the conversation.

"How are you able to manage in such a big place?" Na-Young asked. She had only visited the city once before, and that had been limited to the outdoor market.

"You get used to it. The city is constantly changing. The Japanese have renamed most of the city landmarks and buildings," Boksun said. "Our capital, Gyeongseong, is now Keijō. Japanese architects are redesigning everything using Western-influenced styles, which are considered modern. The Bank of Chōsen looks like a French palace."

Na-Young couldn't picture that, but she understood that even dogs peed to mark their territories; the Japanese were showing their imperial rule. Suddenly, she was no longer in the mood to eat.

She observed that Boksun's face had become fuller and found comfort in her own decision to come to the city. The possibility of having control over her own thoughts, behaviours, and actions excited her, despite the underlying nagging feelings of anxiety and despair.

"I'm planning to stay and find work," she said.

"Won't your family come looking for you?" asked Boksun, raising her eyes to look at Na-Young.

"Which family? As far as my husband's family is concerned, I returned home to my parents. And there's no reason why my parents would think I've left my husband's family. It's the perfect situation."

"I still can't believe you left." Boksun's lips tightened. "Your father-in-law was so fond of you."

Na-Young gestured for Boksun to eat. Yet she herself could only stare at the kimchi on the table. The bright red napa cabbage was darker than she was used to, and the strong umami flavour had caused it to sour. Back in the village such ripened kimchi would be reserved only for stews. Was Father-in-Law missing her, or was he feeling duped by Na-Young and Min-Ho? Should she tell Boksun about the son she had left behind? The kimchi juices triggered images of Boksun's beating, her white chima soaked with blood, and sudden panic startled her into silence.

Surely Min-Ho would be kind to the boy whom they'd passed off as a legitimate heir, she reassured herself.

All the tables were occupied, save the one closest to the entrance. How odd, Na-Young thought, to eat one's dinner surrounded by strangers who had no interest in speaking or getting to know each other. The thought came to her then that anonymity was remarkably freeing. No one expected anything from her or of her. Encouraged by that revelation, Na-Young felt ready to step into any new challenge.

The two of them decided that it would be best to tell everyone that Na-Young was a recent widow and that's why she needed to find work. Boksun knew a lady who ran a teahouse.

"She volunteers at the school," Boksun said. "I think we can trust her. She's helped other girls."

And so Na-Young was introduced to Lady Boss and The Bluebird Sings Here Teahouse. But initially, Lady Boss dismissed the possibility of taking on new employees.

"I don't need any more girls," she said, "I need someone who can keep my accounting books." Her husband had done that job before he left.

They were seated around a low table, the wooden lacquerware inlaid with mother-of-pearl designs of flowers and birds in flight. A rosewood abacus with jade beads rested on top of several books and papers that were stacked to one side.

"I can do it," Na-Young bluffed, thinking back to her lessons with Father-in-Law, who had also taught her to use his abacus. "I used to help my husband with some basic calculations. I can learn anything very quickly."

Lady Boss's face became still. "How would you calculate the profit margins of any business?"

Na-Young recalled a conversation she had overheard between Min-Ho and Sung-Min. "My husband used to worry about this all the time," she said. "The cost of publishing anything and selling it left little profit. His associate wanted to increase ads to make more money." She left out the part about her husband resisting the idea, as the ads came largely from pro-Japanese businesses, and that the associate was really his father.

Lady Boss nodded but did not reply. It was then Na-Young noticed a Bible that looked exactly like Father-in-Law's. Lady Boss noticed her staring at it.

"Do you know what this is?" she asked.

Na-Young nodded.

Lady Boss cocked her head. "Have you read it?" Before Na-Young could respond, she asked, "Are you a Christian?" Her eyebrows twitched, prompting Na-Young to nod. Lady Boss pressed her palms together and looked at Na-Young over her fingertips. "Please share one of your favourite Bible passages with me."

Na-Young's mind drew a blank. She stared down at her hands, aware of the space growing between them. A ticking sound caught her attention. Her eyes darted, looking for its source. A clock hung on the north wall.

"Widow?"

It had been the first time that anyone had called Na-Young by that name. She thought of the calm and poised Widow Oh in Anyang.

"I suppose we could start with the beginning. Genesis and Adam and Eve," Na-Young said.

Lady Boss's face lit up, so Na-Young continued. She hadn't realized just how much she retained from Father-in-Law's lessons as he rambled on, leaping from Joseph and his coat of many colours to the barren Hannah who had begged the Lord for a child. Lady Boss seemed especially pleased when Na-Young talked about Jesus and his ability to heal people, performing miracles such as raising Jairus's daughter back to life. Na-Young felt her body stiffen; the more she spoke, the more ludicrous she felt. But Lady Boss misunderstood her fears.

"I know why you hesitated, but you don't need to be afraid," she said, cupping Na-Young's hand in hers. "We have many practising Christians in the city. Why, the Christian Youth Association is just two blocks west of the teahouse. It was built with American and Canadian money. Their mandate is to promote sports and fitness, but given the organization's Western influence, some great thinking and learning is taking place there. There's even a small Christian college in the same building. I'm happy to introduce you to some of the most prominent missionaries here. I work with the best of them. Of course, we're very, very careful."

Lady Boss elaborated by explaining that a year after the Japanese had seized control of the country, Korean Christians and American missionaries were routinely harassed and arrested on conspiracy suspicions. "They were endlessly accused of treason and assassination attempts against the Japanese governor general. Many were executed. Over six hundred men were arrested and imprisoned."

Lady Boss's ability to remember statistics and historical details allowed her to speak with authority. After all, how could one argue against facts or logic? Still, Na-Young could not fathom how the Christian faith, riddled with so much foolishness and superstition, could possibly be worth dying for. But rather than reveal this, Na-Young lowered her head and nodded.

With this, Lady Boss offered her the job. Lady Boss, Na-Young quickly learned, was a woman of contradictions. While she asserted her authority as Na-Young's superior, she also advised her to set her own goals. "I started with nothing," she said, "but I knew what I wanted."

So Na-Young started studying Lady Boss—observing her movements, her gestures, and how she talked. She appreciated that Lady Boss treated her with a dignity that wasn't afforded to her other workers. After all, Na-Young also wore her hair in a bun, unlike the girls with their braided hair and white hanboks. She introduced her as the Bookkeeper, a title Na-Young preferred over being called the Widow.

"I insist that all my girls know how to read," Lady Boss said. "It's a skill that makes them better employees." A pained look crossed her face as she warned, "The Japanese see Christianity as a threat to their imperial plans. Educating girls is seen as a threat to *every* man. What happens within the walls of our little teahouse must stay here."

Oppa

One Year Later

One spring morning the following year—the Year of the Earth Dragon—Na-Young wrote a letter to her mother. Despite having become quite proficient with the written word, she still struggled to put her thoughts together. She wrote that her marriage had ended but that she was well, managing on her own in the capital. Several weeks later, on a warm July afternoon, Oppa showed up at the teahouse, clad in the black uniform that the Korean aides to the Japanese military police wore.

"What do you make of him?" Twilight whispered, and nudged Na-Young, who had just stepped out of the kitchen.

"That's my brother!" Na-Young said, and in her excitement ran up to him.

An instant tension seized the teahouse. Men exchanged glances as they eyed Oppa standing by the entrance. A regular patron who was about to leave approached him.

"Can't they at least outfit traitors like you properly?" he said. He poked at a patch sewn onto Oppa's sleeve.

Oppa took a step back but didn't say anything. Lady Boss came out of her office, glanced briefly at Na-Young, and was about to say something when Twilight leaned into her and whispered in her ear.

"What? Can't speak?" The man took a step forward to close the gap. "Did they cut off your tongue, too, when they cut off your—"

Oppa grabbed the man's arm but just as quickly released him.

The man looked surprised. "I ought to report you to your Japanese superiors for attacking an innocent man!"

A gloomy shadow crossed Lady Boss's face, but she recovered quickly and led the man out. "I regret that you had an unpleasant visit today," she said. "Have a good day."

"Let's go to the back room," Na-Young said, and ushered Oppa away.

"Why didn't you let Mother know where you were sooner?" Oppa said. "I can't believe we've been in the same city without knowing. If I hadn't visited home when I did, this could have gone on for a lot longer. I've been stationed here for over two years now. I work at the Japanese General Government Building."

How was any of this possible? Na-Young shuddered and paused, unable to speak. Her brother working for the enemy, and all the while, he was less than a thirty-minute walk away.

"Doing what?" Na-Young asked.

"Menial tasks and errands mostly, and I translate for my superiors. Nothing of significance, of course. They draw hard lines."

"You should be back home," Na-Young lamented.

"*You* should be back home," Oppa repeated. "If not to your husband, then to our home."

"Our home?" Na-Young said. The words felt empty to her. "I'm not going anywhere," she said. "Tell Father I'm happy here."

Oppa froze and looked at her. She straightened her back and held her head high, hoping that he could tell that she had matured since he last saw her at her wedding.

"If you didn't want Mother and Father to try and make you go back, why did you write?"

Na-Young felt a nagging need to provide him with some sort

of answer but resisted the impulse to tell the truth: Day-to-day living was easiest on her own. Free from any expectations imposed on her by parents and a husband, she now answered to no one except Lady Boss. But their relationship was determined by their roles as employer and employee. Lady Boss did not ask nor care what Na-Young did outside of work hours. This had given Na-Young time to put aside her old life and instead be entertained by books. The translated play *A Doll's House* had both frightened and delighted her, and had shattered any fantasies Na-Young ever had about a parent or husband knowing what was best for her ever again.

And yet, Na-Young had written to her mother anyway. She wasn't quite sure why. All she knew was that no amount of activity—work or pleasure—could fill an inner emptiness that battled its way into her consciousness from time to time.

"How's Father?" she asked finally. Although Old Man Yang had mentioned that Father wasn't doing very well, she'd hoped that, with the years that had passed, he, Mother, and Second Mother were now well. "And Mother?"

"She's doing remarkably well," he said. "But things aren't as they once were. We should talk privately again," he said hesitantly. "I need to get back to work. I'll let Mother and Father know that you are keeping well."

Later, Na-Young explained to Lady Boss why her brother was working with the Japanese military police—to get them to stop harassing their family farm.

"I understand he's your brother, and he's one of us," she said, "but don't forget our clientele. Tell your brother to wear civilian clothes should he ever visit again."

Na-Young agreed, thinking back to Oppa's encounter with the

rude customer. Sometimes blending in was the best form of protecting yourself and others.

★

A month passed. Oppa returned to the teahouse to tell her that Father was allowing her to stay in the city if he, Oppa, agreed to watch over her.

Na-Young laughed inwardly. The decision was not his to make.

"Maybe I'll visit home in the fall," she said, "for Chuseok. We can both go and play games under the full harvest moon, like we did as children."

Oppa smiled, but Na-Young sensed he was holding something back. She poured another cup of tea and pressed him further about their family until he revealed that while Mother wanted Na-Young to return home, Father had forbidden it.

"But you said he accepted me living here. Has he changed his mind?"

"No . . ." Oppa sighed deeply. "You and I hadn't seen each other in so long—I couldn't bear to tell you that Father demanded you return to Anyang or you would be dead to him."

"He said that?" Her voice was stifled by emotion. Of course her brother would lie to protect her.

"My marriage was complicated," she said, wanting her brother to know that she had tried to make things work. "It wasn't my fault that my husband rejected me." She couldn't bring herself to say that Min-Ho had already been in a relationship prior to their marriage, that his lover was a man.

"But why?" Oppa asked. "He must have had his reasons."

Na-Young bit her lip. Did he think it was her fault? "I gave him what he wanted," she said, thinking about the boy she'd left behind. For twenty-one days after he was born, the boy had been nameless, and she had nursed him. Then, as she and Min-Ho had agreed, she'd passed the boy to a wet nurse and left before the sun rose on the day of the naming ceremony. She had assumed that everyone in the household thought she'd returned to her old village. That was the story she and Min-Ho had agreed upon.

"Clearly, it wasn't enough," Oppa said.

Na-Young was crushed, but she kept a straight face and chose to focus on how nice it was to have her brother back in her life. "What I have here is enough for me."

"That may be, but you can't think of only yourself. Father hasn't been himself since Second Mother's mental decline. She stays in her room all day. We fear she won't be around much longer. Neither will he, for that matter."

What had fate done to her family? Was Second Mother's illness punishment for her vanity and cruelty? And Father, despite all this, had still refused to allow Na-Young to come home. Was that his vain attempt to assert control? Did he not care about her?

"And Mother?" Na-Young asked. "You said she was well?"

"She's running the household again in Second Mother's absence."

Na-Young was pleased to hear that. "I'm so sorry for everything," she said. The happiness she felt at seeing her brother again faded, and the familiar feelings of dread and fear threatened to seize her. She turned away so he couldn't see her face. It hit her again that Oppa was serving their enemy because of her. The same was true for Second Mother's grave health.

"I'll be back to check on you," Oppa said. "You'll stay out of any trouble. Yak-sok?"

"Of course," she said, and locked fingers with him to seal her promise.

Intersection

Every Monday and Thursday, Lady Boss volunteered at Ewha, the girls' school that Boksun attended. Founded in 1886 by Mary F. Scranton, an American missionary, it was located in the west end of the city, at a busy intersection on Jeongdong Street, across from one of the royal palaces, once the home of the royal family.

When Lady Boss was away, Na-Young stepped in as hostess. She even wore hanboks of similar colours. The clothes made her feel confident, as she believed that others accorded her almost the same measure of respect as Lady Boss.

One day in mid-August when Na-Young was in charge, an attractive man she hadn't seen before entered the teahouse. He was the first customer of the day. Something about him caught Na-Young's attention. He was handsome, dressed in a Western-style navy suit, and was tall with good posture. It was only when he squinted to read the wall clock that Na-Young realized he was nearsighted. She seated him and was turning to leave when he said, "Will the fine lady sit with me as I'm served what I hope is the best jasmine tea in the city?" His accent betrayed him. He was Japanese.

A wave of alarm swept through Na-Young. It took her a second to realize that he had mistaken her for Lady Boss. She sat down. Twilight watched, wide-eyed. Although they rarely received Japanese customers, Lady Boss had instructed them to be hospitable.

"Allow me to introduce myself," he said. "My name is Ichinose Tadashi."

"Welcome to our humble teahouse," Na-Young said. She gestured for Twilight to seat him, forgetting that her hand was ink-stained. Determined to perfect her penmanship, she spent her free moments copying out passages from Lady Boss's Bible. It hadn't taken long for her to start memorizing some of them, despite not truly understanding their meaning.

The man looked around the room and turned to Na-Young. "You know what this place needs? Some music to accompany the teas you serve." He eyed the seascape paintings. "Something sophisticated to complement your décor. In the West, jazz is the latest craze."

Na-Young forced a smile. "I'll speak to my husband," she said, mimicking one of Lady Boss's popular phrases.

He laughed. "The old man may want to stick to his old folksy music. Men are often set in their ways. But really, I don't think anyone in the world plays bamboo flutes anymore. What kind of music does he prefer, anyway?"

One thing Na-Young had learned from Lady Boss was to stay clear of responding to open-ended questions. She was already feeling panicked at the thought of her true identity being revealed. She leaned ever so slightly towards him, as she had often seen Lady Boss do, and said, "It appears that you are very knowledgeable in the ways of the world. Have you travelled much?"

His face broke into a smile. "My job used to involve quite a bit of travel. I got as far as America. That's where I discovered jazz—the most powerful, most alive music. I even took up the saxophone."

Na-Young had seen a photo of a jazz band in one of the widow's magazines back in Anyang. The different variety of instruments had amused her, and she wondered how they might sound playing all at once.

Twilight arrived carrying a teapot and two teacups on a tray. The scent of jasmine flowers filled the air as Na-Young poured the tea. She saw the man notice her ink-stained hands and, embarrassed, she said, “Please forgive the appearance of my hands. I accidentally tipped the inkpot when the nib of my pen broke. Ink spilled everywhere.”

“Were you able to save whatever you were writing?” he asked.

“It wasn’t important,” she said. “Please have some tea.”

Twilight returned with a small plate of grilled rice cakes and some of their finest confectionaries.

The Japanese man looked pleased as he gazed into Na-Young’s eyes.

“Where do you purchase your teas?” he asked. He held up a piece of jeonggwa as if to appreciate the vibrant orange of the candied citrus fruit.

Because Na-Young kept the books, she knew all of the companies’ names. She even knew that this particular tea had come from Fuzhou in China, so she told him as much.

“Ah, yes,” he said, and bit into the jeonggwa. “Delicious! Please, I insist you have some also.”

“We never eat while we are working,” she said, “but thank you.”

“I’ve heard that Fuzhou is where the best Chinese jasmine comes from. It’s all in the location, I’ve always said. For the jasmine plant, it’s about the mild climate and abundant precipitation.”

“Yes, you are quite right,” Na-Young agreed absently.

Just then, the flower-painted doors slid open and two men stepped in. Na-Young recognized Mr. Yu, another customer. She excused herself and stood up to greet them when the other man—whom she had never seen before—paused. He whispered something to his companion. Na-Young looked back at the Japanese man, who was brushing candy dust off his suit jacket.

Mr. Yu bowed. "I apologize," he said, "but we forgot about a previous engagement." They left.

Perplexed, Na-Young returned to the Japanese man, who appeared oblivious to what had just happened. Instead, he drank another cup of tea and continued talking about jazz and American music. As more customers started to arrive, he announced his surprise that nearly an hour had passed. He thanked Na-Young for her company and bowed deeply, an unexpected gesture that made Na-Young smile in spite of herself. Given that no other customers seemed to mind his presence, Na-Young tried to forget about Mr. Yu and his companion's abrupt departure.

"He overpaid," Twilight said, counting the Japanese banknotes he had left on the table. "Why did you let him believe that you were Lady Boss?" she asked, sounding more worried than annoyed.

"I don't know, I don't know . . ." Na-Young said, the reality of the situation sinking in.

"Are you going to tell her?"

"What if he never comes back? What would be the point, then?" But an uneasy feeling stirred within her.

Headless Chicken

One afternoon, when Nearby Tree, the cook, and Flower Petal were away sick with the flu, Matchstick told Na-Young they needed chicken to make broth, so she needed her to buy a chicken from the market.

"Why me?" Na-Young asked, somewhat irritated. But she knew that Matchstick, who had long worked at the teahouse, resented Na-Young's privileged status at work. She kept scented handkerchiefs in her sleeves to cover her nose and mouth, a gesture Na-Young came to realize was to manage her nerves more than to catch a sneeze.

"Just because she knows how to use an abacus does not mean her clothes have wings," Matchstick mumbled. Then, quite loudly, she added, "Unless you want to prepare the garlic shoots, onions, spring greens . . ." She inhaled into her handkerchief.

Na-Young reluctantly agreed. Unlike back home in the village, where animals such as chickens roamed openly, their existence in the city was hidden, the eggs and meat they provided insignificant until they had been transformed into real food.

Buckets of clams and sea cucumbers rested by the outdoor market's entrance. When Na-Young reached the chicken stall and gestured that she wanted one bird, the woman running it grabbed the nearest unfortunate chicken. In the split second before the axe fell on the chicken's neck, a queasiness overcame Na-Young, causing her to step back. Her chest heaved as images of Headless

Chicken running in the tall grass flashed in her mind. The smell of burning flesh overwhelmed her senses.

It was in this surreal moment that Na-Young felt, rather than saw, a vision of her own hand tightly gripping a metal object, its blade tearing into a Japanese military policeman's flesh. She saw his body jerking, his arms flailing, before he grabbed at the letter opener that was plunged into his neck. His eyes, two raging suns, locked onto hers. Then, in one sweeping motion, she saw Yeon-Soo kick him so hard that he fell backwards into the fire. A sharp pain coursed through Na-Young's bloodied hand.

She had stabbed the Japanese military policeman, not Yeon-Soo!

How had this truth abandoned her? Unsure of whether the clear blue sky, absent of clouds and birds, was part of a memory from the past or something she was looking up at in the present moment, Na-Young continued to stare blankly upwards, afraid of whatever could come next.

"Are you all right?" the woman at the stall asked. She was holding a package wrapped in newspaper. The bloodstains on her apron triggered a flash of images: Yeon-Soo's head oozing blood after a Japanese military policeman smashed his rifle against it, the blood between her own legs, the blood that seeped around the letter opener lodged in her attacker's neck. For a moment, Na-Young marvelled at how quiet everything around her seemed. But then, as if snapping out of a trance, she tried to restore herself—and some normalcy to the situation—by claiming illness. She asked the woman to have the chicken delivered to the teahouse and, before she could respond, retreated home.

Curled on the floor, Na-Young took herself to a place deep inside her mind: the worn Daegeori mountains where she could hide beneath their many rocky outcrops; the river, where water glittered in sunlight and moonlight. In her mind's eye, she walked along the narrow footpaths. She would venture deeper and farther away until she stood on top of mountain ridges and saw the other side of her world, vast and unending like the sky—and found peace.

When she woke up, the possibility of any other truth felt ludicrous: Yeon-Soo had killed the Japanese military policeman. Of course she had. That was why her friend was on the run instead of Na-Young. Yet, something in her mind refused to release her, and to her horror, the Japanese military policeman's eyes, two raging suns, again flashed in her thoughts. Was it wrong that she felt nothing towards the dead Japanese military policeman? After all, they had, with equal heartlessness, attacked the Korean man and assaulted her and Yeon-Soo. Had it all really happened?

But the baby she had delivered was proof. The child that was born to no father also had no mother. Even if the child grew up amongst his kind, he would always be like a turnip growing in a field of potatoes. Her insides burst with sudden waves of sorrow. She cursed herself. For three years, she had managed to shut down whenever thoughts of her son invaded her mind. Whenever she caught herself covering her ears to the sound of men screaming in pain, or the terrifying blast of three gunshots out in the open sky, or her own piercing shrieks as she gave birth. A fog rushed into her line of vision. She blinked rapidly, and when it cleared, the unthinkable truth seeped in, and she shuddered.

The night passed. She kept her eyes on the door, as if she was afraid someone would break in. When she woke up, her nightclothes were covered in sweat, which she initially mistook for blood, and screamed. She stared at the ceiling, still breathing hard. Na-Young could not undo what had happened. This reality hit her, like a violent slap across the face.

She took a series of deep breaths. She would dress and go to the teahouse, and life would go on as usual. Or . . . could she try to find Yeon-Soo? Should she? Her head throbbed.

But why should she bother to look for Yeon-Soo when she knew that her friend was probably perfectly safe living in the little hut in the middle of nowhere? Na-Young had told herself this so many times, she had convinced herself that she believed it. But the gap was closing between that story and the possibility that everything she had believed was a lie.

A Favour

Na-Young and Lady Boss sat in the outdoor alcove at the back of the teahouse. The garden walls and surrounding greenery created some privacy. Two boulders with flat tops, side by side, served as a sitting bench. Unless the staff needed to tend to any of the drying fruit and vegetables lying on bamboo racks under the sun, they avoided this space, knowing that it was where Lady Boss indulged in her smoking and reading.

As Na-Young poured goji berry tea into two teacups, the scent of dates, ginger, and cinnamon filled the air. She paused to admire the tea's fusion of orange, brown, and pink colours before taking a careful sip. Flower Petal, who could taste and name even the most nuanced flavours, was the one who had started adding cinnamon to this tea, which complemented its lovely essence.

The Japanese man who had visited the teahouse last week had not returned, so Na-Young felt released from any sense of obligation to tell Lady Boss about her deception. Instead, she breathed in the fresh air. She took it as a great honour to have earned her boss's confidence. Lady Boss had moved from sharing simple concerns such as which spices they should experiment with to what should be done with one of the kitchen girls, whom she suspected of overindulging in rice cakes.

"I'm thinking of hiring another kitchen girl," she said. "Business has really picked up."

She was right. Demand for their savory rice cakes and fried

rice cakes with sweet red bean filling had steadily increased as delivery requests.

"Who would have thought that white men could eat such endless orders of rice cakes soaked in soy sauce?" Na-Young said.

Lady Boss nodded. She lit a match and it flared; the air filled with the smell of cigarette smoke. The white men in question were the Americans, a director and executives who worked at the Christian Youth Association. Korean boys were sent regularly to fetch rice cakes from the teahouse for them.

"I think it's great that the organization promotes sports and fitness," Na-Young said. "At least even the Japanese see value in that."

Lady Boss had a different point of view. "It's a calculated deception," she said. She held the cigarette smoke in her mouth for a couple of seconds, then exhaled slowly. "The Japanese are very clever at creating the illusion of freedom."

Na-Young was yet again reminded that people were regularly arrested and imprisoned for following their faith.

Lady Boss glanced briefly at the sky. "The Japanese are keeping a careful eye on the association. Although it would be stupid to house any underground headquarters for revolutionary insurrection there."

Her comment baffled Na-Young, but she said nothing. Instead, she refilled her half-empty teacup and let Lady Boss continue.

"Yes, the Japanese are cunning. They think that by modernizing our sports, we can be distracted from important issues. But there's power—real power—in being part of a team, even a sports team, if it can stir our basic need to belong."

Na-Young sipped her tea. How could archery or wrestling or even a game of tug-of-war, hugely popular in Daegeori, do everything Lady Boss claimed? Other than seeing men rage in anger at a bad call or weep in disappointment, she hadn't witnessed anything so great about sports.

Lady Boss had advocated for a similar athletic association for women and supported the efforts of the women who founded the Young Women's Christian Association of Korea in 1922.

She explained, "Their primary focus isn't on athleticism, but rather, women's rights. Unfortunately, their liberal beliefs clashed with my values on some issues, and we parted ways."

"Liberal beliefs?"

"Brothels, for example. Even if it is properly licenced, I won't condone it."

Na-Young pondered this but felt it was inappropriate to ask any more questions.

A trickle of voices from a nearby alley caught their attention. Some men were arguing, their voices growing louder.

"How about Boksun?" Na-Young asked, looping back to their initial conversation. "As your third kitchen girl?"

"Boksun?" Lady Boss laughed. "No, that work's beneath her."

But wasn't cleaning and cooking what she was already doing at the school to earn her keep? Before Na-Young could say anything else, Lady Boss snuffed out her cigarette and set her teacup down. She looked up at the clouds. "It looks like it will rain again," she said.

They picked up their teacups and the teapot, ready to head back inside.

"My faithful bookkeeper," she said as they stood in the doorway, "I need you to grant me a favour."

"Of course," Na-Young said.

"But it must remain between us."

Intrigued and pleased that she'd earned such trust from Lady

Boss, Na-Young said nothing, determined to help her without question.

★

Na-Young and Twilight were excited to venture out to the large outdoor market by the southern boundaries of the city. Lady Boss had given them a list of items they couldn't purchase in the local market—everything from imported dried fruits to Western-style socks.

Twilight, who usually walked everywhere, including Namdaemun Market, was delighted to ride the trolley car. "I almost feel like royalty!" she exclaimed. They agreed it was better than walking. Twilight didn't know that Na-Young had her own secret reason to be excited. Lady Boss had asked her to deliver a secret parcel.

"This is of great importance," Lady Boss had said, handing her a package wrapped in plain brown ramie. "Tell the girls it's a box of rice cakes I want delivered to an acquaintance who has a small shop. At the market, send Twilight off to buy something so you can go alone."

It was too heavy to be rice cakes. Na-Young suspected it was books, and wondered why they had to be kept a secret from the other girls. It pleased her, though, that Lady Boss trusted her above the others.

Despite being in the city for a few years now, Na-Young still marvelled at how spacious the streets were. She had since learned to read Japanese and could make out some of the shop names.

"I can't believe how modern the city is becoming," Twilight said, ignoring the trolley's jerky movements that jostled them in their seats.

"Glad you like it," said a middle-aged man sitting opposite

them. He had been eyeing them occasionally since they boarded. He was dressed in a blue suit with a pressed, collared shirt. Na-Young suspected that he thought they might be new to the city because of Twilight's enthusiasm. She was always happy to get out of the stuffy teahouse kitchen.

"I remember the day these cars started to run. My old man beat me after finding out that I'd ridden one," the man said, laughing. His dimpled cheeks added a charm to his smile.

"Why?" Twilight wondered.

"A friend of his ran a rickshaw outfit and the trolleys were a threat to his business, but I think he was upset because it was the Americans who brought them here." He brushed some lint off his jacket sleeve. "So, where are you from?"

"We work at a teahouse near Pagoda Park," Twilight answered. Better to state where they work than reveal where they had come from, Na-Young thought.

"Oh?" The man cocked his head. "Both of you?"

"Yes," Twilight said. "We're open six days a week."

Na-Young's pride was injured. She had become so close to some of the teahouse workers—almost like friends—that strangers did not see the class difference that separated them. She looked down at her clothes, a light grey-and-pink hanbok that Lady Boss had chosen for her—a look befitting the hostess of the teahouse. Although Twilight wore good-quality fabric that was perfectly pressed, it was plain white, indicating a lower status. Also, Na-Young was carrying an expensive parasol, a gift from Lady Boss, who considered it an essential accessory to protect the user from both sunlight and rain.

Na-Young used a handkerchief to dab her forehead. Her gaze swept over the people on the street before following a magpie's flight. Was the bird lost? Or merely searching for a tree? The purplish blue of its spread wings was a colour Na-Young associated with luxury and power. Perhaps she should get a hanbok made in the same shade, she thought.

"Anyway, as I was saying," the man continued. "It was pretty rough going the first few months. The old folks thought these trolleys were responsible for the bad drought we were going through. Then there was the kid who got run over and killed by one. Actually, it happened right by your teahouse, by Pagoda Park." He leaned in. "People tried to lynch the trolley driver and conductor. The boy's father went after them with an axe! Some cynical folks thought that because the driver was Japanese, he'd done it on purpose. A mob burned down two trolleys! For a while, no one wanted to work for the trolley company or even ride them."

A lump caught in Na-Young's throat. Since she'd arrived in the capital, her neighbourhood and the small road where the teahouse sat had been quiet and uneventful. How was it possible that such violence had taken place so close by? A chill ran through her.

"But then the Americans sent some thugs to protect the workers. Story goes that they'd shoot topknots off any man who tried to harass the workers or riders. Never saw it myself, though."

Na-Young cringed at the thought, but still wanted to know when it had happened. She asked the man.

"Twenty-five years ago. It's history now," he said.

The shops blurred into each other. Twenty-five years did not seem too long. She was relieved when the man got off.

Namdaemun, the South Gate with its giant two-tiered pagoda that served as the passageway in and out of the capital, looked just as formidable as the first time she'd laid eyes on it with Father-in-Law years ago. The outdoor market was busier than ever, congested with endless rickshaws, carts, and pedestrians criss-crossing each other.

"Let's split up so we can get everything we need as fast as possible," Na-Young said.

Twilight frowned and looked around. The crowd seemed to have grown. "Maybe we should stay together," she said.

"We'll meet back here once we've gotten everything and I've dropped off the package," Na-Young said, and left before Twilight could respond. She walked towards the archway. She knew exactly where she was going: The Peacock with Its Tail of One Hundred Eyes, the shop with no signage, just peacock tails hanging in its doorway.

Off in the distance, she eyed a Japanese policeman and circled around the crowd to avoid him, all the while trying to keep an eye out for him. She bumped into something—someone—and dropped the package. She looked up to see another Japanese policeman.

"What do we have here?" he asked in Korean, and picked it up.

"I don't know," Na-Young said. "My job is only to deliver it."

Without hesitation, he opened the wrapped cloth. "Bibles? In Hangul?" He fingered the letters on one of the covers, opened the book to a random page, and scanned it. Shaking his head, he said something in Japanese.

Distressed, Na-Young looked around to see whether anyone might be able to help her.

"Is there a problem?" a familiar voice said in Japanese. It was the Japanese man from the teahouse! He set the leather bag he was carrying on the ground. With his round, metal-framed glasses, he looked dignified, important.

"Ichinose-san," Na-Young said, trying to hide her relief at seeing him. "I was on my way to deliver a package when I accidentally bumped into this policeman. I've offended him somehow."

The Japanese man spoke with the policeman, his voice calm and even. The policeman squared his shoulders and excused Na-Young with a nod. To her relief, the ramie cloth was draped loosely over the Bibles as he passed the books back to her.

"Arigatou gozaimasu." She thanked the Japanese man and bowed deeply. Did he know what the books were? Should she try to explain?

"It's my pleasure to help you, Lady Song," he said, and bowed. "I'm glad to see you again. There's a wonderful place here that sells the best blood sausages. We should visit it together sometime. Unfortunately, I've got to run. I'll visit the teahouse next Monday when I'm back from some business I need to conduct." He picked up his bag, tipped his hat, and headed towards the train station at the far west end of the market.

He hadn't mentioned the books—and he still thought she was Lady Boss. But there was no time to correct him. She was also in a rush, so she headed towards the peacock tails. Just like the last time she had visited, her legs shook violently as she stepped into the small foyer of the shop, but this time for a different reason. What if the shopkeeper recognized her from years ago? With everything in her, she fought to forget their past encounter and the reason for her visit. A dog entered the foyer, tail wagging. Old Nosey! Again, Na-Young was startled by the dog's appearance but immediately calmed by her sweet temperament.

To Na-Young's relief, a different person was behind the counter—an old man.

"How can I help you?" he asked.

"Are you the proprietor?" Na-Young asked.

The man's expression hardened.

"I have a package for you. From my mistress, Lady Song."

The proprietor's face relaxed. "Ah, you have something for me, then. People call me Master Chang." He came out from behind the table and bowed. Na-Young bowed back and handed him the three Bibles.

"They were wrapped more elegantly, but a policeman opened it," she said.

"Did he give you any problems?"

"Yes," she said, "but it worked out."

The proprietor placed the three Bibles on the counter and picked up the first one. He fanned through the pages, then did the same with the second book. He stopped in the middle of the third book and removed an envelope.

"What is that?" Na-Young asked, then immediately regretted being so forward.

"Nothing. Everything is fine." The proprietor looked up at her and flashed an apologetic smile. "Sorry to have caused you any worry. Please thank Lady Song for her gifts. And thank you." He turned to face the wall of jars. "What do you suppose Lady Song would like in exchange for the books? Maybe some jujube seeds or rhubarb?" He paused for a moment.

Though the proprietor's back was to her, Na-Young saw him slip the envelope into a drawer before he collected an assortment of items that he placed on top of a plain cloth wrap. He skillfully secured the package with string.

The smaller jars on the counter contained roots, seeds, and bark. "I'm sure she would appreciate anything that she could add to her teas," Na-Young offered, distracted by the mysterious envelope and what it could contain.

"And how about the lady here? Is there anything she needs?"

Before she could respond, the proprietor had already begun to pick and choose his medicines for her. With both hands he offered it to her, along with the larger package for Lady Boss.

"What is it?" she asked, this time wanting to know whatever it was that she was delivering, despite that he might think her rude.

"Red ginseng blend for Lady Song. For you, some Chinese medicine they call Xiao Yao Wan."

Na-Young sniffed it and recognized some of the herbs and plants: white peony, ginger, licorice root, and peppermint.

"Thank you," she said, and asked about payment.

"It's a gift," the proprietor said. "Your first duty in life is to take care of your health. We need all the mental strength we can possess to claim our country back." He paused. "It's brave of you to work with Lady Song."

The comment caught Na-Young off guard. Since being in the city, she had learned certain tricks to manage her mind when she perceived a threat: She repressed them or imagined favourable outcomes. Sometimes her fantasies even delighted her, like imagining Yeon-Soo raising chickens and hunting rabbits in the little hut in the middle of nowhere. But Master Chang's words rang with a truth she could not dismiss: While Lady Boss taught her girls to read and write and seemed to protect them, she was also putting them in danger with these secret activities. And in order to gain Lady Boss's confidence and trust, Na-Young had never questioned her. But it was now undeniable that her boss was involved with the resistance activities.

Old Nosey licked Na-Young's hand, and she snapped out of her thoughts. What had happened to the old woman shopkeeper? she wondered. But she decided not to ask. The less she knew, the better.

Back outside, Na-Young wove in and out of the crowd, trying to blend in. She was back at the meeting place, but Twilight was not yet there.

Off in the distance, a Japanese woman dressed in a black kimono beautifully embroidered with red and gold floral designs had caught several people's attention. Her elaborate updo and ornate hair accessories accentuated her mystique. Na-Young ran a hand over her own hair and wondered how long it had to be to get such a high lift. It was at that moment she caught a glimpse of a woman on a prison bus, the sun catching a wisp of the red highlights in her hair. Na-Young did a double take. Could it be Yeon-Soo?

Na-Young jumped when she felt a tap on her shoulder. "Are you all right?" Twilight asked. "You look ill. We need to get back. It'll get busy in the teahouse soon."

"She's being taken to Seodaemun Prison," Na-Young whispered to herself. She knew in her gut that the woman on the bus was her friend. Had their past finally caught up to her? Or had Yeon-Soo done something else?

"The trolley! It's coming. We need to go," Twilight called out.

"Seodaemun Prison . . . where they imprison resistance fighters . . ." Na-Young repeated softly. A bell sounded. She looked up to see the trolley approaching. A sudden pounding in her temple made it hard to think. Twilight grabbed her hand and they ran.

Could Yeon-Soo have joined a resistance group? Had she been in the city all this time, too? Her best friend was alive after all! But her relief faded quickly at the grim realization that Yeon-Soo was the one in true danger.

Bird's-Eye View

A row of persimmon trees grew along the back wall of the boardinghouse. The small yard that separated the house from the wall was crammed with throwaway items: large, cracked kimchi pots, old clothes, and broken furniture. This made it the ideal spot to escape to, as no one else was ever out there. Na-Young often climbed the tallest tree as the sun was setting, and it was there, where she had a bird's-eye view of her surroundings, that she did her best thinking.

She waved at the little boy sitting on the porch of a house two streets over. He waved back and continued playing with his spinning top. How simple life had been for her when she was his age!

Her chest ached with worry. Had it really been Yeon-Soo on the bus? Why was she at Seodaemun Prison? Although she had not seen it, Na-Young was told that the prison stood like a formidable fort, just past the western boundaries of the city. Since the crushing of the independence movement years before, it had been more overcrowded than ever. It was common knowledge that it now held over a thousand activists, despite being built to hold only several hundred prisoners. She thought of Yu Gwan-Sun, the girl freedom fighter, rumoured to have died from brutal torture. Nearby Tree, who was their regular source of neighbourhood gossip and news, had told her that they had ripped out her fingernails and sliced off her nose and ears in an effort to make her give up the names of her accomplices.

"They refused to let her family bury her," Nearby Tree had said. "They didn't want anyone to see what they had done."

"What happened to her?" Na-Young had asked, stunned.

"The Japanese relented only when the American administrators from Gwan-Sun's school threatened to take action."

"And how do you know all this?" Twilight had challenged her.

"Because Lady Boss was there, and she told me. Gwan-Sun was a student at Ewha Girls School, where Lady Boss still volunteers. She was at the funeral."

Na-Young's admiration for Lady Boss had grown after hearing all this. Until she had delivered the package, she hadn't realized the extent of her boss's involvement with the resistance movement.

Could she turn to Lady Boss and ask for help with Yeon-Soo? Her dilemma about whether to tell Lady Boss the truth about the Japanese man seemed insignificant in comparison. Still, that problem gnawed at her. It didn't make sense to confess to both Lady Boss and the Japanese man when only one of them needed to know the truth.

Two birds landed on a nearby branch. Na-Young thought of Twilight and the girls. They knew she was lying to Lady Boss, and by not saying anything, they were caught in her lie, too. So perhaps it wasn't as simple as that. The lie felt bigger than simply misleading someone. They had covered for her, but for how much longer would they continue?

Was misleading someone lying? Wasn't that what Lady Boss did as she mixed truths and untruths about her husband's whereabouts? She was the master of weaving truths and lies together. Still, her lies allowed her business to flourish.

What about lies by omission? Na-Young wondered. Wasn't

that what she was doing by hiding her past from everyone? She thought about Headless Chicken, glad that the giant rocks that littered her grave hid her remains so that her bones would continue to find peace.

Na-Young needed to get to Seodaemun Prison somehow and make sure that the woman she'd seen on the bus truly was Yeon-Soo. But how? Who would help her? Her thoughts turned again to the situation with the Japanese man. He was clearly fond of her, and he seemed to possess some authority. She thought of how he'd dealt with the policeman in the market. The two birds she was watching took flight. In that moment, she decided she would tell him the truth about who she was and then gauge whether she could turn to him for help.

At nine thirty on Monday morning, the Japanese man came back, as he had promised. Monday mornings were usually quiet while Lady Boss was away volunteering. Like on his previous visit, he requested that Na-Young sit with him. A look of uncertainty flashed across Twilight's face, which Na-Young ignored as she told her to bring them some sweet hydrangea tea and their freshest rice cakes.

"I have something for you," said the Japanese man. He placed a small blue cloth roll with embroidered koi fish in front of her. The koi shimmered in the light, mesmerizing her.

"Please open it," he said.

"Of course," she said, realizing that despite the beauty of the cloth, her actual gift was inside it. As she unrolled the wrap, she took her time to observe the fine stitching and indulged in the soft feel of its suede lining. Her jaw dropped when she finished unwrapping the cloth and saw an elegant pen with a red marble design and gold accents.

"The pen has an ink reservoir built in," he said, picking it up to show her. "You won't have to dip your pen into an inkpot anymore. The attachable chain allows you to wear it around your neck if you so choose. I believe it was made in England. I picked it up while I was in Tokyo."

It took her several seconds to find her voice. He had remembered her ink-stained hands. The gesture stirred something deep within her. "It's beautiful, but I can't accept such an expensive gift," she said.

"It's a practical gift. An essential tool that makes writing more effortless and enjoyable. I'm pleased you like it."

Twilight brought over tea and a platter of their cheapest rice cakes. Offended by this gesture, Na-Young held up her new pen. Twilight nodded blankly and walked away.

Na-Young wished the light in the teahouse was brighter. The Japanese man looked better out in the natural sunlight.

"Do you frequently visit Namdaemun Market?" he asked.

"No, it's hard for me to get away from this shop," she said.

"Oh? I'm in the area quite often for work but I go to the market whenever I get cravings for blood sausage. We should go to the place I mentioned."

She tried to imagine him indulging in pig intestines stuffed with minced meat, barley, vegetables, and pork blood.

"Don't look so surprised," he said, leaning in. He whispered, "My maternal grandmother was Korean."

Whether it was the precious gift of the pen or the knowledge that the man was partly Korean, Na-Young exhaled, feeling an unexpected sense of pleasure.

Twilight looked over at their table. Desperate for some privacy, Na-Young asked the man to follow her out to the alcove. They took their teacups and settled on the boulders. She had been right: In the morning light, there was a glow to him that added to his charm. Even the gold, black, and white embroidery thread made the koi sparkle more vividly under the sun.

"May I?" he asked, taking out a pack of cigarettes from his jacket pocket. He had lovely hands, his nails neatly trimmed. She imagined the feel of his hand on hers and felt her cheeks grow warm. "Would you like one?"

"I've never tried smoking."

"Oh? Would you like to try?" He offered a cigarette. "I'm happy to teach you."

Her heart was racing. Would it help calm her? She had observed Lady Boss's demeanour change by deeply inhaling a cigarette—as if it allowed her to release her frustration and anxiety. Na-Young tried her best to mimic the way she held a cigarette.

"Why, you're a natural! Let me light it for you."

She placed the cigarette in between her lips.

"You need to inhale to ignite it. Just a little . . . then inhale again." As the flame of his lighter touched the cigarette, a wave of excitement flowed through her.

"Now, exhale." His eyes were fixed on her lips. She did her best to copy what she'd seen Lady Boss do. She coughed at first, but after a few puffs, it was effortless. She basked in his full attention.

"Tell me," she said, feeling quite bold, "something about your work."

"Although I was never an important man, my duty long ago was to protect important people." He chuckled. "My job was to guard the prime minister."

"That sounds rather important," she said, intrigued. The likelihood of his being able to help Yeon-Soo seemed more promising than ever.

"I was on security detail when Prime Minister Hara was assassinated inside Tokyo Station." Her look of confusion prompted him to explain. "He was stabbed to death by an ultra-rightist."

"When was that? What was he doing at the train station?" Such an open public place would have made him an easy target.

"I'll never forget the date—November fourth, 1921. He was on his way to Kyoto."

"Did you like him?" It may have seemed like an odd question to ask, but her initial reaction to his death wasn't a sympathetic one. After all, it was his government that had chosen to oppress Korea.

"He was loved by some people because he was the first commoner to become prime minister. I personally supported him. He was an outsider and the son of a samurai-class family that fought against the Meiji Reform to restore an old form of imperial rule. Even if one didn't agree with his political inclinations—which many didn't—he was a good man at heart. He understood the will of the common man because he was also a commoner." The Japanese man paused and added, "He was also a Christian like you—the first Christian prime minister."

"What makes you think I'm a Christian?" Na-Young asked, concerned.

"You were carrying copies of the Bible when I met you in the outdoor market."

He had seen the books after all! She sipped some tea and contemplated a plausible response. The taste of the cigarette in her mouth had somehow tainted the tea's gentle sweetness from the mountain hydrangea leaves.

"I did everything right and yet everything went wrong," he said. "I guess you might say that I've spent the past few years trying to redeem my name. Right now, my work with the government involves promoting the radio."

"Radio?" Na-Young asked.

"Radio," he repeated. "It's the next step to modernizing Keijō."

She hated how he called the capital by its Japanese name.

"Think about it—a centralized medium for everyone to receive information. Not just news, but music and entertainment. That's what radio would bring. Our government has spent a lot of time and effort trying to modernize this place. Part of my role is to oversee the building and operation of the transmission facilities." His eyes sparkled with enthusiasm. "I'm sorry, this is all probably over your head, Lady Song."

Offended, Na-Young regretted bringing him out to the alcove. She hated how he believed that his people were "helping" rather than oppressing her country.

"Forgive me," he said, seeing her face. "The last thing I would want to do is to upset you." He started again: "Our commitment to your people should be embraced. Why, do you know the number of newspaper and magazine publications that have sprung up in only a couple of years? There are more political, cultural, and academic activities happening now than ever. And yes, yes, it was harsh in the beginning, but good came of that. Even the whole police system has been expanded and reorganized."

Na-Young thought back to the conversations she had overheard between her husband and his companion back in Anyang. Indeed, they had said that the Japanese were granting permits more freely now. The family's printing press could grow by publishing new things. But at what cost? The flowers that the Japanese offered, while seemingly attractive, had seeds that were poisonous. *The man's partly Korean*, Na-Young reminded herself, but it did little to settle her nerves.

Since there was no ashtray, she stubbed out her cigarette on the side of the boulder. When she looked up, the Japanese man was reaching towards her. For a split second, she thought he might be trying to touch her face. Her stomach tightened. She followed his hand with her gaze and watched as he caught a mosquito. He took out a blue handkerchief to clean his hand, and simultaneously checked the time on his watch.

"It's lovely," she said, admiring the watch. "I still marvel that something so small can do the same job as a giant sundial."

"And do an even better job at that," he said. "I need to go. Thank you for today's visit."

"Thank you for my gift." Na-Young had a brief impulse to tell him the truth about who she was and ask for his help, the way she'd planned to do, but she was still upset with his arrogant assumptions about Japan's need to reform Korea.

"Besides the Bible, what else do you enjoy reading?" he asked, not picking up on her mood. "I can likely get my hands on some popular Western novels for you. I've noticed that Tolstoy is very popular here."

Na-Young recalled what the widow had said about the Russian author and how writers like Kim Seok-Song had written about him and his works in magazines for modern women.

"Do you enjoy Russian literature?" she asked.

He laughed, clearly delighted. "You're familiar with his works!" he said. "I read some of his popular novels when I was studying abroad in America."

"You studied in America?"

"Yes, at Harvard, a prestigious American university. There were quite a few of us, mostly sons of diplomats." He stood up. "I suppose, then, that you've read the Tolstoy book I was going to recommend?"

She recalled that the widow in Anyang had a cat with a Russian name. "*Anna Karenina*?" she wondered aloud.

"Of course you'd be attracted to a strong female protagonist!"

She had no idea what he was talking about. How long could she keep up these false pretences?

"I don't want to make you late," she said, and hurriedly stacked the teacups. Then, realizing that her opportunity was about to be lost, Na-Young finally mustered the courage to ask when she noticed him checking his watch again.

She changed her mind. She would need his full attention, and she would need more than a few minutes.

"Perhaps we could pick up our conversation next Monday?" he asked, and added, "Lady Song, if I may say, I find you thoroughly enchanting." He left, smiling.

"What are you doing?" Twilight demanded. Na-Young ignored her and stepped back out into the alcove.

Na-Young had forgotten what it was like to yearn for a man—or maybe she'd never really known. She closed her eyes and saw mountains. A hot sun. Rivers. She unrolled the koi cloth and admired her pen again. She thought back to Daegeori, when she and Yeon-Soo were doing laundry by the river. Back then, she could not have imagined such a fine gift. How far she had come since then!

The koi roll slipped behind the boulder she was sitting on, and when she reached for it, her hand landed on something hard and metallic. Something was buried there! She rolled up her right sleeve and sifted the dirt away from the object. It was a container. Several rolled-up copies of paper were stuffed inside. Another container, buried beside it, was filled with small Korean flags mounted on wooden sticks. And in another, copies of different maps. She unfolded one. It showed the city with several circles drawn all over it. The fibres of the paper were weakened from being repeatedly folded.

This surprise discovery snapped her thoughts into sharp focus. When Lady Boss had first told her that all that happened at the teahouse was to remain a secret, Na-Young had presumed that this was to hide that Lady Boss was teaching girls to read and write. But now she wondered: How deeply was Lady Boss involved with resistance work? Could she be more than a mere supporter? And what was in the mysterious envelope in the package Na-Young had delivered? Maybe it contained information far more sensitive than she could have imagined. She contemplated the possibility that Lady Boss was not who she appeared to be.

"It's easier to go with the wind against your back than in your face," she recalled someone once telling her. Perhaps she shouldn't try to discover the truth if she didn't want to know it.

Bamboo Forest

The teahouse was empty and Lady Boss was away. The staff members retreated to their break room. Na-Young was still preoccupied with what she had found in the alcove. She played out different scenarios about how she could approach Lady Boss, but ultimately decided to avoid a confrontation. Instead, she sat and practised her penmanship to keep her mind busy.

"What's the point of copying out passages over and over again?" Twilight said. "If you're going to waste time and ink, why not write something original?"

The idea caught her attention, although she doubted her ability to be creative and write something others might find interesting. Besides, writing the same thing repeatedly, like chanting a mantra, allowed her to enter a quiet state of mind where the silence was more important than understanding the meaning behind anything she wrote.

"You could interpret my dreams and write about them," Flower Petal said. "I've been having the oddest ones. Last night I was wandering through a bamboo forest when I was overcome with such intense pain, I thought I was going into labour—which was impossible, because I wasn't with child. I remember Mother telling me that on the night I was conceived, she dreamt that a sea dragon came to her, and by the grace of the Buddha-sun, she would have a healthy son. She got me instead."

They laughed. Even Matchstick, who usually kept her distance, was friendlier, and had brought a small plate of their finest rice cakes and cut melons to the table for them.

"A bamboo forest represents immortality and supernatural powers," Nearby Tree said.

"If that's the case, I'd wish that I could turn this teahouse into a bamboo forest and grow a thousand trees," Flower Petal said.

Na-Young recalled wandering into the bamboo forest back in Daegeori—the village name itself meant bamboo. There was something magical about being there. In the heat and humidity of summer, the canopy of bamboo stalks, shielding her from the sunlight with its green leaves high above her, offered a cool escape. In the spring and fall, the lull of leaves blowing in the breeze made one feel part of the forest itself, and the snow-covered ground in winter felt like walking on clouds. And in all seasons, the bamboo leaves stayed green—unchanged, like other trees in nearby forests whose leaves turned colours and fell to nourish future generations.

When she was five, she had mistakenly told her mother that her brother had carved his name into a bamboo tree—and somehow the word got back to Father, who had whipped him for foolishly defacing the tree.

"I didn't mark it to own it," Oppa had told her, suggesting that that was what Father had thought. "I did it because I had learned to write my name and liked seeing it."

"At least you know what your own name looks like," she had said, wondering about everything else he was learning in school.

"Why should that bother you? No one will ever call you by name aside from everyone in our family."

"That's not true," she had said. "My friends."

"What friends?" he teased. He was right, of course.

Was it etiquette, tradition, or simply habit that caused everyone to call upon each other by rank, which reminded each person where they stood in their family, social groups, and society? Husbands and wives never called each other by name; her mother's friends always addressed Mother as "Mi-Young's mother," following the usual custom of calling friends by their children's names. Thankfully, everyone at the teahouse simply called her "Bookkeeper."

"Maybe I could write something about bamboo. Bamboo shoots are delicious," Na-Young said. "They fill your stomach so you never grow hungry. Bamboo, like wise men, is strong yet not strong. Bamboo can be bent and shaped to make baskets and containers, cut down to make doors. Why, you can even make hats out of it."

On tiptoe, Na-Young swept the air with her hands and arms to show the trees' height. "Yet they grow tall and strong, strong enough to hold up walls. Like a person of integrity, the bamboo does not change with the season—it maintains its integrity. Their transformation can be compared to that of a wise man."

"But bamboo is hollow. What does that say of men?" Twilight said, crushing Na-Young's enthusiasm.

"Why don't you write about famous or important people?" Nearby Tree suggested. "Everybody wants to read about a hero," she said.

"Yes! Write about the One with Fire Hair! They say she's the new Yu Gwan-Sun, the next girl hero, and that she has hair the colour of fire," Flower Petal said.

"That's ridiculous!" Matchstick scoffed.

"It's true," Flower Petal said. "They say that under the afternoon sun, her hair is the colour of red fire, that in her presence, one can actually feel the heat she radiates. She also possesses an eagle owl's keen vision and wisdom and has translucent white skin."

"She sounds more like a demon than a hero," Matchstick said.

Na-Young's heart raced. Could they be talking about Yeon-Soo? Yet her friend was blind in one eye, and the other girls hadn't mentioned that.

"She sounds more mythical than real," Nearby Tree said. "Although I suppose that's what we do when we need someone to look up to—they have to be larger than life."

"Have you seen this person?" Na-Young asked.

Flower Petal shook her head. "But my sister did—when the wind took the girl's hat and exposed her hair."

Images of Yeon-Soo in the city drifted in and out of Na-Young's thoughts. It had to be her on the bus. Or was she simply tricking her mind to believe that her friend was still alive? Na-Young pushed herself up from the table so quickly that she almost lost her balance. The rush of excitement became fear for Yeon-Soo and the struggles she must be facing.

Her head ached terribly. Perhaps she should somehow write about the chaos, anger, and sadness within her. Could releasing those thoughts onto paper allow them to escape her mind—like trapped birds in a house, finally finding the way out? *Maybe my brain isn't trying to kill me,* she mused. *Maybe it's trying to help me.*

A Bit of Jazz

On an afternoon when Lady Boss was out, Na-Young overheard a conversation between two men. They were talking about the new broadcasting station that had been built by the Japanese.

"What better way to spread Japanese bullshit!" the bald man said to his companion. "It's bad enough that the bastards are in our country, they'll soon be in our houses, too, jamming their damn propaganda down our throats!" His voice was loud and slurred.

"Yes, now they'll be able to disseminate their version of the news as it actually happens all over the country," his friend agreed.

"Sons of bitches!" The bald man slapped the table.

"Hush!" his friend said.

"Why? Are there pro-Japanese spies amongst us?" He looked around the room, but everyone was ignoring him. He drank from a flask.

"This is why you shouldn't drink on an empty stomach," his friend said. He signalled for Twilight and asked her to bring more heotgae-cha. Flavoured with raisin tree fruits, it was the best tea to relieve hangovers. When it was ready, Na-Young took it over to the table herself.

"But couldn't music be played on the radio? A bit of jazz might lift everyone's spirits," Na-Young said as she poured the tea.

The bald man looked at her. "Are you stupid?" he asked. "Where am I? I thought we were at The Bluebird Sings Here Teahouse, not a makutsu. Does Lady Song know you're a dimwit? Likely a Japanese sympathizer, too!"

The man's companion stood abruptly and pulled his friend up with him.

"Of course this is a fine establishment! And you are a fine lady." He apologized profusely, paid, and dragged his friend outside.

"I can't believe he talked to me like that," Na-Young said under her breath.

The expression on Twilight's face turned from anger into a forced smile as Lady Boss entered the teahouse.

"Special treat," Lady Boss said, holding up two bundles of left-over Chinese food that she had brought back from her meetings at the Christian college. "Put it in the kitchen for later." She passed the bags to Twilight. Then, noticing the tension between them, she cocked her head.

"We just dealt with a rude customer," Na-Young said. "Everything is fine now."

"Then let's get to work." Lady Boss clapped her hands.

"I need to talk to you," Na-Young said, the pressure of everything on her mind weighing heavily.

"Can it wait? I have something to tend to."

Na-Young sensed a note of urgency in her voice—or was it avoidance? Na-Young nodded. What else could she do?

Despite her desire to stay out of the alcove, the Japanese man and Na-Young returned there because it was the only place that offered privacy. He had another gift for her: a watch this time.

"It's too expensive. I can't accept it," she said. Despite the thrill of such a valuable possession, something in the grey clouds told her that she had to draw a line. She thought of Father-in-Law and his many gifts.

"It gives me pleasure to indulge you," he said. "You admired my watch so much."

A rumble of thunder in the distance left Na-Young feeling more unsettled. The weather had grown cooler. Fall had arrived.

"Have you noticed it hasn't rained once during your visits?" Na-Young asked, thinking anxiously about the buried containers. Rain would force them back inside the teahouse, where they'd be safely away from the evidence of Lady Boss's rebellion.

"No, I can't say that I have."

"I used to like the rain," she said. "I liked playing in it as a child."

"My boy does the same!" he said.

"You have a child? You're married?" She suddenly felt stupid. Of course he was married. Why else did he only visit once a week?

"No, I'm widowed. My wife passed away during childbirth. My son is in Japan with my parents."

"I'm very sorry to hear that. What's your son's name?" Na-Young said, surprised at how relieved she felt that he was no longer married. Clearly, he had forgotten that Lady Song was married. A pang of guilt shot through her, but she chose not to remind him.

"Hideyoshi, but we call him Yoshi. He was born deaf. He's seven now." The man showed her a photo of his son standing next to a huge man with a topknot, dressed in a robe.

"That's Miyagiyama Fukumatsu," he said. "He's my son's favourite sumo wrestler. Miyagiyama-san won two consecutive championships but had to sit out for some years due to a hand injury. We were lucky to meet him in Tokyo last year. The sport is hugely popular. There's another sumo wrestler he admires—his name escapes me—but Yoshi claims that that wrestler's success is his powerful left-hand grip. He believes it's his secret weapon. My son also prefers using his left hand."

"Your son is clever," she said, "to be so observant." His name reminded her of the Japanese general Toyotomi Hideyoshi, considered one of Korea's oldest enemies. Old Man Yang used to tell her that he'd never go up north again after hearing that the general's dead spirit haunted the mountains there.

The Japanese man blushed with pride. When she told him that she didn't know anything about sumo wrestling, he excitedly shared that Yoshi aspired to be a wrestler.

"Initially, I was skeptical, but given his disability and all the discrimination he'll face in life, what better job than to be a professional wrestler?"

"He looks adorable, far too adorable to fight," she said.

"Unfortunately, boys have to start at a young age, and get into a good stable that offers the best training. The men follow a very strict code of behaviour. Everything, from what they eat to what they wear, is dictated."

"It sounds like a harsh life. I'm not sure I'd want that for my child."

"That's because you're a warm, compassionate person," he said. "Yoshi still has several years to think about this. Apprentices are usually fourteen to fifteen years of age, I believe." He paused. "You should visit Japan one day. Many of your people do nowadays."

Again, the way he referred to Koreans triggered an instant annoyance in her, and she fought to control it by staying quiet.

"All you'll need are your residence registration papers," he continued. "Tokyo is a big city, but the transportation system in Japan is excellent."

Finally, angry at her own inaction and at the thought of thousands of her people imprisoned, she felt compelled to ask, "What do you know about Seodaemun Prison?"

"Why do you ask?"

"I overheard some men talking about it in the teahouse."

"I don't know much about the prison other than it has far exceeded its capacity with anti-Japanese criminals."

"How would one go about finding out if someone is there?"

"That wouldn't be difficult. If my people are known for one thing, it's our thorough recordkeeping." He smiled as if he had told a good joke, then turned serious. "Is there anyone there that you might know?" His voice dropped and she knew to be cautious.

"No, but a customer was telling me about it, so I wondered."

"Lady Song. You don't want to know anyone inside that prison. As liberal and as fair as our government is trying to be, they will spare nothing to go after anyone deliberately trying to sabotage their efforts."

He had finally crossed a line that their conversations hadn't permitted before. Her anger and indignation energized her. "Don't you mean 'your' efforts? After all, you are part of that government. I think *your* government is deliberately imprisoning everyone they perceive as a threat. It's the fastest way to kill one's spirit. And that's what your government wants. They imprison women and children. They even killed a seventeen-year-old girl. You have a child. What do you think of that?"

Na-Young could see by the Japanese man's face that any warm feelings he'd had for her in this moment were gone. She cursed herself for speaking so boldly and realized that she had to act quickly if any hope of regaining his affection was possible.

"I'm sorry," she said. "You probably think I'm just a naive, simple girl, and maybe you're right." She lowered her head and turned away.

"No, no . . ." he said. "I don't want to argue with you."

"Can you help me find someone?" she asked. "Her name is Yu Yeon-Soo."

The look of vulnerability on his face told her that he could be swayed. She met his eyes and held his gaze. Confident, she leaned over and pressed her lips against his.

He drew into her, his arms wrapping around her. "I'll do my best to help you," he said, and kissed her back.

Thorny Bushes

True to his word, the Japanese man returned with news to share.

"Yes, the woman you asked about is at Seodaemun Prison," he said, accepting the tea Na-Young passed him. They were sitting on the boulders in the alcove, at his insistence. He preferred to smoke outside when possible. "She's being detained on charges of organizing an anarchist group."

Na-Young almost dropped her cup, hot tea spilling on her chima. She braced herself for the inevitable news that Yeon-Soo was also charged with murdering a Japanese military policeman.

But the Japanese man said nothing else. That was her only charge. Overcome with relief, Na-Young forced herself to stay composed.

"I need to get her out," she said.

"The charge is quite serious."

"Then we'll have to break her out."

He laughed but stopped when he saw that she was serious. He lit a cigarette and offered her one. "Is she a relative? If so, I could arrange a visit."

Na-Young passed on the cigarette and hesitated, unsure of how much she should tell him. "No, but she's like a sister. She's not much older than me."

The Japanese man took a long drag from his cigarette. "I've thought quite a bit about what you said. About how prisons kill one's spirit. I agree that it's not right what happened to Yu Gwan-

Sun. I didn't know all the details until I asked around. The official story is that she was a ruthless threat, but I find it hard to believe that a young girl could be so dangerous that she had to lose her life."

"She lost her life fighting for this country's freedom."

"Lady Song, you speak with so much passion. Please, I can't stress this enough. Do not get yourself involved with anything that would compromise your reputation. Don't underestimate the sophisticated intelligence network that is in place here in this country."

Was that supposed to intimidate her? She thought of the metal containers buried behind them. The tall hedge that separated the yard from the back alley made her feel boxed in, especially since there wasn't a separate way in and out. When he got up and started to pace, her anxiety grew.

"Yes, I accept your offer to help me. I want to see her," she said.

He handed her his empty teacup and nodded. "I'll see to it immediately."

Her heart skipped with joy, but she kept her emotions steady. She wanted him to leave now that she had gotten what she needed, but he seemed in no hurry to go.

"Did you know that some of the best books ever written were done so in prison?" he said. "Yoshida Shōin, a brilliant intellect, wrote some of his most powerful essays while confined. One of my professors at Harvard even devoted an entire lecture to the subject. I didn't have the language skills to get through the books he recommended, although I did manage to get my hands on a translated copy of *The Pilgrim's Progress*, my professor's favourite."

He really has no idea I'm not listening, thought Na-Young as she sipped her tea. Then, remembering the high stakes at play, she forced herself to pay greater attention.

"So you're saying that prison is a space of confinement, but not for the imagination?" she chimed in, trying to recall a similar discussion she'd had with Father-in-Law. He had once argued that a loss of some form of freedom or even one's senses hadn't stopped the deaf German composer Beethoven from creating masterpieces and the blind English poet John Milton from writing over a thousand lines in his epic biblical story about the Fall of Man.

"John Milton's loss of sight surely did not compromise his brilliance," she added, mimicking Father-in-Law's tone and authority.

"Yes, I've read *Paradise Lost*," the Japanese man said. "Lady Song, if I didn't know better, I'd swear we studied together in America. You never cease to amaze me."

Na-Young felt an instant warmth. "For all we know, your son could become a combination of Beethoven and Miyagiyama—the world's first classical-composing sumo wrestler."

Hearing this, he pulled her up and kissed her. In spite of herself, she pressed against him, giving in to an overwhelming urge to be with him.

"Sorry to interrupt," Twilight said. "Lady Boss is asking for you."

Na-Young pulled away to see her coworker, an unmistakable look of amusement on her face. Rather than leave, she continued to stand, watching the Japanese man's look of confusion at her mention of Lady Boss.

"Tell her I'll be right in," Na-Young said, annoyed. She tossed the two teacups she was holding behind the boulders.

"My mother—our boss—is here," she said to the man. "She's very old-fashioned. It would be highly inappropriate for me to be out here with a customer. You need to hide!"

The Japanese man nodded and scanned the tiny yard for a

place to go. He dashed towards some thorny bushes that wrapped around the teahouse wall.

"There you are," Lady Boss said. "What are you doing out here?" She sniffed the air.

"I've been smoking!" Na-Young said, fanning the air. "It's a terrible habit. I didn't want the girls to know, so I've been coming out here."

Lady Boss nodded. "I suppose it's my fault. I should quit. It's affecting my sense of smell and taste, not to mention my breathing."

"You're back early." Na-Young tried to sound casual.

"I wanted to talk with you to see if you might join—" A fat raindrop landed on Lady Boss's head.

Na-Young's heart was about to burst. Was Lady Boss going to ask her to join a resistance group within earshot of the Japanese man?

Lady Boss used a handkerchief to dab her forehead. "It always seems to rain whenever we step out here," she said, and gestured for them to go inside.

The teahouse had quickly filled with customers who had stepped in to avoid the rainfall. Na-Young racked her brain, trying to figure out how to smuggle the Japanese man out safely. Knowing that he was hiding in the very place where Lady Boss had hidden containers full of things that could implicate all of them in an anti-Japanese conspiracy scheme was enough to make her vomit.

"You look ill," Lady Boss said, and insisted that Na-Young lie down in the back room. Na-Young seized the opportunity to slip out into the yard.

But the Japanese man was gone. He'd probably climbed over the tall hedges somehow. If he was good enough to work as security for the Japanese prime minister, then maybe getting out of a tiny backyard was easy, and she had worried for nothing. Her relief lasted only a moment, though, as she recalled how sad he had looked when he'd told her he had failed to do his job. The prime minister, after all, had been killed on his watch. She went to collect the two teacups she had tossed behind the boulders. It was then that she noticed the lip of one of the containers poking through the dirt. Her imagination went wild. Could the Japanese man have discovered them? Or had the rain simply washed away the dirt covering them?

"I can't keep doing this!" she said aloud, sure that her head and heart would soon explode and nothing would matter because everything would be lost.

Back home, the persimmon trees were still damp from the earlier rain, but Na-Young climbed the highest branch to find the late evening sky a deep blue. The wind had picked up and she was glad that she had a thick shawl.

She was certain that Lady Boss was going to ask her to join the resistance cause, and she thought about how she should react and what she should say. Na-Young couldn't say no without jeopardizing her relationship with Lady Boss, not to mention her job at the teahouse. And then there was the Japanese man. She had a huge opportunity to secure his help in finding Yeon-Soo, but how could she ever reconcile his role in the oppression of Korea with her loyalties to Lady Boss? How could she ever make things right? One lie, like a single mosquito joining a swarm, now threatened to harm her in ways beyond her imagination.

The little boy from across the street came out and waved good night. Tonight, more than ever, he reminded her of Yeon-Soo's son, Su-Bin. She regretted again that Su-Bin's nickname had been Chicken Boy, and that he had played alone and had largely seemed lost in his own world. Despite his oddities, he'd had a wisdom about him. After all, he was the one who had refused to let a headless chicken die, and in turn, that headless chicken had saved Na-Young's life.

In her mind, she called out to Su-Bin, asking, "What's the opposite of a lie?"

He answered, "The truth."

"Can telling the truth make things right?"

"But isn't the truth subjective?"

"Yes. Your mother truly believed you were wonderful, bright like the sun, while an entire village mocked you because you flapped your arms and chased after your beloved Headless Chicken."

Did the truth require more than one person to believe it in order to be right? Na-Young thought about all the lies she had told Mother to protect her. When Father had brought Second Mother home for the first time, she had lied and told Mother that the new wife looked hideous. Mother had agreed, even though they both knew that Second Mother was tall and radiant like a sunflower. If two people, or an entire group of people, believed something to be true, was it? The Japanese believed the Koreans were a backward people, while the Koreans believed the Japanese were ruthless with only one goal: to advance their imperialistic power at all costs. If you asked an American, what might be said?

Could one be honest without telling the truth? In her heart of hearts, she hadn't meant to lie, deceive, or hurt anyone. This, Na-Young knew to be true about herself, even if no one might agree.

Could there be something in between—a half-truth? She was a hostess at the teahouse, just not *the* hostess who the Japanese man thought she was.

Na-Young thought back to the bald man in the teahouse, the one who had accused her of being stupid. He'd said that the Japanese would use radio to spread false information and propaganda—lies to promote their political cause. She imagined her own lies, spreading like wildfire, and the grave danger that followed.

Then she recalled Father-in-Law stating the importance of working with the "right" people, even if they were Japanese. How critical was it to know the "right" people? The ones whose "truth" had the power to impose life and death over others? Unfortunately, she didn't know anyone with power other than the Japanese man, so her hopes rested with him.

Shadows

Desperate and alone, Na-Young turned to Twilight, who was the closest thing to a friend she had. They were in her boardinghouse room, taking turns eating Chinese fried rice and vegetables out of small bowls, and discussing how to help Yeon-Soo. Oppa showed up with rice wine.

"Even if we find a good lawyer, Yeon-Soo might be stuck there for a while," Oppa said. "There are over two hundred guards who work in that prison, including some thirty chief guards. I'm sure one or more of them could be persuaded to help, but where would we get that sort of money?"

"Be serious!" Twilight said.

"How much do you think we'll need?" Na-Young asked.

Twilight whistled, eyebrows raised, when Oppa started guessing at the amount they needed.

"Again, where are we supposed to get that sort of money?"

"We've got to hurry," Na-Young said. Her heart raced at the thought of the prison guards discovering that Yeon-Soo had killed a Japanese military policeman. She added, "We have to get her out." She was about to say, *It's my fault she's in prison,* but caught herself. Instead she said, "She's my best friend."

Oppa shook his head and rested a hand on top of Na-Young's.

"Do you think Lady Boss might be willing to help?" Twilight asked cautiously.

How much did Twilight know about Lady Boss's political agenda? Na-Young wondered. Did she dare ask? She shook her head.

"I know whom I can ask," Na-Young said finally. "I need to go to Anyang."

★

Despite the short time she had lived in Anyang, Na-Young had never ventured beyond the suburbs or the neighbourhood she lived in. The area was still largely rural and agricultural, but had a downtown with shops and restaurants as well as the usual traditional markets. This was where she found Min-Ho's office.

"When my secretary told me you were waiting to see me, I almost didn't believe her. How did you know I was here?" Min-Ho asked, and offered her a seat.

She took a deep breath, pleased with herself for having gotten there. While surprised, he didn't seem unhappy to see her. "My brother went to your home. One of your house servants told him."

"He came all this way?"

"Yes, I need your help," she said.

"You must be desperate if you've come to ask me."

"Yes," she said.

"So you know about Father?"

She shook her head.

"He died last year."

The news took Na-Young's breath away. Her body stiffened and she fumbled for something appropriate to say.

He lowered his head. "It's fine. He died. It's what old people do."

"But he was still young." Na-Young thought about her own father.

"Do you believe someone can die of a broken heart?"

"I don't know."

"Yeah, well, I think I broke the old man. When Sung-Min came back and his father disowned him, I let him stay with me."

And here I thought I'd broken Father-in-Law's heart by leaving him, Na-Young thought. Guilt had a fascinating way of claiming people.

"You love Sung-Min. Being with him didn't kill your father," she said.

"You don't think it's wrong?"

"Not if you really love him."

"Aye, stop being a martyr. Judgement is a natural instinct. We do it without thinking." Min-Ho reached for a pack of cigarettes on his desk. He offered her one, which, to his surprise, she accepted.

"Love is complicated," she said. "I've yet to feel love in that special way, so perhaps I'm wrong in believing that it's hard to find. If your heart has taken someone who loves you back, I think you're very lucky."

She was tempted to add that Oppa, too, had once said to Sarwon that he'd wait for their father to die if that's how long it took for them to marry. She also thought of the Japanese man and the complications that could come from being with him.

"If I may, I'd like to give you one piece of advice," Na-Young said. She tapped her cigarette against the lip of the ashtray on his desk. "Treat Sung-Min better than you once treated me. If you care deeply for him, focus on being kind and giving."

"You're teaching me how to love someone?" he asked, looking amused. His eyes, once hard as black onyx, reflected a light that drew Na-Young to him.

"So, how can I help you?" His demeanour was relaxed.

"I need to borrow money, but it will take me a long time to pay you back," she said breathlessly. "I work at a teahouse in the capital."

"I see," he said, and paused. "What's the money for?"

"To get a lawyer for a friend in Seodaemun Prison. She's been imprisoned for organizing an anti-Japanese group. We grew up together. She's like a sister to me. I want to get a lawyer, but Oppa thinks that's pointless. He suggested I figure out a way to possibly bribe a guard."

"Your brother's not wrong," he said. "But your best bet is to look for a crooked judge. That way, she won't be on the run—she'll be free." He stubbed out his cigarette and was silent for several moments. "I'll need a few days to get the money together," he said. "I have some business that will take me to the capital. How about I bring it to you next Thursday?"

"You'd do that?" For a second, she didn't know how to react. Finally, she rose and bowed deeply to him. She rejoiced at her double luck. Lady Boss would be away volunteering at the school that morning. They could meet at the teahouse.

He nodded. "Anything to help a freedom fighter stick it to the damn Japanese."

Na-Young stood a moment, glancing around, wondering whether she had the right to ask about her son.

"Anything else?" Min-Ho asked.

A lengthy pause followed.

"The boy's well," he said finally. "He and Sung-Min are inseparable. Sung-Min thinks he'll make a wonderful scholar one day."

"He's still so young," Na-Young said. Her heart swelled at the thought of sunlight reflecting off the boy's cheeks. She tried to slow her racing heart and quickly shut down her thoughts. Drawing in three quick breaths, she focused on the ashtray and exhaled slowly. *Stay focused on why you're here,* she reminded herself. *On present matters.*

"He is more than well cared for. I promise. Life is easier, believe it or not, without Father interfering in my personal and professional affairs."

As harsh as it sounded, Na-Young understood and nodded. Anxiety grew inside her like brushwood near an open fire: She wanted to know the boy's name. But she was too afraid to ask. *It's better this way*, she reasoned as she stepped outside. A name would only give power to past decisions and memories, allowing them to exist beyond their shadows.

Hangul

On the Monday four days before Min-Ho was supposed to come with the money, Na-Young went over the teahouse's accounting books. Business had grown even more, and a boy had been hired to deliver rice cakes, confections, and loose teas. It had been Na-Young's idea to package the treats in the elegant, handmade masu boxes that she had learned to fold years ago. Suddenly, she was struck by a possibility: What if the rice cakes held coded messages? Perhaps sending written messages or envelopes like the one she had delivered was now too dangerous. The sheer outlandishness of the thought made her question whether her growing anxiety was making her foolish.

"I want you to come to Ewha with me on Thursday morning," Lady Boss said. "Your writing and reading skills have much improved. I have a great surprise for you."

"Who will serve as hostess?" Na-Young asked, knowing already that Twilight could easily cover.

"The teahouse will be fine for just one morning without us. Besides, Boksun's been looking forward to seeing you again."

Was Boksun a secret resistance fighter? Was that why Lady Boss had laughed when Na-Young suggested that she work at the teahouse? How had she risen to such important work? Na-Young stopped her heart racing by holding her breath and then exhaling slowly. Perhaps Boksun was merely studying and aspiring to be a translator—which in itself was quite remarkable, given that she'd once been an illiterate maidservant.

Her thoughts turned to Min-Ho. What would happen when he came with the money and she wasn't there? What would Twilight say when he asked for her?

As much as it troubled her, she had no choice. She wrote a letter to Min-Ho and sealed it in one of Lady Boss's envelopes.

"A gentleman will be here on Thursday morning asking for me," Na-Young told Twilight. She scanned the room and saw that their two customers were distracted with a card game. "Please give this to him. It's a matter of life and death that he gets it." She showed her the envelope and slipped it under the red place mat on a table where a potted plant sat. "In exchange, I'll grant you whatever favour you want."

"This is about the money to help your friend, right? Did you figure out a solution?"

"Keep your voice down!" Na-Young tugged on Twilight's sleeve.

"Relax. Of course I'll help." Twilight gestured for Na-Young to lean in. "I'll get back to you with my request," she said, and smiled.

On Thursday morning, Na-Young and Lady Boss took the trolley to Ewha Girls School.

"Isn't it sad and lovely that the school was built so close to an important part of our history?" Lady Boss said. She was referring to the royal palace, which sat just east of the school.

She rambled on about the palace's history. Na-Young was amazed at how much Lady Boss knew, but her mind was distracted and her stomach in knots at the thought of attending her first resistance meeting.

"One day, perhaps the royal family will grace the palace again."

Na-Young gazed at the massive palace grounds and the different buildings that made up the palace, with its fancy painted wood and stucco and spacious gardens.

"Don't look too closely," said Lady Boss. "The Japanese have been slowly stealing everything inside and destroying whatever parts of the royal estate they want. There used to be many, many buildings surrounded by ornate botanical gardens." She gazed up at the clouds. "I still remember the day Queen Min was killed by Japanese assassins. I was a student here at Ewha. My teachers were sobbing. It happened on a Tuesday. I remember that, because by the time we got word of what had happened, a whole day had passed. On Wednesdays, our teachers used to make us recite Bible passages in front of the principal but on that Wednesday, we were told to go outside and play. The girls and I were so happy, until we found out the reason why: Our queen was dead. Then we all started crying."

Na-Young had not known that Lady Boss had attended Ewha. Her continued devotion to the school suddenly made more sense. And if Lady Boss was organizing secret anti-Japanese meetings inside the school, that was another layer of danger. Or perhaps that was a clever ruse. Who would suspect a girls' school? Then Na-Young remembered Yu Gwan-Sun.

"Never underestimate the potential of a single girl," the widow in Anyang had once said.

Lady Boss had started walking towards the school.

"So what happened to the king?" Na-Young asked.

"All this happened just before the Japanese officially declared ownership of the country. Her husband, King Gojong, fled the palace. He was our last king. And now the Japanese have the audacity to use the palace to hold their grand affairs and official events."

Boksun greeted Na-Young warmly upon their arrival. During

her first visit there, when she had sought out Boksun upon arriving in the city, she had thought the building, with its red bricks and three aboveground levels, looked majestic. A place of learning dedicated to women. Today it looked menacing, as if it concealed inescapable danger. Boksun led her into a room where a group of women had already gathered.

Lady Boss introduced Na-Young to a white woman. "This is Ms. Alice Appenzeller," she said.

Na-Young bowed to her.

"It's a pleasure to meet you," the woman said in perfect Korean.

"Don't look so surprised," Boksun said. "Ms. Alice was born here. Her father was among the first Methodist missionaries to work in Korea. She's the school's current president."

"Your father wasn't by chance Horace Newton Allen?" Na-Young asked, recalling past conversations she had had with Father-in-Law about the American medical doctor and Protestant missionary who'd founded the university hospital where he had studied.

"No, his name was Henry Appenzeller, but Mr. Allen worked closely with him to introduce Christianity to Korea. Mary Scranton, who was among them, started this school and served as its first president." She took Na-Young's hand. "It's lovely to welcome you." Turning to Lady Boss, she thanked her for bringing Na-Young.

More women started arriving. Boksun passed Na-Young a cup and told her it was coffee. She took a tentative sip and was surprised that it was both sweet and bitter. They joined a conversation. A woman was talking about the challenges of translating literature from Chinese to Korean. "You wonder how much meaning gets lost if one translates a work into Korean from Chinese that has already been translated once from the original Norwegian."

"I've only translated one foreign work—one of Maupassant's books," another woman said, "but it was from the Japanese language to Korean, so I think it was easier."

Na-Young felt like a moth amongst butterflies as the women enjoyed their coffee and foreign biscuits. Just then, they were interrupted by another white woman, who clapped to get everyone's attention. She spoke in English and the woman next to her translated for them.

"I'm so delighted to welcome all of you," she said.

"My name is Joyce. I'm honoured to be here to welcome so many distinguished guests. We are very fortunate to have with us some of the most prominent Korean women writers, translators, and editors. It is my hope that you will get to know each other and that friendships will be formed as we work towards bettering the status of women in Korea. It is our belief that the representation of women in literature plays a vital role in bringing about social and political change."

Then Lady Boss, who was standing amongst the women at the front of the room, spoke.

"Until recently, those of us who were privileged enough to know how to read and write were taught for a single purpose—to fulfill a prescribed role imposed upon us by men. Women weren't allowed to use the same writing system as the ruling-class men, who claimed Hanmun, the script of the Han Chinese, and denied us access to it. I would argue that women have since embraced the true Korean writing system, Hangul, and we are now primed to use it to express our views and help Korea to become a modern and independent nation."

The room broke into applause.

"And now it is my pleasure," said Ms. Alice, "to unveil our first library dedicated to showcasing women's writing!" She gestured for everyone to turn to the back of the room. Boksun was there, standing next to a bookshelf lined with books.

"Korean women have been writing for centuries, but very little of the writing has survived," Ms. Alice continued. "By preserving, collecting, and organizing women's work, we can help transmit knowledge of earlier generations to the next and help with women's spiritual and intellectual awakening. We hope our work here can play a central role in creating a new vision for what the modern woman can do here in Korea."

More applause. This time, Na-Young clapped, too. She was still trying to understand how all of this connected with resistance work when Lady Boss came up to her again, this time to introduce her to a woman named Yang Paek-Hwa.

"She's a talented writer, but more importantly, an excellent translator," said Lady Boss. "It's because of women like her that we're able to read books by some of the world's best writers and be introduced to new ideologies."

"Oh?" Na-Young said, intrigued. "May I ask what you have translated?"

"Perhaps you've read it," she said. "*A Doll's House.*"

"By Ibsen?" Na-Young said, recalling the widow's fascination with the play.

"You've read it!" The translator looked pleased. "Although it's been translated by two others. Do you recall the translator's name?"

Na-Young shook her head and asked, "Are you working on anything now?"

"To be honest, I wasn't prepared for the attention the play's been getting. Ibsen is also very popular in Japan right now, so we've been able to access a wealth of information about him and his work. I just wrote another article on him. I'd be interested in your thoughts. What is your opinion about Nora?"

Na-Young took a sip of coffee and thought about what the widow had said about the play. "I think Nora appeals to Korean women because she dares to challenge the establishment." She was pleased that she was able to recall almost word for word what the widow had said.

"Have you read any essays about the play?" the translator asked. "Some state, quite convincingly, that Nora represents everything that women in Korea need to acknowledge and change if we want to create a new identity."

"I find it fascinating, the anguish women face around the world," Na-Young said. "But it's different for us. Unlike Nora, we are twice oppressed. Once by the men in our country and then by the Japanese. The struggles and the barriers we face are much more challenging." She was delighted that she had come up with an original thought. The room came into sharp focus.

"Would you ever consider writing an essay on your thoughts? We could have it published. I know the editors from *New Woman* and *New Life* magazines," said the translator.

Na-Young was so flattered, she was speechless.

"Who knows," the translator added. "If women writers are properly encouraged, perhaps our stories will be translated into English one day and the Western world will learn from our history and ways of life." The women nodded and laughed, but Na-Young's brows drew tight. Did she have it in her to rise to their expectations?

When Na-Young and Lady Boss were about to leave, Ms. Alice came to them. "I'm so glad you brought this lady to us," she said. "I do hope you will return again soon." She loaned Na-Young some books, which were carefully wrapped in plum-coloured cloth. Thrilled to explore books that went beyond Lady Song's Bible and other religious texts, Na-Young promised to read and study them carefully.

The moment felt surreal. What if she'd been wrong about the school's secret resistance activities? Na-Young thought about the new possibilities for women that the school and its bookshelves offered. Maybe all Lady Boss wanted was for her to become one of these women, like Boksun.

She glanced at her watch. Had Min-Ho already visited? Had Twilight done as she'd asked? Despite the joy she had felt seconds earlier, she was relieved when Lady Boss expressed her regrets yet again at having to leave so they could return to work.

Smoke

Early Sunday morning, the one day that the teahouse was closed, Na-Young quietly let herself in. The letter she had left with Twilight had asked Min-Ho to meet her there with the money.

Relying on the little light that shone through the window, she made her way into the kitchen to boil water for tea. She had just stepped back into the main tearoom when someone grabbed her from behind. Terrified, she used the coin pouch she carried to land a solid blow to her attacker's face. The man moaned as he crumpled to the ground.

"Who are you?" Na-Young demanded.

"Who are you?" he asked.

"I work here," she said.

"So do I. This is my teahouse." The man struggled to stand back up.

Lady Boss's husband? "You're bleeding," she blurted out awkwardly, and handed him a handkerchief. She turned on the light. Although she had never thought about what the man might look like, she was surprised to see that his hair and beard were silver and his face was marked with faded smallpox scars.

"You're not one of the regular girls. What are you doing here?"

"What are *you* doing here?"

"I just got back from Manchuria."

It was then that Na-Young noticed the containers from the backyard, covered with dirt, sitting on a table. "Where did you get those?" she demanded.

"What do you mean?" he said, looking equally alarmed.

"You found them?"

"*You* found them?" he repeated her question.

"Yes—buried in the yard."

"They're my containers."

"You left them there? It wasn't your wife?" Na-Young marvelled at the revelation.

"My wife! All she cares about is women's affairs. Do you know what's in these containers?" he asked, wide-eyed.

"Yes."

Tossing the bloody handkerchief aside, he popped one open and scattered the maps on the table. A few fell on the floor.

"What are you going to do with all of that?" Na-Young asked.

"We're making plans. We need to rid this country of the damn Japanese sooner rather than later."

"Does Lady Boss know?"

"My wife and all her damn foreign missionaries. They want the Japanese government to exercise a more liberal policy in Korea. They're urging them with their 'prayers'—they don't know that all the bastards want is to enslave us and bend us to their will!"

"I agree with you," another male voice chimed in. It was Min-Ho! "We need to drive the bastards out before they spill more blood on Korean soil."

How long had he been standing there? She hadn't heard him arrive. Min-Ho reached down, picked up a map, and studied it.

"Who the hell are you?" Lady Boss's husband demanded. He teetered a little as he took a step sideways to shield the tabletop, which was covered with maps.

"This is—" Na-Young stopped. Uncertain of how to express their unique relationship, she settled on the easiest response. "This is Park Min-Ho, my husband."

"Well, my name is Lee Jung-Myung and this is my teahouse. What the hell are you two doing here while it's closed?"

But before she could answer him, Na-Young smelled smoke. "My boiling water!" she said. They ran to the kitchen. It was filled with dark smoke. Min-Ho grabbed a towel and threw the burning pot into a nearby metal basin.

"I can't believe I almost burned the teahouse down," Na-Young said between coughs. Wiping the smoke from her eyes, she stumbled out to the alcove.

"Stop overreacting!" Master Lee said, and propped the door open to let the smoke out. When she looked up, she saw that the swelling and bruising around his nose and eyes had grown worse. She was about to mutter another apology when she saw that the lawn had been dug up, leaving holes and mounds of dirt. How many containers had Master Lee buried back here? Realizing the depth of his commitment to freedom fighting, Na-Young took a bold chance and told him about Yeon-Soo.

"That's why he's here." She turned to see that Min-Ho had lit a cigarette. "He's loaning me money to get her the best lawyer possible."

"You shouldn't be focusing on getting the best lawyer but greasing the greediest judge," Master Lee said. "I've seen enough good people go down to know that much."

"That's what I said!" Min-Ho exclaimed.

"The judges are all Japanese. No way they'd listen to one of us," Na-Young said. "But they might be tempted by one of their own." Could the Japanese man be persuaded to help again?

The Truth

Na-Young resolved once again to tell the Japanese man the truth about everything and what she needed from him. A month and a half had passed since she'd first seen Yeon-Soo at the market. Time was passing quicker than she could move.

She made the bold decision to visit him at work, at the newly built Gyeongseong Broadcasting Station headquarters, which was a short bus ride away. To Na-Young's dismay, the man was stuck in a meeting, and his secretary could not tell her how long he would be. She chose to wait, despite knowing that she was expected back at the teahouse later that afternoon. The pressure in her head sharpened as she watched the minute hand on the clock tick. Two hours passed.

Finally, his office door opened, and a small group of men left.

"What are you doing here?" the Japanese man asked when he saw her. He showed her into his office and closed the door behind them.

"Sorry," she said, "I needed to talk to you." The air was thick with cigarette smoke. She added, "Your office is very nice." It was larger than Min-Ho's office, with Western-style furniture. Perhaps it was the brightness of the room and the Japanese flag hanging on the wall, but Na-Young felt her body tensing.

The Japanese man sat behind his desk and poured sake into two glasses from a bottle he pulled out of his desk drawer. "It helps me think," he said, and offered her a glass.

She looked outside at the horse-drawn carriages, rickshaws, and automobiles on the streets, the sound of their movement dulled by the closed window. A strong wind rattled the glass; winter would come soon.

Suddenly, the Japanese man stood up from his desk and embraced her, catching her off guard. His white shirt was freshly pressed. She feared it might wrinkle if she fell into his arms, but her knees went weak, and she couldn't help it. He looked into her eyes as if spellbound. She felt ashamed to be enticed so easily by his touch. He traced her cheek with a finger and smiled teasingly.

Just as he was about to kiss her, she pulled back and blurted out, "I lied! I'm not Lady Song—I'm her bookkeeper. I should have told you when you first mistook me for her, but I was so taken by you."

He looked at her, confused. "What's your name?"

"Kim Na-Young."

He took a moment to let the news sink in.

"I wanted to tell you each time we met but it just got harder . . . and then I grew fond of you and your stories about your sweet little boy." She looked over at his desk, at the framed photo of his son. It was easier to confess her affection for his boy than for him alone.

His face softened at the mention of Yoshi. She seized the moment and said, "I need your help again . . . with my friend."

His smile turned into a smirk. "I guess it's true what they say about your people after all."

Despite his wounded look, Na-Young couldn't let him off the hook. "What do you mean? What's true about my people? We're not the enemy."

"You throw words around like you know what they mean.

Have you ever wondered how strong the word 'enemy' is? I work with many of your people who see value in a merger of our two countries."

She didn't know what to say and let him continue.

"Organizations like the Iljinhoe existed before our countries *agreed* to the 1910 treaty. Tens of thousands of your people realized that this country could not develop on its own. Iljinhoe's leader was a high-ranking official in your government! Would you call these fellow countrymen your enemy, too?"

Na-Young had no idea about such organizations. The thought of people in important positions collaborating with the Japanese was beyond comprehension. Of course, there could always be one or two traitors, motivated by money or personal power, but thousands? Still, Na-Young couldn't let him believe he was in the right.

"Japan has always been an enemy to Korea. Your son even shares the name of one of our greatest enemies."

The colour drained from his face. He downed another shot of sake. "Consider this for a moment: Japan, as the more advanced nation, economically and culturally speaking, is obligated to ensure the progress of our neighbours."

Na-Young laughed.

"How is this any different from the foreign missionaries who bring their white religion into Korea?" He went on, "Surely, my line of reasoning holds. Anyone in a superior position has a moral obligation to ensure that they help elevate their fellow man. It's no different from a father teaching his son. I assure you I am not an enemy, and Korea can be saved."

"You mean conquered," Na-Young said stubbornly, although his comments about foreign religions and pro-Japanese Koreans had compromised her conviction. For as long as she could remember, she'd heard nothing positive about the Japanese. Father had complained endlessly about how hard everyone had to work to meet their demands and feared that their family would end up becoming tenant farmers. Chills ran down her spine as she thought about the little house in the pine grove and how the Japanese military police had killed the mother and the little boy and girl who had played with Headless Chicken. Then, images of the Japanese military policemen attacking her and Yeon-Soo flooded her thoughts.

"Ichinose-san, my reluctant enemy, you demean me without even knowing it because you've bought into your country's propaganda. You may not actually try to kill your enemies, but what you do is far more dangerous. You're setting up radio and telecommunication systems here. What do you think your government intends by investing so much time and money in that?" Na-Young was so enraged, her body shook.

The Japanese man drew a sharp breath. "I think you should leave," he said.

As Na-Young headed back to the teahouse, her anger gradually subsided. She hated feeling ignorant when he spoke of things like foreign religions and the Iljinhoe. She'd need a greater depth of knowledge to make him see her point of view, although Na-Young realized this might never be possible again—a thought that brought a wave of unexpected relief. But then, realizing it was a minor victory with an enormous cost, she berated herself: She'd ruined any chance of having the Japanese man help free Yeon-Soo.

Inventory

It was midmorning and quiet in the teahouse. Na-Young and Lady Boss were in the back room going over inventory.

"Have you ever heard of the Iljinhoe?" Na-Young asked.

"Why do you ask?" Lady Boss said, cocking her head.

"I overheard some men talking about it. The conversation got heated." Na-Young didn't know why she'd added that last bit. "Do you know the name of the organization's leader?"

Lady Boss hesitated, then picked up a pen to start filling out a form. "His name was Song Byeong-Jun, but he went by a Japanese name, Noda Heijiro. That's how I'll always remember him." She broke into a coughing fit.

"You talk as if you know him," Na-Young said.

Lady Boss stopped writing but didn't look up.

"What does he do now?" Na-Young pressed on. "If he goes by a Japanese name, he must hold a place in high office."

"He died three years ago. And I prefer never to talk about him."

The Japanese man had failed to mention that the man was dead.

"Some Koreans willingly aided the Japanese? It sounds complicated," Na-Young said, thinking about her conversation with the Japanese man.

Lady Boss gave a slight nod but did not reply. She rang her little bell and asked Twilight to bring them some tea and a fresh handkerchief.

Na-Young thought of the tin containers in the backyard. Did Lady Boss know that her husband had returned home? Perhaps she wasn't even aware. But how could Na-Young ask her such a question? It would be impudent to ask about such a personal matter. A sense of mounting doom haunted her.

Na-Young decided to toss aside the usual social etiquette. She said, "Your husband. I need his help. My best friend, Yeon-Soo, is just like Yu Gwan-Sun. She's been detained for leading some sort of resistance group. I don't want her to suffer Gwan-Sun's fate. I don't want her to die in prison."

Lady Boss stiffened. "I see. You never mentioned my husband or this friend before." She looked up at the ceiling, and then back at Na-Young. "Why didn't you tell me you knew people engaged in independence work? Do you know how dangerous that is? The Japanese police have eyes everywhere."

Na-Young sighed. Hiding secrets was hard work. But she wasn't the only one who was hiding something. Lady Boss was a master.

From the doorway, Twilight said, "Flower Petal isn't feeling well and is asking if she can leave now."

"Now? We have several orders that need to go out this afternoon." Lady Boss was visibly agitated. She dismissed Twilight with a wave of her hand.

"I can help cover in the kitchen," Na-Young offered.

"Thank you, but no," Lady Boss said firmly. "I'll do it." Then she added, "I'll ask my husband to meet you at Pagoda Park early tomorrow morning. It's Sunday, so no one will miss us here."

Na-Young nodded. "Thank you so much. Please let him know that I got the money we needed. He might wonder—"

Lady Boss raised a hand to stop her. "Share only what I need to know. I extended the same courtesy when I needed your help."

Na-Young's look of confusion led Lady Boss to remind her about the Bibles she had delivered to the shop, The Peacock with Its Tail of One Hundred Eyes.

"You put me in danger," Na-Young said, recalling the envelope that the proprietor had discreetly removed from the book's pages.

To Na-Young's surprise, Lady Boss didn't deny it. "You delivered a secret list of words needed to decode sensitive messages. The words were cleverly disguised as a poem about the first full moon of the New Year, so it looked innocent, but nevertheless, knowing the truth would have only caused you unnecessary worry and distress. Not knowing served you."

An instant pressure at the back of her head caused her body to tense. Na-Young opened her mouth to question how Lady Boss could have put her in harm's way, but then, remembering that she needed her help, said nothing.

"Tell the girls I'll be right there." Lady Boss dismissed her.

Na-Young's heart raced. She had to stay focused on her mission to help Yeon-Soo. A poem about the moon was a good omen, she thought. Unlike the blazing sun that saw everything, the moon was discreet; it knew how to keep secrets. As she closed the office door, she saw Lady Boss light a cigarette—something she never did indoors.

"The kitchen's a mess," Twilight said. "Have a look."

A large table was overcrowded with assorted rice cakes that needed to be boxed and labelled. Hunched over another table, Matchstick decorated a tray of freshly steamed rice cakes with tiny flower petals. Na-Young noticed that each flower had a different number of petals.

"Wouldn't they look better if they all looked the same? The ones with five petals look so much prettier than the ones with three," Na-Young said.

"We just do as we're told," Matchstick said without looking up. "We don't want any more trouble." She pulled out a handkerchief from her sleeve and breathed deeply into it.

Seeing Na-Young's puzzled look, Twilight said, "When Matchstick and Flower Petal mispacked some boxes and the boy delivered a box to the wrong address, Lady Boss shrieked so loud, you'd think they'd killed someone."

Na-Young, who had never heard Lady Boss yell before, found it difficult to imagine.

"You were off that morning. Lucky you."

Could all of that have happened while she was visiting Min-Ho's office? As Na-Young welcomed customers for the rest of the day, her head swirled with questions. Why hadn't Lady Boss seemed surprised or reacted in some way when Na-Young asked for her husband's help? It bothered her that she had agreed not to ask any questions. And what messages were being sent using the rice cakes? She had suspected earlier that the rice cakes contained coded messages, but had laughed it off. How foolish that felt now. Her eyes closed in anguish. Maybe knowing too much was the real danger.

Pagoda Park

The next day, Na-Young met Lady Boss at the park's entrance. As they climbed up the steps of the octagonal pavilion, Na-Young saw Master Lee gazing up at the sun.

"I heard you had the money?" he asked.

Na-Young discreetly passed him a small pouch stuffed with the money Min-Ho had given her. She wondered why they were meeting outdoors instead of back at the teahouse. But she had promised not to ask any questions. Last night she had lain awake, anxious with fear but excited at the possibility of reuniting with Yeon-Soo again. Free from everyone who ever sought to control them, they would be accountable to no one. They could both study at Ewha and perhaps even go to university one day. Yeon-Soo would understand the decisions Na-Young had made, and the knowledge that they had both lost sons would only strengthen their bond.

"I have to warn you: You're asking me to do something dangerous," Master Lee said. "My source says Judge Ito is our best bet. But once your friend's name becomes known to him, who knows where else it may lead. If things go badly, we could be putting your friend in grave danger. Are you sure you want to go ahead with this plan?"

In a daze, Na-Young closed her eyes. Instantly she realized that a series of *her* decisions had brought her to this distressing moment. It had been her idea for Yeon-Soo and her to run away to the mountains, her idea to leave her son behind in Anyang. And now she was about to gamble with someone else's life, no matter how good her intentions.

But what choice did she have? It was one thing for Yeon-Soo to be in prison, one of thousands fighting for freedom—but how much worse would things be if the Japanese ever found out she had killed one of their own? Na-Young's insides felt like they were unravelling. Could the truth extend to implicate her, Na-Young, as well? Terrified by the thought, she agreed.

"Very well, then," Master Lee said. "I'll see what I can do."

Instantly, she felt ashamed for worrying about her own safety when her friend sat in prison, and turned away.

Na-Young recalled the first time Lady Boss brought her to this park. It had been the meeting place for the largest-ever protest against Japanese rule. Thousands of people, including children, had turned out on the first of March in 1919.

"I was standing next to Chung Jae-Yong when he passionately read out the words to our Declaration of Independence," Lady Boss had told her. "He was just a student, but using the simple power of his voice, he stirred the spirit of a massive crowd who wanted to reclaim our country. Our protest was just one of hundreds taking place across the nation. We were marching peacefully through the streets when the Japanese military police brutally attacked everyone. My husband and I fled to the teahouse, grabbing as many people off the streets as possible to hide them. We barricaded the door with tables."

Nine years later, tens of thousands of these protesters were still locked up in Seodaemun Prison. Others, like Yu Gwan-Sun, the seventeen-year-old girl whose story and courage had come to live inside Na-Young's heart, had lost their lives fighting for something they believed in.

Convinced she had made the right decision, Na-Young turned back to thank Master Lee, only to find that he had already left.

When she arrived back at the teahouse, Lady Boss said, "All you can do now is wait and hope."

Na-Young dropped her gaze. Having hope suggested people had control over their lives. They believed that something good would happen—or, at the very least, that something terrible wouldn't. But having hope could also be passive. One could simply wait for fate to bring what she hoped for and abandon control. She quickly tired of thinking.

"Hope is a virtue. Christian hope is better than hope alone because of God's grace." Lady Boss began quoting from the Bible and Na-Young stopped listening. Her thoughts returned to the Japanese man's argument that foreign missionaries were no different from the Japanese in Korea. What about her country attracted such foreigners and their will to control what wasn't theirs?

Yeon-Soo

A week passed. The tiny boardinghouse yard seemed smaller yet as Na-Young and Oppa waited.

"I wish I could have gone with him," Na-Young said. The plan was for Master Lee to escort Yeon-Soo back to her place.

"Just be grateful that Master Lee managed to bribe a judge. I still can't believe he pulled it off."

Na-Young sipped her tea and looked out for the little boy across the road. She hadn't seen him lately and hoped he was all right. The midmorning sun made the air seem hazy.

"My room here will be too small for both Yeon-Soo and me. We'll have to move, of course," Na-Young said. "I'm hoping Yeon-Soo will agree to go to school. Or maybe we'll start again somewhere else. We were originally supposed to go to Pyeongchang and stay with Mother's cousin at Woljeongsa. Can you imagine the two of us living as monks in a Buddhist temple?" Na-Young chuckled and started to pace. "I'd have to take Twilight along . . . She made me promise her if I ever left the city, she could come."

When Twilight had told her that she was tired of the monotony of working at the teahouse and wanted to go somewhere else, Na-Young had thought she was joking.

"You don't know how good we have it here," Na-Young had said. The teahouse had just closed so they were sweeping and tidying up. "Where else would we be paid to work? Taught to read and write? And after work, who are we accountable to? No one."

Twilight had angled her head and looked at Na-Young. "We do the same thing, day in and day out. I send the money I make to my parents so that my brothers can go to school."

Na-Young lowered her head. Despite the years they had spent working together, she knew very little about Twilight's life outside work.

"I don't even want to get married," Twilight said. "At least we get paid to cook and clean here, like you said." She laughed, but her voice was laced with melancholy.

"Okay, if and when I leave, you can come with me, but we might end up at a temple."

Twilight blew out a breath, frowned, and said, "Sure. Why not? Just promise me I can go with you."

"Promise."

And now, Na-Young thought, she might have to keep that promise. She stopped pacing and stretched out her back. "She even made me yak-sok and you know how I feel about that."

"I can't believe you actually believed I'd cut off your pinky finger if you broke your promise!" Oppa said, and chuckled loudly.

"I was a kid! Promises meant something to me back then." Na-Young leaned against the wall and slid down to a sitting position. "Forget the temple. I want to go to school." She and Twilight had been reading the translated poems of an English poet, Elizabeth Barrett Browning. It was one of the books that Ms. Alice had loaned her. Barrett Browning was a woman, yet she was fearless enough to write about the injustices that existed all over the world: exploited children in English mines and people traded like cattle in America. Sadly, women everywhere seemed to suffer the same fate of oppression at the hands of men.

"You should visit Mother," Oppa said.

Na-Young shook her head.

But Oppa continued, "Father's health won't allow him to live much longer, and I'll be able to return home once I've finished the ten years I agreed to serve. Hopefully the Japanese will be long gone before then."

Ten years? Na-Young's heart dropped. She had always assumed he could leave his job sooner rather than later. As she remembered why he had agreed to work with the Japanese military police, her heart raced, and she winced, knowing that it had been choices she'd made that had led to his sacrifice.

"Then you can finally be with Sarwon." She hesitated a moment, trying to lighten her burden. "Yes, I've known about the two of you for a long time now. I'm very happy for you both."

Oppa's eyes twinkled, but his expression was incredulous. He leaned against the wall and listened quietly as she poured them more tea and continued to speak.

"The estate will become yours. You and Sarwon can live in peace. If you really want, you can even sell the farm and go to university like you once dreamed. It's not too late. If I can dream as a woman, surely you can do even more as a man."

Before he could respond, Master Lee appeared at the door with a woman Na-Young didn't recognize.

"Who is she?" Na-Young asked Master Lee.

"Yu Yeon-Soo," the woman replied, her voice low and tentative. She was emaciated, the yellowing of her skin and the whites of her eyes adding to her sickly appearance.

"This isn't *my* Yeon-Soo!" Aghast, Na-Young looked at Master Lee.

The woman bit her chapped lip. "There were two of us with the same name," she said. "Your friend, did she have red highlights in her hair?"

Na-Young nodded.

The woman opened her mouth, then closed it.

"Speak if you have something to say," Master Lee said. His face was red.

Nodding, the woman said, "We were both called before a judge. He seemed confused when he saw that we shared the same name. He read some lengthy charges against us and found your friend guilty of high treason and sentenced her to an immediate death. I was released."

How could that be? Na-Young had never considered the possibility that another person in the prison could share her friend's name. "What have I done?" she said, horrified at the realization that her friend might be dead. Her knees buckled. Oppa grabbed her arm to ease her onto an upturned pot.

"Who told you that Yeon-Soo was at Seodaemun Prison in the first place?" Master Lee asked.

Na-Young struggled to think clearly but sensed everyone waiting for a response. She was about to tell him about the Japanese man but stopped herself. Would he have suspected that she'd try to get Yeon-Soo out without his help? Could he have somehow been responsible for the "lengthy charges" against her? Or was she just losing control of her imagination?

"I'm very sorry for your friend. But I'm grateful for your help. I was told I could stay here with you—" the woman said.

"How did she look?" Na-Young interrupted. "My friend Yeon-Soo, I mean. Did she look all right?"

Tears filled the woman's eyes, but she remained composed. When she accepted a cup of tea from Oppa, Na-Young saw that her wrists were badly discoloured.

"What did they do to you?" Na-Young hadn't meant to be so blunt.

The woman drank her tea. "They chained me to a wall and forced me to kneel on bricks for hours at a time. They wanted me to confess to being a traitor, but all I did was steal melons from my employer."

Na-Young blinked hard and willed herself not to cry.

"Your friend, I'm sorry to say, was limping, so I imagine she endured some of the worst beatings. She is what my mother used to call foolish and brave. Brave, because she kept yelling 'man-se'—long live our country!—even before the judge. Foolish, because that's likely what sealed her fate."

Overcome with confusion and the unexpected twist of fate, Na-Young grabbed her teacup and threw it at the wall. The porcelain smashed to pieces and tea seeped through the broken pieces and into the cracks on the ground. The air hung still. It was then that she glanced out the window and spotted the little boy from across the road. Squatted on the ground, he was watching his spinning top and drumming the air with his fingertips. His presence helped settle Na-Young.

"Can we still save Yeon-Soo? Do we have time?" Na-Young asked.

The woman shook her head. "I can't say that she's still with us even as we speak. I'm very sorry, but the judge ordered her to be taken away to the south compound."

"What does that mean?" Na-Young demanded.

"The execution site." Master Lee wiped his forehead with his sleeve.

“Then we’ve got to go there. Now.”

“We can’t just show up. It’s heavily guarded,” Oppa said. “You’ll end up in prison, too, and that won’t help matters.”

If you can’t make something better, then try not to make it worse. The words came back to her in Yeon-Soo’s voice.

“Do you have any other place you can go?” Oppa asked the woman.

She nodded and asked whether she could leave.

Master Lee suggested that he and Na-Young return to the teahouse and seek his wife’s counsel. “She’s better connected than anyone else in this city.”

Na-Young and Master Lee were on Jongno Street, a block away from the teahouse, when they heard a great commotion, a noisy collection of unintelligible voices. It grew louder as they neared.

“Stay here,” Master Lee said, and gestured for her to stay back. She could feel his panic. He slipped around the corner. Japanese police were barking orders: “Keep back! Keep back!”

Alarmed, Na-Young peered around, hugging the building that sat at the corner.

A small crowd Na-Young recognized as mostly regular teahouse patrons was standing outside the teahouse. Japanese police were directing them across the street. Then, to her shock, she saw Twilight, Nearby Tree, Matchstick, and Flower Petal being dragged outside by the police.

Na-Young turned away and came face-to-face with Lady Boss. “You’ve got to get away! The police have raided the teahouse!” Lady Boss said.

“But what about the girls and your husband?”

"They'll be fine. The Japanese won't find anything at the teahouse. I made sure."

"How?"

Lady Boss shifted her weight and raised her chin. "Twilight told me about your Japanese man. Luckily, I had someone watching him as he watched us."

The gravity of this revelation and Twilight's actions made Na-Young's knees buckle.

"We knew everything. My husband and I have been doing this work since the Japanese invaded our country. He's been away in Manchuria working on several anti-Japanese campaigns. When he told me that his love for our country outweighed his love for me, I told him I felt the same way. We kept all this from you and the girls because the truth is a heavy burden."

Na-Young was lost for words. Her suspicions had been right. Master Lee had lied when he'd said dismissively that his wife was only interested in women's affairs and her Christian faith. He'd been protecting her.

"But I understand. I know what it's like to be forced to keep secrets. I've made mistakes, too," Lady Boss said.

"We make mistakes when all we live for is to survive," Na-Young replied.

"Run and don't look back." Lady Boss's tone was severe. "The Japanese man will surely keep looking for you, even if you know nothing of our work."

Suddenly, it occurred to her: Lady Boss meant for her to run right now.

"What about you?" Na-Young asked. "After everything you've done for me . . ."

"It's what women do for each other," she said.

"Yeon-Soo! My friend—" Na-Young's eyes welled with tears.

"Right now, you've got to focus on saving just one person, and that's got to be you."

"But I didn't even get to say goodbye to the others. I promised Twilight something."

"Life is about making the best choices we can at any given moment, and right now you must choose to not look back. You must trust me."

The noise outside the teahouse was getting louder; the Japanese police were moving towards the main street. Na-Young started running.

Promises

After packing what few possessions she owned, she wrote her brother a farewell letter—without disclosing her destination plans—and left it with the boardinghouse owner. She would flee to the little hut in the middle of nowhere near her village, the one where she'd imagined Yeon-Soo living peacefully for all these years.

Early the next morning, she went out to the backyard. She hoped the little boy would be out playing. She wanted to say good-bye and see him one last time. To her surprise, she found Twilight slouched against the wall, fast asleep. Disturbed by Na-Young's touch, Twilight woke with a start.

"I was told Lady Boss wanted me to find you," Twilight said, rubbing her eyes. "Your room was locked by the time I got here last night, and I didn't want to make any noise." She pointed to her satchel. "Wherever you're going, I'm going with you. You promised."

"What happened to you and the others? I saw the police take you away."

"They never arrested me or any of the girls. All they did was ask questions. I went back to the teahouse, but it was closed. The shopkeeper next door said that Lady Boss had left a message that you were looking for me."

"Where are the others now?"

"I don't know."

"I need to leave. I promised Lady Boss." *Save yourself so you can help others.* The idea swirled in her mind like a fallen leaf.

The little boy was nowhere in sight. Na-Young's heart ached, but she knew it was time to go.

They walked for several days, stopping to eat and to rest along the way. But rather than stay at the little hut in the middle of nowhere, Na-Young led them to Daegeori. She'd realized that running away from her problems had only led to even bigger ones, so she'd decided to return home. No longer the naive and fearful young person she'd been when she'd left years ago, she resolved to face her father and her mother, and to deal with the consequences that awaited her. "Sometimes we need to go backwards before we can move forward," she told Twilight.

PART IV

village

Lunar New Year

Two months had passed, and Na-Young and Twilight had settled into village life. Father, frail and bedridden after losing Second Mother only a month prior, barely recognized his daughter, so he wasn't angry that she'd returned against his wishes. When he called her by Second Mother's name, rather than be irritated, Na-Young found herself pitying the man who had once forced her to marry and then banished her. He died shortly after, whispering Second Mother's name—a gesture that moved Na-Young, in spite of all the pain their love story had caused her family.

With both of them gone, Na-Young came to terms with the realization that, like most women, Second Mother had been doing the best she could with what life had offered her. *I'm no different*, she thought, and forgave herself for her part in Second Mother's decline. Guilt, often self-imposed, was pointless because the past could not be changed. Dwelling on it only made the present painful. Yeon-Soo had been wise to say: If you can't make something better, then try not to make it worse.

A rooster crowed in the distance in anticipation of sunrise and a new year, the Year of the Earth Snake. Na-Young returned from a walk to the nearby bamboo forest, and the cold air, smelling faintly of earth and trees, entered the room with her.

Back in the main house, Mother stirred at her presence and woke up. "Is it morning already?"

"Yes, it's the beginning of a new day," Na-Young said. Beginnings were better than endings, just as light was better than darkness, and faith was better than doubt. "I've been so angry and afraid," she confessed. "I even blamed you for letting me get married, and you did nothing wrong."

"Is it so hard to think we want the same things?"

"It's taken me a long time to figure out what I want."

"Patience granted me what I wanted," Mother said, and looked around. She had outlived both her husband and his lover to reclaim her rightful place in the household.

"Are you going to be okay today?" Na-Young asked. Mother dreaded the morning ceremonies of the Lunar New Year. When she was a child, Na-Young had asked, "Why do we have to honour four generations of dead relatives?" The prayers had seemed endless, and no matter how hard she tried to meditate like the grown-ups, her mind always drifted. A few times, she had even fallen asleep, only to be severely scolded by Mother. While she understood why they cared about those whom they had known and lost, such as her grandparents, she wondered why they needed to go back so many generations. Things changed, of course, when they lost her sister, Mi-Young. Na-Young wanted to pray for her. She thought back to what Mi-Young had looked like just before her death. Her skin was pale like white sand, her face looked sunken in, and she had large, blotchy patches on her cheeks. The terrible gurgling sounds she made as she tried to breathe had scared Na-Young, and it had been a relief when her sister finally passed. *She isn't suffering anymore,* Na-Young had consoled herself.

And now, they had to pray for Father and Second Mother, too. Na-Young made sure Second Mother's four boys were properly dressed and had practised the bowing rituals. She told them about Yeon-Soo, referring to her as an aunt whom they also had to remember in their prayers.

★

Unlike the sombre morning prayers, the afternoon's celebrations were loud and festive. The whole village, including all the house servants, had come to the square, dressed in as many layers as possible to stay warm. A noisy group of little boys was chasing another boy, waving a slingshot in the air. Twilight sat by a small fire, weaving colourful ribbons into some of the girls' hair as they listened to traditional folktales told by Lady Ko, the apothecary. Na-Young smiled, seeing the woman's ancient collection of puppets, which even as a child she had thought were old and battered. The puppet she'd loved most was a tortoise, its shell made of bamboo strips. She still remembered how her favourite story began: "Long ago, the Dragon King of the East Sea became so ill, he had to eat the raw liver of a hare to survive." Na-Young continued to smile, remembering how the clever tortoise, who moved slowly but deliberately, had tricked the fast-moving hare to get what he wanted.

Musicians, who carried their drums and string instruments, settled into their favourite spots near the main campfire, a giant blaze that burned wildly to block any evil spirits from entering the New Year. In the centre of the square, three men struggled to secure a pig on a spit. The little boys stopped playing and came running, lured by the giant pig.

"Idiots!" Old Man Rhee said, and slapped one of the men hard on the head. "You need to tie its feet together!" He was still the village's unofficial leader after all these years, and was responsible for overseeing the pig's roasting. Now, almost blind, he'd been gently set aside by the village elders.

"Let them do their job!" his wife said. She was the only one in the whole village who dared to stand up to her husband.

"Where is the firewood?" her husband demanded, ignoring her. "Do I have to do everything around here? Where the hell is my good-for-nothing son?"

Na-Young spotted him, Hyun, huddled around a group of men drinking. Suddenly Old Man Rhee lost his balance, crashing into the side of the pig. His wife let out a cry of surprise.

"My head!" Old Man Rhee cried. He wiped the coarse salt that had been smeared all over the pig from his forehead. When his son rushed over, he grabbed his father by the shoulders but fell down as well, so that both men were rolling around on the ground. The children burst into laughter and chanted, "Chubby, chubby piggy, who is your master? Chubby, chubby piggy, you have no master."

"Get back!" the wife yelled, her voice raspy and sharp. She kicked snow at them, and they scattered away from her.

The sun climbed higher in the sky. It was getting warmer. Na-Young bowed and greeted everyone politely; the women bowed their heads. As far as they knew, Na-Young was a widow like many of them.

"It's good to have you back," Sarwon said. Her lips and teeth were blue from the dried blueberries she had been eating. When Na-Young didn't say anything, she took Na-Young's hand and led her through the crowd. As they both reached for some apples spilling out from burlap sacks, Na-Young bumped into Yeon-Soo's mother-in-law. How had the woman been, Na-Young wondered, without Headless Chicken around to amuse her? She bowed deeply, but before she could say hello, the woman threw her such a hateful glance that Na-Young's jaw dropped. The woman cursed at Na-Young and called her horrible names, just loudly enough for Na-Young to hear.

Shocked, Na-Young kept her eyes low and followed Sarwon. They climbed a tree and settled onto its branches as they ate apples and watched a bird pecking at the ground a few metres ahead of them. Beyond that were the familiar rolling hills off in the far distance. Na-Young imagined the river where she and Yeon-Soo used to do laundry, and she longed to dip her feet into the water, despite the chill in the air.

"Did you see the way Yeon-Soo's mother-in-law looked at me?" Na-Young asked. "I thought she was going to attack me!"

Sarwon looked around cautiously. "It's okay," she said. "She's still raging about everything that happened since her daughter-in-law ran away with her magical headless chicken."

Instantly, Na-Young's chest tightened, then relaxed slowly. Yeon-Soo was at peace now.

"She also hates that your brother was working with the Japanese. But if you must know, that's all my fault. I told him that you and Yeon-Soo had run away. I panicked, but he kept pressing me for details. He figured something bad must have happened, but we refused to believe that you could have killed anyone, let alone a Japanese military policeman. You, of all people . . ."

Na-Young looked away. In the distance, men gathered to play tug-of-war. "All the men living on the west side of the river on this side!" someone yelled as they milled about, trying to organize themselves. Amongst them was Old Man Yang, who had decided to stay in the village to welcome in the New Year, his hwangap year. As a visitor and not partial to either side, he served as the referee.

"People keep saying I look good for sixty," he had told Na-Young when she'd greeted him that morning. "They think they are complimenting me, but it's a bit insulting—the idea that at my age I should be wilting away. Maybe once upon a time sixty was old, but I've travelled all over our land, walked almost every road that connects this village to its neighbours, and beyond that, towns, and the capital. My age benefits me because I know how to travel by sunlight and moonlight and what roads to avoid. I alone choose how my days will unfold."

Na-Young had been so sure she'd be happy back home, but hearing about Old Man Yang's adventures caused a deep heaviness to settle in her chest. But what choice did she have but to stay in the village? She felt an apple seed on her tongue and bit down on it, even though Mother had always warned her never to do so, claiming it could kill her.

Nearby, Second Mother's boys were shooting snowballs at a tree using their slingshots.

"Can I show you a trick?" Na-Young asked, joining them.

One of the boys passed her his slingshot.

"Turn your body slightly sideways and make sure your feet are facing forward and even with your shoulders. Remember, the more you go back like this," she said, pulling the band as far as possible, "the farther it'll go." Her snowball shot far past the tree. Everyone cheered.

Despite her misgivings, Na-Young knew that returning to the village was the first step to redeeming herself, and now, in her father's and brother's absence, she would run the farm. She knew how to read and write in Korean and in Japanese. She also knew how to keep the farm's books and run a business. When her brother came home, he and Sarwon would marry and take over, and Na-Young would be free to go back to Anyang. She could watch her son grow, even if from a distance. Furthermore, she could continue to study and write. Her insides ached, thinking about Boksun studying multiple languages and training to be a translator, and how fate had allowed her to transform into a person of potential importance.

"I could teach you to read and write," she had suggested to her mother. "I wrote an essay inspired by the bamboo forest." She recalled what she had said in the teahouse about men and their integrity. That bamboo was the same, that the trees had their own integrity, remaining unchanged throughout the seasons. Yet Twilight had pointed out that bamboo was hollow, suggesting that that mirrored man's nature. Na-Young's visit to Ewha had taught her that it wasn't only men who wrote and thought about important matters such as philosophy, psychology, and ideology. Women were not merely focused on surviving and serving others. It had hit her then: Why was she thinking about the nature of men instead of women? After all, women needed other women, much like how a single bamboo could only do so much, but the collective strength of bamboo stalks could be used as scaffolding for the biggest temples and the most treasured palaces.

"Your talking is giving me a headache," Mother said. "I was born to be a wife and a mother, not a thinker. And I've fulfilled both roles. I can rest. You write if you want."

Yes, but without a reader, what would be the point? Patience had never come easily for Na-Young, but perhaps village life, where one could not rush cabbage to grow or melons to ripen, and where not even the most delicate flowers harboured grudges when monsoon rains drowned them, would allow her time to contemplate. A new essay idea came to her about the beauty of acceptance: when giving up means giving in to something closer to the truth. Words and ideas rushed through her thoughts. She had learned it was futile to fight her urge to write.

Most of the villagers had gone home. Some of them lingered, mostly drunk, by the campfire, which still burned brightly, casting shadows that looked liked demons and night spirits. Jung-Su, Yeon-Soo's brother-in-law, staggered into the fire's glow, flask in hand, and, losing control, crashed down beside her. He fumbled through his coat and pulled out a rag full of walnuts. "I could crush these with my bare hands for you."

"You're drunk," Na-Young said.

"Drunk enough to want you."

She swiped vainly at his hand.

"Your brother's a damn traitor," he said.

"Oppa had his reasons," Na-Young said defensively.

"What possible reason could there be? He's just a farm boy."

Na-Young felt a need to protect her brother's honour. "Oppa's the bravest person I know!"

"Helping the Japanese certainly doesn't make him a hero," Jung-Su said. He took a swig and wiped his mouth with the back of his coat sleeve. "I'm tired of hearing about how wars and fighting make heroes out of stupid people. It makes us no better than animals."

"Animals fight. They can be just as violent. Our neighbour's cow crushed the leg of my sister's dog once."

"Yes, but their hearts aren't evil. They fight to survive and protect what is theirs."

"Isn't that what Oppa's doing, too?"

"In a Japanese-issued uniform?" He downed the last drops and tossed the empty flask aside.

Na-Young's insides boiled. She bit her lip to stop herself from saying any more and accidentally revealing too much. She stood, ready to leave. Jung-Su stumbled to his feet as well. His eyes were bloodshot. He grabbed her arm.

"You're angry. Good!" he said. "Once the weather breaks, I'll start my search for Yeon-Soo again. I'd be happy to turn her over to the Japanese after all the hell she's put us through, reward or no reward."

Na-Young shook her arm free and walked away.

"I'll split the reward with you," he said.

Na-Young whirled around. Pulling the rag back out, he squeezed the walnuts in his hand, and to her amazement, they cracked open. He popped a piece into his mouth.

Na-Young couldn't help but laugh at his display, recalling how Yeon-Soo had once stood up to him. A strange sensation ran through her. A thought flashed through her mind. Could Yeon-Soo's spirit be out there in the darkness, watching? She shook her head; the thought was ridiculous. Her eyes scanned her surroundings and stopped where the moonlight broke through the treetops. Na-Young became aware of all the noises around them: the crackling of twigs and branches as people moved about, the popping of the fire, and the song of a woman echoing faintly in the background.

Jung-Su pulled her to him. Something brushed against her hips, and suddenly his tongue was in her mouth. His breath reeked of alcohol, roasted pig, and walnuts. She tore away.

"We should have killed you, too," she said. She only realized what she'd said after the words had slipped out.

Jung-Su scoffed. "You don't have it in you. Yeon-Soo, though . . ." He traced his hand over his nose as if to recall the time she had hit him with his own rifle when he'd tried to kill Headless Chicken. "Yeah, I can't wait to get my hands on that bitch and her stupid chicken again."

Na-Young exhaled. Thankfully, he was too drunk to realize what she had said. Then a realization came to her: She hadn't been the only one looking for Yeon-Soo.

Rag Dolls

Two days passed. Na-Young heard footsteps outside Mother's door. It was still dark out. Sarwon passed her a small satchel that was stuffed to its capacity.

"That should be enough food to keep you going for the day. Are you sure you don't want me to go with you?" Sarwon asked. "Where exactly are you going, anyway?"

Na-Young had said nothing about her plans to revisit the hut in the pine forest. If Old Man Yang could create his own adventures, so could she—and perhaps going back to the hut could satisfy her growing restlessness. Truthfully, she didn't know why she needed to go back. For all she knew, she could be walking back into a nightmare, three dead bodies rotting, their stench keeping even the mice away. Or perhaps she'd find Yeon-Soo there, skinning a rabbit she'd trapped. Impossible, but still . . .

The last time Na-Young had trekked this path, it had been summer, and she'd been fleeing from an unwanted marriage and the Japanese military police. The same threat of violence hovered over the treetops, unseen yet ever-present. Was it memory that was causing this? Could her past leave such a lasting imprint on her body?

She walked through ankle-deep snow. Her determination waned as exhaustion caught up with her. At midday, she stopped at a river. The shock of the icy water jolted her. An image of Yeon-Soo in the cabin flashed in her mind's eye, but sadly, she shook her head to let the picture go. Would Yeon-Soo be upset with her for breaking her promise never to search for her friend? Na-Young exhaled heavily. Her attention shifted when she sensed that someone was watching her. Struggling to remain calm, she assured herself she was alone.

The absence of the dirt paths troubled her. She relied on the rows of evergreens and the mountains to guide her, recalling the narrow paths that ran alongside them. She reached a partial clearing and realized she was unsure where she was. The cold seeped through her. Looking above at the clouds, she saw hazy images and caught wisps of memories: Yeon-Soo smoking under a tree, Headless Chicken strutting and exploring her surroundings, and she, Na-Young, staring up at the clouds before falling asleep.

Then, she saw it. Smoke drifting in the distance.

Just as she was about to knock, Na-Young heard the rustling of movement and caught the outline of a familiar figure. Jung-Su.

"You followed me?" Suddenly she understood the eerie feelings she'd had—her instincts had been right. She was being watched.

"I knew you'd lead me to her."

What had she done? "Please go," she begged.

"Are you kidding? After everything that's happened?" The desperation in his voice matched hers. "I'm not even doing it for the money—I just want to see the sight of her pathetic face when I'm feasting on her stupid headless chicken."

She slapped him. He slammed her against the door. Snow on the rooftop fell in a plume of white dust. The door opened and they both fell inside. A man stood over them.

"What's going on?" the man demanded. "Who are you?" A beard and mustache covered his face; a tangle of hair had been pulled into a clumsy topknot. Na-Young stood up and thought he looked familiar. He caught her gaze, and when their eyes met, she recognized him as the man assaulted by the Japanese military police, Yoon Chun-Heh. When she saw that he, too, recognized her, her eyes widened in a plea for him to stay silent. She watched his eyebrows twitch and looked for any sign that he might have understood her need for him to keep her secret.

Jung-Su was back on his feet, scanning the one-room home. Dust particles floated in a stream of sunlight by the window. A black pot bubbled in the fireplace. Magazines and paper cluttered the table where Na-Young and Yeon-Soo had once feasted on roasted yams and rabbit.

Jung-Su ran his fingertips along the paper. "Anti-Japanese newspapers?" He stopped to look at the ink stains on his fingers. "I'm looking for a girl," Jung-Su said. "She's wanted for murdering a Japanese military policeman."

At the mention of this, the man turned to Na-Young.

"You live here alone, old man?" Jung-Su asked.

"This is my house, but I've been away since last fall. My wife and children weren't here when I got back. I believe they went to visit my wife's oldest aunt in the north and will return once the season becomes friendlier."

He didn't know! Who had buried their bodies? Surely not the Japanese. It must have been Yeon-Soo. But when had she left? And why? Was it to join the resistance activities in the capital? Na-Young's head was spinning. Should she tell the man the truth and expose herself to Jung-Su?

The man was quiet. In his eyes, Na-Young could see a mutual understanding that the man knew Jung-Su was a threat.

"What were you saying about your wife?" Jung-Su asked, distracted by what he was reading.

The knowledge of the man's family's death shamed Na-Young.

The little girl's rag dolls rested against a wall. She saw an image of the child playing with Headless Chicken on her lap.

Jung-Su placed the newspaper back on the table. "I guess Yeon-Soo's not here after all," he said. "Sorry to have wasted your time." He left without acknowledging Na-Young.

With Jung-Su gone, the man asked, "Do you know what happened to my family?"

She was overwhelmed by the dilemma of whether to tell him the truth. She could say nothing and leave the man as she had found him, filled with possibility and hope. But that hope was false, an illusion. Surely, not knowing was worse than knowing the truth, regardless of how painful it was. Only the truth would allow him to move on—a lesson she was still learning.

Na-Young shook her head ever so slightly and squeezed her eyes shut as tears fell. When she opened her eyes again, the sudden explosion of pain on the man's face told her he understood. "They're dead," he said finally. "Maybe it's better this way."

Na-Young removed the walnuts and rice cakes from her satchel and put them next to the rag dolls.

Gently, she asked, "When you got back . . . how was the state of your home? I'm trying to figure out if my friend ever made her way back here."

"Everything looked as always, but my wife's clothes—she didn't have much—but everything was gone. That's why I thought my family had gone away."

She was beginning to walk out when the man caught her arm. He whispered, "I did notice something odd, though: the magazines, newspapers, and notes I'd hidden under the floor by that wall—someone had gone through them."

"What were they about?"

He pointed to the papers on his table.

Could this be where Yeon-Soo had first discovered rebellion work? Was this why she had gone to the capital? She had found a new purpose, one that gave her a sense of direction and meaning.

Na-Young was back at the village's edge again. From a distance, everything looked the same, but she knew better now. When morning broke, she would find Old Man Yang and ask him to deliver her essays to Boksun in the capital. Perhaps she could share them with others at the school, including Ms. Alice, with whom she hoped to study one day. The idea of others reading her own work both thrilled and scared her. The calming sound of wind gently blew in her ears, a glorious chorus to welcome new possibilities.

Harmony

One Year Later
March 1930

On the third month of the new calendar in the Year of the Metal Horse, when the courtyard was slowly beginning to smell of sweet earth, Old Man Yang returned to the village.

"I have something for you from Boksun," he said to Na-Young. He handed her a magazine.

"Just one?" she asked. Her friend had sent magazines, notepaper, and books ever since Na-Young first shared her essays with Boksun last year.

"Here's the letter that goes with it," Old Man Yang said.

As villagers gathered around the cart, inquiring about the items Old Man Yang had, Na-Young read the letter.

My writer friend,
Congratulations on your first publication!
Your faithful servant, Boksun

She flipped through the magazine and stopped when she saw her name: "The Bamboo Forest" by Kim Na-Young.

"You look like you've seen a dokkaebi!" Old Man Yang said.

"No, not a goblin—on the contrary, this is my name," she said, pointing. "This is something I wrote."

"Why, that is remarkable! How proud your father would have been to have such an accomplished daughter!"

Just the thought of her father knowing that she could read and write made her heart jerk. Would he be proud given that he refused to let her attend school? Did it even matter now?

"Will you return to the city? Are you finding village life dull after living there?" Old Man Yang asked.

"I miss the capital—I miss the people I knew there."

"You're going to be famous now! A peacock surrounded by common magpies."

Na-Young blushed. "But magpies are auspicious—they are the messengers of good news."

"A messenger, that's me," he said, and chuckled. "And you are the writer of messages!"

A deep, chaotic joy overcame her. Her essay was perfectly typeset and claimed back-to-back pages of the magazine she was holding. Just like Lady Boss and Yeon-Soo, she had found her own way to contribute to society and empower other women.

Later, as she hiked up the mountain to Su-Bin's grave, Na-Young recalled the three promises she had once made to Yeon-Soo when they'd parted years ago: Let her best friend go, visit her son's grave to say goodbye, and under no circumstances would she look for her friend.

She had kept two of her promises.

The winds were stronger now and pushed her along until she finally stood at the gravesite.

"I'm back," she said, "and I brought something to read to you!" She pulled out her magazine. Tugging at her shawl, she settled cross-legged on the ground.

At least you're a captive audience, she thought with a laugh. She knew that Yeon-Soo would have appreciated such a joke. It was then that she noticed a fluttering piece of cloth caught in the dirt near the grave. Curious, she gently pulled on it. Buried under a layer of earth was a tiny package bound by several strips of faded, stained white cloth. It was the gold-and-jade lotus-blossom brooch!

When had Yeon-Soo buried it here? She looked around in vain, as if for a clue, but saw only the ancient trees and a cloudless sky in the distance. It took her several moments to steady her hand so that she could pin the brooch on her shawl.

"Jade is a living stone. It will protect you on your journey," she whispered. She said it again. And again. And soon a chorus of voices flooded her mind: her mother, her sister, Mi-Young, Yeon-Soo, and, finally, her own, repeating the phrase like song lyrics in harmony.

Author's Note

Thanks to my daughter, who chose to do a double major in French and East Asian studies at the University of Toronto, I was exposed to Korean studies for the first time at the age of forty-nine. All throughout her undergraduate years, I read every article and textbook she read and got a crash course on Korean, Chinese, and Japanese history.

I became especially interested in the years that my great-grandmother was a young woman, the 1920s. To this day, some of my fondest childhood memories are of my great-grandmother. She was a vivid storyteller. The first time I ever heard of the rabbit and turtle tale, it was not about a race, but rather a turtle tasked with cutting out a rabbit's liver so that it could be used as healing medicine for the Dragon King, who lived under the sea. Each of the stories I heard unconsciously taught me Korean culture, customs, and traditions. They stayed with me long after I left the country in 1975 for Toronto, Canada.

I learned as an adult the reason why my great-grandmother never read to me. She was illiterate. Did she ever want to know how to read and write? As bizarre as it sounds, I wanted to gift her that, especially after hearing about how heartbroken she had been when her husband took a second wife—a practice that was legal then. And so, this novel is a reimagining of her story, inspired by a core message that runs throughout the narrative: Women need other women to survive.

AUTHOR'S NOTE

The novel begins in 1924, fourteen years after Japan formally seized control of Korea and imposed its own governor-generalship, suppressing Korean culture and national identity. Books, articles, and other resources about Korea under Japanese colonialism, which ended with Japan's defeat in World War II, need to be explored and discussed in order to fully grasp the impact that that period continues to have on present-day Korea.

All Things Under the Moon is a work of fiction that blends imagination and history, inspired by a young woman's symbolic journey of sacrifice, moral ambiguity, and self-discovery. In my desire to recreate my protagonist's world as authentically as possible, my daughter and I travelled to South Korea and visited each location mentioned in this novel, from Seodaemun Prison, where seventeen-year-old Yu Gwan-Sun was tortured and killed for being a freedom fighter, to my great-grandmother's old home, to the mountains of the tiny village not found on any map that serve as formidable bookends of this novel.

To learn more about Korea during this time period and about the books and resources that were used to tell the story of my protagonist, Na-Young, visit my website at annykchoi.com.

Acknowledgements

An author once told me, "Use the acknowledgements page wisely. Some readers actually read them."

This novel began as an idea in the editorial room at Simon & Schuster Canada. I had just told Phyllis Bruce, who had acquired my first novel, *Kay's Lucky Coin Variety*, about my great-grandmother, who, as a child living in Japanese-occupied Korea, was constantly getting into mischief that threatened her and her family's safety.

"That's your next book," she said. Years later, despite the many flaws in my new manuscript, Phyllis saw through to the heart of the story and offered to publish the new novel. I will always be grateful for her unwavering belief and encouragement throughout the writing of both my novels.

Brittany Lavery took over as my editor after Phyllis retired. Luckily for me, she not only saw and understood the story I wanted to tell, she knew the path to get us there. A big thanks to her for her invaluable insights and guidance, and to everyone at Simon & Schuster Canada who helped shape the novel, including Sarah St. Pierre and Janie Yoon. I would also like to thank and acknowledge the expertise of Sophie Bowman, whose knowledge of Korean literature and history helped inform the factual accuracy of the novel.

In appreciation for the support and feedback provided by members of my writing community, a big thanks to Adam Pottle, David Iggulden, Tina Dealwis, Thomas Allen, Tali Voron, Shane

Clodd, Maureen Lynch, Andrew Fruman, Saad Omar Khan, and all the members of my former writing group, the 11th Floor Writers. Thanks again to Lee Gowan at the University of Toronto School of Continuing Studies for connecting me with Phyllis and helping to kick-start my writing career. Many thanks also to Frank Montesonti and Bryan Hurt at National University in San Diego, who read the original manuscript and provided critical feedback as part of my master of fine arts in creative writing studies.

A special shout-out to my mentoring group, Writers in Trees, especially Chelsea Kowalski, for her keen editorial eye and enthusiasm for this story.

To Jackie Kaiser, my brilliant literary agent, who makes everyone she represents feel like her most valued author, thank you for encouraging me through the often daunting writing and publishing process, and for championing the stories I want to tell.

Lastly, thanks to my mother and father; my brothers, John and Martin; and their families for their constant support throughout the many years that it took to get this book out into the world; and to Patrick, my husband of twenty-seven years, for his love and encouragement to keep pursuing my endless writing goals. And my deepest gratitude to our daughter, Claire, who patiently and meticulously researched, edited, and read through countless drafts of this novel—you're awesome.